EVERYDAY MOVEMENT

EVERYDAY MOVEMENT

Gigi L. Leung

Translated by Jennifer Feeley

RIVERHEAD BOOKS NEW YORK 2026

Riverhead Books
An imprint of Penguin Random House LLC
1745 Broadway, New York, NY 10019
penguinrandomhouse.com

Book design by Alexis Sulaimani

LIBRARY OF CONGRESS CONTROL NUMBER: 2025035482
ISBN 9780593855379 (hardcover)
ISBN 9780593855386 (ebook)
ISBN 9798217183487 (international edition)

Originally published in Complex Chinese in hardcover in Taiwan as 日常運動 by ECUS Cultural Enterprise Ltd., New Taipei City, in 2022

First United States edition published by Riverhead in 2026 by arrangement with ECUS Cultural Enterprise Ltd., Taiwan through New River Literary Ltd.

Printed in the United States of America
1st Printing

The authorized representative in the EU for product safety and compliance is Penguin Random House Ireland, Morrison Chambers, 32 Nassau Street, Dublin D02 YH68, Ireland, https://eu-contact.penguin.ie.

For all who carry anger and sorrow

Contents

PART ONE

New Town *3*

Vendetta Train *26*

Life During Wartime *49*

Sai Mui, Baby Girl *72*

Terrain of Skin and Flesh *101*

PART TWO

Panda *137*

PART THREE

The Final Class *185*

Snoopy Friends *215*

The Outside World *236*

Be a Girlfriend *261*

PART ONE

New Town

No one could have imagined how events unfolded last Sunday. It was like drinking warm water every day, so habitual that you never questioned the nature of the liquid. There was no need to cautiously stick out your tongue to test the temperature. Who would ever suspect that the routines of an orderly life might quietly conceal an invisible poison? One day, scalding white steam curled from your cup. But still, no one noticed. The water slid past your lips, waves of searing heat engulfing the soft flesh of your mouth. Before you could react, the pain had scorched every inch of its tender surface. It was too late to spit it out. Your entire respiratory tract was ablaze. Everything was on fire.

It was the end of July, the height of summer. The sunlight was so brutal that even the birds sought shade among the trees. At the end of a tree-lined lane overlooking the university sports ground was Ah Lei and Panda's dorm building. Inside their double room, space was tight. A ceiling fan stirred. Ah Lei lay sprawled on the bed, her face slick with sweat, her body leaving a damp, oily imprint on the sheet. All sticky and bothered, she felt like a piece of fish jerky mid-cure. Her eyes still foggy with sleep, she didn't want to get up. She reached for a bottle of water and took a sip. It made her throat prickle. On the other side of the room, Panda was meticulously putting on makeup in front of a mirror. Her hand stayed steady as she traced her lash line.

"Don't drink it," Panda warned Ah Lei. "It's from the protest. It might be contaminated." Ah Lei didn't utter a peep. Snuggled under the covers, she subconsciously touched the back of her neck, as though the stinging still lingered. It had been days since their ill-fated visit to New Town Plaza, but Ah Lei still had vivid nightmares of what happened.

"I'm having lunch in New Town Plaza with my cousin Ah Mak. Remember him? You should join us!" Panda moved on to her eyelashes, lifting them upward with a mascara spoolie. Ah Lei shook her head, limp as a broken-winged insect, with no will to go anywhere. Panda couldn't take it anymore. She yanked the covers off Ah Lei and pulled open the curtains. Sunlight poured into the room.

Ah Lei shielded her eyes instinctively. She couldn't help but wonder how her roommate could go on living so merrily, with such ease. After the terrifying ordeal they'd just gone through together, Panda appeared to have no trouble eating or sleeping, just like any carefree university student.

"No matter how painful it gets, life must go on." Panda shoved toiletries into Ah Lei's hands as if she had heard Ah Lei's thoughts. "Get ready and join us! Besides, you really need a new phone. It's been such a hassle these past few days."

These words persuaded Ah Lei to comply. She got out of bed. The broken phone had been a gift from her older sister, who was studying abroad. It had a cute little bunny charm dangling from it. Had she held on a bit tighter that day, would it have made a difference?

But there was no way to go back in time to change what took place in the mall. In her dreams and waking moments, she kept thinking about that severed finger covered in blood, tumbling onto the cold, glossy marble floor.

When Ah Lei stepped into the shared bathroom, two young women were brushing their teeth by the sink. Behind the sink were several toilet stalls. At the other end, there were four shower booths. During the semester, sometimes dormmates had to wait for their turn to wash up. Ah Lei made her way to the far end of the sink and fixed her gaze on the mirror. She might've been imagining things, but she felt the young women were stealing glances at her.

The women were mainland students who lived in the room at the end of the hallway. They stayed in Hong Kong over summer break for their internships. Once, after returning from a rally,

Ah Lei and Panda washed their helmets and goggles and left them to dry in the common lounge. The two mainland students had just finished making breakfast. Upon catching sight of Ah Lei and Panda, they immediately gathered up their bowls and chopsticks and retreated to their room.

"Maybe they're nationalistic Little Pinks. Maybe they'll secretly snap photos to post on Weibo so they can put us on trial in the court of public opinion!" Panda said with a grimace. "Do you want to talk to them? Try to win them over with love and peace?" Ah Lei removed the filter from her face mask and said, "It's not like that." Things weren't so black and white.

It wasn't always about taking sides or trying to change someone's mind.

It was a more intricate and elusive dynamic, like a metronome swaying back and forth. You never knew which way it would lean at any given moment. She noticed the way the mainland students looked at her; it probably wasn't disgust or disdain, but she couldn't quite name it. Lately, she hadn't been able to figure out some of her own feelings. After that lounge encounter, she started drying her protest gear in her room, so as not to bother anyone.

For the past two months, Panda and Ah Lei had also stayed in their dormitory room instead of returning to their homes for the summer. In hindsight, it was a wise decision. This way, they didn't have to report every outing to their families, who were especially nervous given the ongoing street demonstrations. It spared everyone unnecessary family friction.

The two had been classmates in junior high, although they could hardly have been considered friends back then. Panda's outspoken and carefree personality had always made her popular at their all-girls school. Ah Lei, on the other hand, was quiet and reserved. She agonized over every decision, needing to think through different angles before finally making up her mind, only to second-guess herself all over again.

Before becoming roommates, the only time they'd ever spoken to each other was back in ninth grade when the government tried rolling out national education in schools across Hong Kong. A few senior students formed a concern group, going from class to class to explain how the proposed curriculum was a thinly veiled "brainwashing" attempt at stuffing students full of patriotic ideology. They had prepared a petition letter against it and collected signatures. Panda was the first in their class to sign it and rushed up to the blackboard to rally her classmates to do the same.

"A single spark can start a prairie fire. Adults think we're still just kids, incapable of using our own judgment. They tell us to stay out of politics and focus on schoolwork, but that's just wrong," she said.

She mimicked the tones and expressions of those parliamentary candidates on TV, clenching her hand into a fist and waving it in the air. She spoke with such conviction that it was as if she caught those dazzling yet slippery terms such as "right and wrong," "justice and righteousness," in her grasp, where they swelled into a scepter and struck the ground with a resounding thud.

"We aren't old enough to vote yet, but isn't it high time that we practice what we learned in Civic Education class and show society that we care?" she asked.

At first, the students passed the petition around like a hot potato, afraid of getting into trouble. But Panda's impassioned speech echoed in the hushed classroom like the luring tunes played by the Pied Piper of Hamelin. One after another, her classmates offered their signatures.

When the forms reached Ah Lei's desk, she kept twirling her pen as the pages fluttered under the fan. She was struck by the lightness of these sheets. Could signing them really make the proposed policy go away? Did her fellow students truly grasp the weight behind words like "righteousness" and "justice," and the price that came with them?

She wasn't sure if she herself fully understood these ideas.

"Are you hesitating out of fear?" The two classmates were not even familiar enough to address each other by their names.

Panda leaned in, her body blocking the sunlight from the classroom window. Her question was really a statement: Anyone who hesitated to sign was a coward.

To Ah Lei's relief, the class bell rang.

"Let me think it over," she mumbled, sidestepping Panda's question. She hastily shoved the form into her drawer just as class began.

No one had imagined that the petition and the students' newly kindled passion would end up like an unlucky paper airplane, trampled and forgotten before it had a chance to take flight. The very next day, when the members of the concern group were handing out flyers, they were called into the principal's office.

It wasn't clear what the principal said. Rumor had it that when the students came out of his office, some were sobbing miserably, some were red-faced with anger, and others, apparently stunned, wore blank expressions. The concern group disbanded that very day. Their Facebook page was wiped clean. From then on, there wasn't any voice of dissent left on campus. On the bulletin board put up by the Civic Education Society, there were more pictures than words.

Two years ago, when Panda and Ah Lei started university, they were assigned to the same dorm. Even then, they didn't become particularly close—their personalities still differed, and their schedules rarely aligned.

This changed in June when they went to Tamar Park for a peaceful rally to protest a proposed extradition bill. Since its sovereignty was transferred from the UK back to China in 1997, Hong Kong had been self-governing and maintained its own legislative and law enforcement systems. This was the era when Ah Lei and Panda grew up. Ordinary citizens were alarmed by the new bill because they suspected it would open the door to mainland law enforcement and feared scenarios where their fellow Hong Kong residents might be secretly arrested and transferred to the mainland for trial.

Ah Lei hadn't been the most political person, but even she understood it would be an infringement of civil liberties in Hong Kong, so the night before the rally when Panda invited her to join her, she agreed immediately. That day, the peaceful gathering turned into turmoil when police fired tear gas at the crowd. Some rallygoers were arrested. In the months that followed, as they shared more unthinkable experiences, they came to realize it was at the park—when they linked arms and ran together—that their lives became entwined like vines, winding tighter and denser as time went on.

That summer, it felt like they had each begun leading two different lives. On weekdays, they worked part-time jobs; on weekends, they took to the streets. A few of their friends always led the way at the front, while Ah Lei and Panda trailed behind to provide support. They each carried a large bottle of saline solution, with smaller bottles in their pockets. After tear gas struck, they were ready to help people rinse their eyes or wounds.

Out there, Ah Lei's nerves were always stretched tight, like a rubber band pulled too far but unable to snap. Every scrap of update or conversation she heard left her on edge. Her hands were so sweaty that more than once she fumbled the saline bottles and had to go after them as they tumbled down the street. In the aftermath of a clash with the police, it was always a mess. People sprawled face down on the ground, vomiting; some had swollen, bloodshot eyes that couldn't stay open; some of them were injured on their legs or arms with blood streaming down from fresh wounds. Cries and moans blended with the sharp cracks of gunfire nearby. In the first few weeks, Ah Lei always stood frozen on the sidelines, unable to chip in.

The Hong Kong she knew emphasized instrumental rationality—a "first-world" materialistic city ruled by capitalism. An elite education had drilled in her that this city ran on cool-headed speculation, analysis, and salesmanship.

But none of these things explained how, on a recent outing, human blood trickled on the ground, streaming past her half-dirty Nike sneakers.

That day, when the police began closing in to clear the scene, protesters fled into the metro station, found a spot without CCTV, and changed out of their black outfits—a sort of protest uniform—before boarding a train.

As their train left the station, friends traded information. A few people gossiped about celebrity news: who was hooking up or breaking up with whom; someone suggested grabbing a late-night snack. Occasionally, a fellow passenger shared updates on protests in other areas—where bullets had been fired, where fires had broken out. Most riders hunched over their phones, lost in their own information feed.

Ah Lei found a quiet corner and sat down with Panda. She wryly noted that the most obvious benefit of the movement thus far was that weekend-night train cars were no longer jam-packed, and one could easily find a seat. She leaned against the grease-smeared glass, the reflections of her companions indistinct. Now and then, a burst of laughter or an impassioned curse drifted over.

Before heading back to campus, several classmates stopped at an all-night cha chaan teng. It was already past ten, but all five round tables in the modest dining room were still fully seated. A few elderly men picked their teeth and cursed at the newspapers in front of them. Ah Lei guessed they must have lost their horse bets. Diners sat almost back-to-back. A waiter sailed through the space to refill the teacups. A waitress retrieved various dim sum delicacies from the steamer pot. Fire flared up from the wok as the chef stir-fried beef chow fun in the open kitchen.

The owner ushered the group outside where he had set up some tables and chairs for them. They ordered a few small dishes to share. In the sweltering weather, the air was thick like a layer of plastic wrap clinging to everyone, squeezing them tight, making them sweat without end. Ah Lei couldn't stop scratching the back of her neck, fearing that the poisonous gas had left a rash blooming across the skin she couldn't see. Panda asked if she wanted to ice it. She shook her head.

The young men at the table were starved and tore into the food like ravenous wolves. A sexy barmaid sidled up to promote beer, and they ordered several bottles right away. Suddenly, Ah Lei felt a cold sensation creeping across the back of her neck and yelped.

She turned around and saw Panda and the others popping open the chilled bottles. A guy immediately began chugging his beer.

Panda pressed one of the icy bottles against Ah Lei's neck and asked, "Any better?"

"Are you even supposed to drink alcohol after being teargassed? Isn't it just adding poison to poison?" Ah Lei responded.

The guy sitting next to her stiffened. "Don't be scared, it's fighting poison with poison!" he said.

Panda chimed in. "C'mon, alcohol gets the blood flowing—maybe it'll flush out the toxins faster."

Ah Lei silently picked up a bottle and poured drinks for the others. As she watched the foam rise and overflow, she realized she wasn't able to join her friends' banter.

Her thoughts returned to a recent encounter at a metro station. She and her friends hadn't had a chance to change and were still dressed head to toe in black when they brushed past a family. A little boy wearing a cartoon animal headband, clearly just back from a theme park, excitedly pointed at them like he'd spotted some exotic beasts. "Mommy, protesters! They're protesters!" he shouted. His mother panicked and rushed to cover his mouth. Ah Lei and her friends were flustered and scrambled away.

In the days that followed, she replayed the starkly different reactions in her mind: the child's innocent elation, the mother's fearful misgiving, and their own jittery anxiety. "Why did we panic and run away?" Ah Lei asked Panda. "Were we doing something wrong?"

"People who think too much usually aren't very happy," Panda said.

When Ah Lei returned to their dorm room, Panda had put on a new sleeveless sundress. She twirled in front of Ah Lei, asking if she looked good, and considered which pair of shoes would go well with it. The swish of the dress radiated such energy, Ah Lei thought. It was like a colorful little whirlpool.

In contrast, she was still in her wrinkled T-shirt, looking terribly disheveled. She felt barely human. It had been like this the entire summer break. Often, she stayed in and languished in bed all day, doomscrolling on her phone. She stopped meeting up with friends and skipped her part-time job shifts.

Panda, meanwhile, was as vivacious as ever. Every day she was out and about: going on dates, going to work, and going shopping. Everyone called her Panda, but she was really more like a fluttering, vibrant songbird. She seemed to be doing great—no, no, better not say "great," which sounded too much like blame. Better to say "normal." She ate three meals on time, followed a set routine, and kept track of everything. She even squeezed in beauty treatments at the salon now and then and invited Ah Lei to come along for a couple's discount. Not that there was anything wrong with that.

Ah Lei couldn't free herself from being preoccupied by the movement. The blood-soaked reality of it consumed her. Before going out, she needed hours to mentally prepare herself; after coming back, she needed another few hours to process it all. Ah Lei felt like a broken, lopsided spinning top. Just staying upright took everything she had.

Even though several days had passed, she was still unable to process what had happened on Sunday. Whenever she thought about it, the spinning top inside her tipped off-balance.

Watching Panda organize her handbag, Ah Lei said, half-mocking, "Be honest with me. When you walk by those boutiques in the mall, checking out the maxi dresses, don't you ever think about the bloodied floor from that day?"

"It's the bags that bring things together." Panda pointed at a black backpack and a pink handbag in the wardrobe. "From the right, life looks soft pink, the black splotch an accidental smudge; from the left, the world appears solid black, the pink an indulgent swipe of lipstick. But is it really? The truth is, they're just two different bags, sitting side by side on a shelf."

"What if there's only one bag, both black and pink, mixed together?" Ah Lei asked.

"Sure, but when you think about it, the colors don't really go together. They kind of clash."

"Like New Town Plaza last Sunday?"

"Like New Town Plaza today," Panda said.

Last Sunday, Ah Lei and Panda were just going out for dinner. There were protests and clashes happening across the city, but they wanted to give themselves a day off from the movement. And so, they went to the nearest upscale mall—just two metro stops from campus—for a nice meal, a little window shopping, and maybe even a spontaneous movie.

Was a shopping mall supposed to be a haven for all? Back in mid-June, when the movement had just begun, a video clip went viral: several protesters, fleeing the police on a main road, suddenly darted around a corner and dashed into a nearby luxury mall. They stumbled straight into the bewildered gaze of shoppers and tourists. After a few steps, the protesters looked back and saw the police hadn't followed them in. Instead, they clamored at the other side of the glass doors, hurling insults, trying to draw the protesters back onto the battlefield outside. The glass doors, it turned out, formed a sacred border.

From then on, many protesters developed guerilla tactics, strategizing for a game of hide-and-seek. These glossy halls of consumerism—malls, shopping centers, commercial complexes—became temporary ceasefire zones. No matter how desperately they ran on the sweltering streets, how the chase began to seem like a matter of life and death, if they could make it in time and fling open one of those glass doors before being caught, a blast of cold air would embrace them, chilling them inside and out.

That pleasant coolness meant safety.

Gradually, the open spaces in these shopping malls were transformed into miniature civic squares. Crowds gathered there to sing and chant; they put up slogans and posters on the wall. And so, people began to think that, somehow, capitalism protected them. Yet this sense of security was as fragile as those thin, crystal-clear doors, offering no real defense. A single flick, and they'd shatter.

That day at New Town, however, when Panda and Ah Lei emerged from one of the shops, they saw broken umbrellas, masks, and used first-aid supplies strewn across the floor. Screams and sobs were coming from all directions. In the distance, a mass of black-helmeted, heavily geared security officers closed in.

Ah Lei and Panda processed the new reality: Riot police had breached the mall.

Many shoppers were stunned. When they pulled themselves together to flee, some of them collapsed on the floor. Others tried to retreat into the individual shops for shelter, but the staffers swiftly hit the automated door buttons, and the shutters came crashing down, shattering everyone's belief in their presumed protector.

As the police advanced, people scattered toward the exits. On the first floor, at least a dozen protesters in black shirts were pinned to the ground, their limbs twisted into grotesquely unnatural postures.

Multicolored spotlights illuminated the ornate displays of luxury goods. In a shop window, mannequins in evening gowns and cocktail dresses bestowed their smiles on two policemen as they jumped a guy in khaki shorts. One of them clenched the man's shoulder, forcing him to kneel. When he struggled, the other cop held his head with both hands. His thumb dug at the poor man's eye, as if ready to gouge it out.

Ah Lei, Panda, and a few concerned bystanders shouted for the officer to stop, begging for the man to be left alone. But it only made things worse. As if to demonstrate his authority, the officer pressed down harder. A struggle ensued.

All of a sudden, an ear-splitting, bone-chilling shriek drowned out the other noises, echoing through the almost empty, cavernous mall.

Everyone paused to look. The kneeling man was now let free, his eye red and swollen.

He spat out something. A bitten-off finger. The one that had thrust into the soft issues of his eye socket. Dripping with blood, it landed on the pristine marble floor.

That evening, the men and women in search of transactional happiness fled for their lives. Clutching the latest fashions, electronics, cosmetics, dried seafood, and herbal medicine, they rushed into the metro station connected to the plaza.

The mall had just betrayed them, so they shifted their faith to public transit. They needed to believe that there were still places of order in this city, places that were undisturbed by the chaos on the street, or the threats of crumbling society and an authoritarian takeover. If they managed to get there, maybe they could carry on as usual, pretending it was just like every weekend in the past, returning home with the spoils of their consumption.

Ah Lei and Panda had been among the first to duck past the metro turnstiles. Soon, the police officers came charging into the station, swinging their batons and shouting at the crowd. Their roars echoed throughout the space. Ah Lei and Panda saw the officers menacing the crowd outside the turnstiles like herders corralling livestock. The two of them hurried down to the platform. Ah Lei trembled as she gripped Panda's hand. She could feel the soft fibers of her mask tickling her nose, but she didn't dare lower it to scratch. Her body was all tense. Panda squeezed her hand, their palms damp with sweat. Ah Lei imagined that under the mask, Panda's face must be pale, but she managed to whisper, "Don't be afraid. We'll be okay." This gentle assurance triggered more grief. Ah Lei's chest tightened. They both teared up.

More people surged toward the platform, nearly toppling over on the escalators, pushing one another. In this tumult, Ah Lei dropped her phone. When she picked it up, she saw the screen was shattered and the bunny charm from her sister was gone. They crammed into a full train car. A few passengers were holding the automatic doors open. The announcement repeated in Cantonese, Mandarin, and English: "Please stand back from the doors." The doors began to shut like massive jaws. Inside, passengers clawed at the doors, shouting, "Wait! Many people haven't made it on yet."

The metro staffers on the platform kept reassuring the riders, almost pleading: another train was approaching. They just had to believe it and release the doors. This train needed to depart.

But Ah Lei didn't believe it, nor did her fellow passengers. How could they trust any place anymore? She used to believe in the plaza, comfortable and stylish, full of people busy enjoying the cheer and peace of consumerism. Now the police had barged in here. They deployed pepper spray at the shoppers' faces, slammed batons on their foreheads, and gouged a man's eye. They left the mall bloodied and haunted by resounding wails. In the metro station just now, they prowled, like farm owners inspecting their livestock. No one could make it stop.

If Ah Lei and other passengers trusted the staff and let go of the doors, what would happen to those stranded on the platform?

In this city, was there any public place that she could feel safe in?

This was their first time back in New Town Plaza since Sunday night.

The place had been restored to its stylish and comfortable environment. The seven-story glass building was like a glistening gift box. Air-conditioned and showered in bright light, the plaza was oblivious to the shifting of the seasons, or day giving way to night. They walked across the spacious lobby toward the restaurant area in the back. It was lunchtime, and every corner of this global village—eateries serving Japanese ramen, Southeast

Asian curry, Italian pizza, and Taiwanese hotpot—was packed with well-dressed diners, chatting, laughing, and eating with elegant manners.

When they arrived at the bistro, Ah Mak was already seated at a booth. Ah Mak had ordered for himself and was eating soup. His left forearm and half of his hand were wrapped in gauze. Panda greeted him and ordered risotto for herself and a cheddar cheeseburger for Ah Lei.

"How come you're free on a weekday?" she asked Ah Mak.

He pointed to his arm. "Sick leave. I'm off for two days."

"My cousin works maintenance at a train depot. He lives alone," Panda said, winking at Ah Lei.

Ah Lei knew exactly why she added that last detail. Ah Mak had recently gone through a breakup. Apparently, it had something to do with the movement. Panda was scheming to fix them up. She was making things very awkward.

Ah Lei had only met Ah Mak once before, at a rally in early July. He'd been dressed head to toe in black, with a gas mask strapped on, looking like a member of the Valiant Faction—protesters willing to be on the front lines during clashes with the police. Normally, the mask should have protected him from the worst of the tear gas, but when he staggered over to the first-aid station, he was coughing uncontrollably. Ah Lei helped him sit down, and immediately she understood what was wrong. He had put the mask on clumsily without properly sealing the plastic rim tightly around his mouth and nose. The gap allowed the gas to seep in. He didn't have much frontline experience after all, Ah Lei thought to herself.

As Ah Lei helped him take off his mask to flush his eyes, Panda exclaimed, "It's you?" Ah Lei had no clue who he was, but she knew that calling out the name of someone you recognized at the scene was taboo. Without asking any questions, she instructed him to open his eyes wide, tilt his head, and keep blinking.

He was so quiet. No crying out in pain or putting up a struggle.

At the bistro, Ah Lei sat off to the side, listening as the cousins talked. Their conversation mostly revolved around Panda complaining about her mother while Ah Mak tried to gently defend his aunt, saying nice things about her and urging Panda to be understanding. This annoyed Panda so much that she barely touched her appetizer. "Of course you think she's was nice. She never nags you," she snapped at him. "As people say, it's easy to be pleasant with people you only occasionally meet; a different story if you have to live together. You have no idea how I feel. Who gives you the right to play peacemaker?"

Ah Lei was taken aback. Panda was usually all jokes and grins, never taking anything too seriously. She rarely saw Panda lose her temper. Watching Panda and Ah Mak, Ah Lei thought of her older sister. In the months since the movement broke out, Ah Lei had spoken with her a few times over the phone. In those calls, Ah Lei went on about her fractured everyday life. "The bloodshed is real, but so is drinking beer and cracking jokes. The resistance is real, but so is the mundane routine of life," she vented.

"As the question goes, would you rather be a happy pig or a miserable Socrates? But right now, I feel like a miserable pig."

Astute yet kind as always, Ah Lei's sister comforted her. "When conflict becomes part of your daily life, it's natural that you need some getting used to. You know, each person has their own way of coping, and not everyone can allow themselves to fall apart. Maybe maintaining order is the only way Panda knows how to survive."

Their food arrived. Ah Lei cut off a piece of her burger and popped it into her mouth. Her eyes widened.

The pillowy bun was paired with a richly aromatic beef patty that was crispy on the outside, tender on the inside. Juice burst forth in her mouth. Ah Lei was suddenly awakened by the sensation. This must be the best burger in the world, she thought. She closed her eyes and swayed her head gently as if to prolong the pleasure.

Seeing Ah Lei's reaction, Panda smiled smugly and patted her roommate on the shoulder. "Told you! I wouldn't steer you wrong. That's Angus beef. With food this good, haven't you regained the will to live?"

Ah Lei glared at Panda, feeling a flash of self-contempt at being overcome by a mere burger. Nevertheless, she grabbed the rest of the burger, abandoning any care for etiquette, unconcerned with the strangers around her. Her nails dug into the soft bun, her fingers slick with grease. She opened her jaw wide to take a big bite and chewed it forcefully. Melted cheese and tomato juices dribbled down her fingers onto her wrists. It was a feral mess. But she didn't care. She clutched this delicious burger like a drowning man hanging on to a piece of wood.

As she ate, her guilt lessened, and she felt like everything might be okay. Perhaps life was supposed to be this way. She, too, surrendered to material desires and cheap satisfaction.

After settling the bill, Ah Mak asked the women to be careful out there. "Auntie really does care about you. Go see her when you get a chance," he told Panda. Not at all her usual cocky self, she responded with a hug, saying softly, "You're the one who really needs to be careful."

Briefly, Ah Lei met Ah Mak's eyes. He still looked so calm. She was a little embarrassed. Ah Mak had paid for the meal, even though she had barely said a word to him. She had sheepishly accepted his generosity but was still struggling to justify it to herself. She found the courage to hand him a paper bag. It contained some dressings and a packet of pink antiseptic solution she had carried with her. Ah Mak nodded in thanks and waved goodbye.

Panda linked arms with Ah Lei, and they went to look for a new cell phone. Ah Lei tried to block out her memory from Sunday. The electronics store had been so quick to kick out customers and slam its shutters when things went down. It was now jam-packed with shoppers again. There was no trace of trauma.

On prominent display was the latest smartphone model. It was advertised to be sleek, ultra-thin, and featherlight. Its dual-lens camera promised crisp photos. It looked glossy and beautiful. Its price tag was nearly ten thousand Hong Kong dollars.

Ah Lei had never bought herself a new phone. In fact, she rarely spent money. Her sister's hand-me-downs had served her well. She had never wanted bells and whistles on a phone. She wasn't one for trendy extravagances. The salesman stopped by and patiently walked her through the merits of the new model: a wide screen, high-resolution photography, high-definition video playback. The camera even had a portrait mode. He snapped a shot of her for demonstration. In the photo, the background receded into blurriness, and Ah Lei looked striking and sharp.

Ten thousand was a serious sum, Ah Lei calculated. It was nearly a month's pay when she hadn't skipped her part-time job; enough for a decent trip. It could pay for laser eye surgery—well, probably just for one eye, anyway.

Nevertheless, an impulse overrode all these considerations. She ran her fingers over its shiny body, as if it would help her forget everything that had come before. She absolutely had to have this perfect phone.

Vendetta Train

A battered train rattled into the depot, looming before Ah Mak like a bloodied, dying figure straight out of a B movie. He had just arrived at work this Monday morning, and the sight of the rickety train lumbering forward gave him a jolt. Instinctively, he took a half step back.

After it came to a halt, he stepped inside. All the display screens had been shattered, and the CCTV cameras had been spray-painted black and bashed broken. Between the handrails, electrical wires dangled. They had been yanked out like entrails ripped out of a wounded body.

Taking care of the trains was Ah Mak's job. On recent weekends, however, Ah Mak belonged with those who wrecked trains. For weeks on end, millions of people had marched in demonstrations, but the government barely responded. Many protesters became convinced that it was time to escalate their actions. This included damaging the metro system, which was partially publicly run.

Before this moment, Ah Mak had never imagined crossing paths with a train he might have intentionally damaged. It felt like an abandoned doll from one's childhood turning up out of the blue in one's living room; or an ex-girlfriend who had been comatose for years, showing up in a yellow tracksuit with a katana sword in hand.

Was this something out of a James Wan flick, or a Tarantino plot? Ah Mak loved watching films, finishing even the crappy ones. He found that when people asked about his circumstances or opinions, it was easier to borrow scenarios from films that mirrored his own experiences than to search for some abstract words to express himself.

His girlfriend, Chan Yuek, was a few years younger than him and still a sophomore in university. She wore her hair in a long bob and Ah Mak thought she looked like a young Maggie Cheung. She studied the humanities and approached the world with unyielding idealism. She believed that if everyone were brave, honest, and willing to act, society would become a better place. Her mantra was "Change starts from you." When they went on dates, for example, Chan Yuek refused to dine in chain restaurants because she was boycotting big corporations.

"Just think—if one person boycotts a chain store, it means a little less profit and a little less influence for the corporation. All that power capitalists have? It's given to them by consumers." Chan Yuek laid out her case while she and Ah Mak sat in an artisanal cafe that only served single-origin pour-over coffee. Ah

Mak found this coffee unbearably bitter. All he could think about was grabbing a Coke from the convenience store across the street.

Chan Yuek often behaved like an older sister. She complained that Ah Mak was too comfortable with borrowing other people's words to express himself. Using them as stand-ins, she said, would only pull him further and further away from his own intentions. It was no different from dressing in someone else's clothes—he would end up a shadow.

Ah Mak didn't disagree. But he also didn't know how to change. He knew this was related to the two things that really got under her skin. One was the craze of reposting out-of-context literary quotes online; the other was the cabinet. Every time she visited his place, to reach the light switch, she had to take off her watch before slipping her hand into the narrow gap behind the cabinet.

"Your mother doesn't even live here anymore. Why can't you just put the cabinet elsewhere?" Ah Mak imagined that Chan Yuek had an old-fashioned balance scale in her head. She liked to measure how much she mattered to him. She sat on one side of the scale, and on the other, it was sometimes a cabinet, sometimes his family, sometimes the entire world.

When Ah Mak had just started at a vocational college, his mother informed him that she was getting remarried, apparently to a mainlander. She laughed at the irony of life—after a decades-long detour, it turned out she was returning to China. Her years in Hong Kong, she said, felt like nothing more than a dream.

Fortunately, Ah Mak was already all grown up, and he could stay in their apartment. When they moved in more than a decade ago, this had been a studio. A few years later, she remodeled it into a one bedroom so he could have his own space. This public housing estate was about thirty years old and was home to hundreds of families. Its hallways were chronically wet and dotted with mold. Its walls were thin. Over the years, the neighbors endured one another's noises and quarrels. But they were lucky to be here because the units were rent-controlled.

Since her second marriage, she came back each year to spend a month with Ah Mak. Near the end of her stay, she always busied herself shopping for baby formula, mobile phones, medicine, cosmetics, and cigarettes at the request of her mainland friends, who still believed that products sold in Hong Kong were better.

A few months before Ah Mak's mother moved away, she carried out an annual ritual: a grand reshuffling of the entire apartment—adding this, tossing that, moving things from left to right, front to back. She had always said this ritual was her prerogative. That year, she was especially ambitious with her project. She called it a parting gift for her son.

She replaced the old fluorescent bulbs with dimmable LED ones. She brought in a large flat-screen TV and a sofa bed. When Ah Mak was at school, she measured the distance from his bedroom door to the edge of his bed. One day, he came home to find a sleek modular computer desk with a built-in cabinet, perfectly slotted in by his bedroom door. What happened to his old desk, Ah Mak asked. It was an old secondhand desk that he had covered with movie-themed postcards and cutouts from magazines. For years, he did his homework among a mashup of his favorite films: *The Godfather*, *Breathless*, *A City of Sadness*, *Trivisa*, and *Tokyo Family*. His mother, beaming with pride, said she'd slipped the carpenter an extra envelope of cash to haul the worn-out old thing down to the garbage, sparing her the trouble of moving it herself.

Ah Mak didn't say anything. He understood that his mother needed this. She had to give up on too many things in life. When she was young, she had reluctantly left her hometown for Hong Kong, where she reluctantly married, and later, also reluctantly, settled in this rundown flat. She needed to prove that she had control over something. He had come to this understanding when he was thirteen when, without any warning, she cleared out an entire box of video discs he had stashed under his bed. He was shocked when he discovered the box was gone. But he accepted it. He allowed his mother to exercise these powers. The old desk was only Ah Mak's latest sacrifice for her.

The wall cabinet was meticulously designed: on the top, there were two glass display windows; the middle section was taken up by adjustable shelves; the bottom half was a computer desk with a sliding keyboard tray. On the lower left side, a rolling platform made it easy to move the computer tower in and out. Despite all her careful planning, Ah Mak's mother had overlooked one detail: the cabinet was built flush against the wall, blocking the light switch by the door.

The narrow gap between the cabinet and the wall was barely enough space for a hand to slip through.

Chan Yuek had often complained to Ah Mak how she had to keep her hand completely flat going in and coming out. If she made a fist or twisted her wrist, her hand would get stuck in the gap or scraped by the rough wooden splinters on the back of the cabinet. Several times, in a hurry, she pricked a finger on the wood. It wasn't that Ah Mak had been oblivious to the problem all this time. But he felt that the cabinet had claimed its place in his room. Instead of moving or dismantling it, he'd rather live with this inconvenience.

One day, she reached in without taking off her pink crystal bracelet, and when she was pulling her hand out, a sharp splinter snapped the bracelet, sending the crystal beads flying everywhere. He would never forget the frustrated, pitiful look on Chan Yuek's face.

That was when Ah Mak began to realize that his willingness to endure and his inability to act could hurt the people around him.

In July, after spending a few days under the harsh sun, Ah Mak recognized that a complete, irrevocable rupture had taken place. Back in June there had been a hint of breeze in the air and a touch of ease in his mind. During the marches, he was relaxed enough to observe the strangers on the sidewalks, having lunch or waiting in line for a table. Since then, so many unforgivable injuries had been inflicted on his fellow protesters. There was no turning back. He was no longer the version of himself who had believed in the popular principle of "Peaceful, Rational, and Nonviolence."

On weekdays, Ah Mak was a quiet worker. He went through the motions and felt somewhat detached from it all. The mood at the depot was laid-back. His coworkers took it easy when they could, so he didn't feel guilty and enjoyed his downtime as a kind of rest. Weekends, by contrast, were a lot more stressful. Out on the streets, every moment demanded concentration. Amid the chaos of tear gas canisters being hurled in all directions, he calculated where to set up barricades, when to advance, and where to retreat.

In those moments, he was so alert that his senses were heightened. He thought he could feel his blood flowing in slow motion. He could feel it coursing through vessels, and he could almost hear its steady, pulsing rhythm, like the *whoosh* of a train charging through a tunnel.

Last year, Ah Mak graduated from technical college. In the months leading up to it, Ah Mak busied himself making the most of his soon-to-expire student ID. As often as possible, he went to the cinema with Chan Yuek. He didn't put much effort into job hunting, and the peak hiring season slipped by. He didn't mind. His rent was only 10 percent of the market standard, and he had the savings from his years of working part-time jobs. He spent his time watching Netflix on a friend's account. Occasionally, he went to job interviews, but nothing ever came of them. He wasn't in a hurry. Three months after graduation, a friend offered to refer him to a railway maintenance company. Ah Mak asked about the workload and nature of the job, then accepted it.

The depot was like a deserted train station frozen in time. A few railway tracks ran through it. Sometimes there was a parked train waiting for inspection or repair. This spacious place was occupied by few employees. Ah Mak, as a contractor, did the most physical labor for the lowest pay. Each day, he walked back and forth through the empty train cars, inspecting the equipment. His supervisor, Uncle Gin, was a full-time employee of the railway company. He started here when he was young and steadily climbed the ranks to become a train conductor. After reaching middle age, he grew tired of the strain and transferred to the maintenance department as a supervisor. Uncle Gin often showed up late and spent the day idly scrolling on his phone, shaking his leg as he sat around. However, his salary was the highest. That said, apart from his pro-establishment views, he was a decent guy. Sometimes, he lent Ah Mak his employee ID so he could enjoy a discounted lunch at the staff cafeteria.

There were also three young engineers, all mainlanders who had graduated from Hong Kong universities. They usually kept to themselves, chattering away in a dialect no one else understood. Uncle Gin didn't think much of them, grumbling that they should have learned Cantonese. Uncle Gin didn't speak Mandarin, so when he needed to communicate with the mainlanders, he made Ah Mak act as a go-between. At first, Ah Mak worried they might be Chinese nationalists who looked down on Hong Kong, but they turned out to be more open-minded and talkative than he had expected. Sometimes they sarcastically called themselves "people from the Great Country." They even volunteered to teach Ah Mak how to service the trains.

When Ah Mak was still new at the depot—before everything had begun on the streets—he told Chan Yuek that the people at work weren't bad at all.

Chan Yuek shot back, "Just a few small favors—getting you discounted lunches, teaching you some skills—makes them good people? So only convicted criminals, murderers, and arsonists count as bad?" Ah Mak let it slide, eager to avoid confrontation. He knew Chan Yuek had a set of much higher standards for what it meant to be "good." She was argumentative, hungry for conversations. She clearly believed that communication led to progress, that absolute truth emerged from debate. Usually, her pointed comments didn't bother Ah Mak because he knew she had good intentions. Also, the last thing he wanted was to engage in a debate about the merits of debating.

In early June, Ah Mak came across a social media post calling for a general strike on Wednesday, June 12. Protesters hoped to use the shutdown to put pressure on the government. A rally would be held around the Legislative Council Complex from the morning onward.

Chan Yuek wasn't going to class and urged Ah Mak to join her at the rally. After careful deliberation, Ah Mak called in sick. At noon, the two of them arrived at Tamar Park, the patch of waterfront greenery next to the Legislative Council Complex overlooking Victoria Harbour. The air was cool, and they could have easily passed for tourists thanks to their casual getup and the camera Chan Yuek carried around her neck.

There were already a lot of people there, lounging on the grass or the benches. Some had spread out picnic mats and were eating sandwiches. People were chatting, reading, and singing hymns. The atmosphere was like a cultural festival. Ah Mak, however, wasn't able to enjoy the peaceful optimism in the air. Chan Yuek was displeased with him again: What was he thinking when he took a sick day? Why didn't he have the courage to make his stance clear to his employer? Didn't he know taking leave was completely different from walking off one's job?

"Do you feel ashamed for going to a rally?" Her interrogation was relentless.

In the next couple of hours, Ah Mak reflected on these questions as they helped organizers distribute bottled water to participants.

Around three o'clock, suddenly, banging noises broke out from a distance. A commotion erupted. At the far end of the park, a wave of people surged forward, shouting, "Run! Quick, run!" In all directions, people who, just a minute ago, had been lounging around, picnicking, or reading, leapt to their feet and bolted in panic, leaving their belongings behind.

Still caught up in Chan Yuek's admonishment, Ah Mak didn't immediately grasp the situation: tear gas and rubber bullets had been fired to disperse the crowd. From the edge of the park, a squad of riot police in helmets were advancing toward rallygoers, wielding round shields and long batons. It wasn't until the sting of tear gas assailed his nose that Ah Mak, wearing only a basic face mask, came to his senses. He grabbed Chan Yuek and ran away from the park. They kept going west along the waterfront, passing the nearby Ferris wheel, and finally ducked into the International Finance Centre mall.

Like a movie trailer, what happened on that day became a prologue, heralding the scenes that would repeat endlessly throughout the summer. The frames were always filled with smoke, flames, and sweaty running bodies. In the pitch-dark cinema of Ah Mak's mind, the concept of time dissolved. When he was alone, he paused, replayed, and fast-forwarded these scenes in a loop.

With many things in life, Ah Mak came to sudden realizations of what had transpired well after the incidents.

When his mother quietly carted her things out of the apartment each day, her effort gradual and persistent like an ant moving house, Ah Mak just sat around watching movies. He never thought to ask her any questions. At last, one day, she dragged out the large suitcase they'd used on their one and only trip to the mainland. When her heavy luggage thumped against the front door, the movie Ah Mak was watching had just reached its climax and he finally snapped to attention. When he looked up, his mother asked, "Will you walk me downstairs?" Only then did it dawn on him—she was leaving. The burly man who had driven his mother back here several times in a truck was waiting downstairs.

Maybe Ah Mak loved watching movies so much precisely because as long as his eyes were locked on the screen, he was an audience member, someone untroubled with the need to justify or explain himself. He was safe. It helped him tune out his mother's chitchat on the phone. It allowed him to ignore his aunt's sympathetic words when she came to visit. It gave him license to shut out the expectations from Chan Yuek—and from the world.

The only problem was that, sooner or later, a movie always came to an end.

The lighting in the depot was dim, a sallow yellow like a lemon about to rot, its juice splattered across the walls in mottled shadows. The place had a high ceiling and a vast echo, as if it were the inside of a giant's lair. Between the pillars, numerous slim cables crawled like worms. On the tracks, trains sat like elongated, winding coffins. Employees and contractors were not required to clock in at the depot. Sometimes Uncle Gin didn't show up until eleven, but the mainland engineers always arrived on time at nine. Ah Mak came in even earlier. His responsibilities included testing and replacing circuit boards; hooking up screens to computers; punching in commands to simulate the standard train schedule; making sure the central broadcast announced the arrivals; checking if the system's small red lights lit up correctly and if they flashed at the right frequency. The tasks were tedious but manageable.

His aunt had asked him, why not find a steady office job with opportunities for promotion? He wasn't interested. In an office, he would have to socialize with coworkers, pandering to them and chiming in tactfully during group conversations. If he weren't careful, he might get caught up in some petty drama of office politics. Ah Mak was no good at that sort of thing. The depot gig was a blue-collar job, but he preferred the company of a bunch of guys a little rough around the edges. They didn't need him to fake niceties.

Back then, Ah Mak's biggest frustration here was the weak Wi-Fi. The depot was semi-outdoors and had spotty network coverage. On top of that, the mainland guys loved using Douyin. They liked to lay out the oversized packaging foam to make a temporary sofa, stretching out on it, and watching short videos one after another. Ah Mak was often off to the side playing games on his phone, quietly competing for that feeble signal. Often, when Ah Mak logged on to his game, the coworkers'

Douyin videos froze; other times, the engineers queued up new videos, crashing Ah Mak's connection mid-game, and his hard-earned ranking tanked instantly. Under their breath, the Wi-Fi rivals cursed one another. But there wasn't any open confrontation.

Nowadays, Ah Mak's worries were more complicated. He could handle practical tasks, but abstract ideas challenged him. Activists encouraged the public to integrate resistance into everyday life. They suggested that advocacy shouldn't be confined to the streets: one should bring it into the home, the workplace, and social occasions. The goal was to educate, persuade, and spread the message, breaking out of echo chambers and building broader support. Many people around Ah Mak earnestly put this into practice. Panda organized campus events and invited professors to speak about social responsibility and civil disobedience. Chan Yuek rallied a team of university students to return to their alma mater and connect with high school students. They formed small groups for civic education and emotional support.

Meanwhile, Uncle Gin and a few other older guys spent their days cursing the protesters, accusing them of being bankrolled by the Americans, of pushing for Hong Kong independence and destroying the city. Ah Mak had assumed the mainland engineers would join them in this criticism, creating a united patriotic front—"Glory to Great China!" "Long live the motherland!"—But they said nothing. Showing no interest in taking a stance, they went on lounging around, watching Douyin. Ah Mak felt a kind of kinship with these young men from the north. They shared a need to stay silent.

Chan Yuek, however, continued trying to lure Ah Mak out of his shell. Lately, on dates, she took to pressuring Ah Mak to carry "the spirit of resistance" into his everyday life. He should, she insisted, work on his colleagues and supervisors and preach the ideals of the movement like gospel. When he heard rumors about the protests, it was his duty, she said, to quash the falsehoods and denounce the liars. He needed to draw a clear line, she said. He needed to demonstrate his loyalty.

Chan Yuek took his ambivalence to be indifference. She couldn't stand it.

One evening in early July, Ah Mak met up with Chan Yuek at a restaurant after work. Between work and protests, he hadn't managed to get any rest. Sitting at the table, he was so exhausted that he could barely keep his eyes open. However, her words stung him awake. "Why don't you ever say anything? I want you to talk to me, to tell me what you're thinking," she pleaded.

"We have nothing left now. All we can hope for now is that everyone contributes a little. If everyone takes a small step, it will make a big leap for civil society. But Ah Mak, why couldn't you even bring yourself to join the strike?"

Ah Mak knew how Chan Yuek drew her lines. On that day, calling in sick to join the rally was the best he could have mustered. He tried to explain this. But it was not good enough for her. By giving notice, he had failed to stand up against the system.

He recalled how, when they were newly in love, they used to excitedly dissect scenes and storylines after finishing a movie. Little had he known that two cinephiles could love movies in vastly different ways. He enjoyed losing himself in the music, the sound effects, and the way the camera moved through a scene; Chan Yuek, however, was devoted to evocative imagery, reasonable plot development, and whether the content of the story aligned with the format of storytelling. Their perspectives were related, but never quite meshed together. After talking past each other for a while, they learned to leave the cinema quietly and to head to a restaurant for a peaceful dinner.

Did these distinctions create an unbridgeable gap between lovers? Ah Mak wasn't sure. That evening, at the restaurant, he searched within himself but found no response to her exasperation. He didn't feel entrenched enough to put up a defense; neither was he ready to nod along in appeasement. So he kept his head down as if focusing on his borscht. Each spoonful was as salty as the last. They finished the rest of their meal in silence. Later that night, she broke up with him over a text message.

A few days after Chan Yuek broke up with Ah Mak, he decided to join a peaceful demonstration downtown by himself. Born and raised in this orderly city, he believed the clashes in Tamar Park to be a one-off accident. He put on a plain T-shirt, jeans, and canvas shoes, as if he were heading out for a leisurely afternoon. He wasn't completely wrong. When he followed the crowd and marched down the wide, car-free boulevard, he admired the bustling businesses lining up on both sides: a dried seafood store steeped in a briny scent; a record shop playing '90s Cantopop on repeat; a newsstand owner dozing off at his post.

The crowd turned off the boulevard onto a bar district. Ah Mak was struck by how sleepy this place appeared in daylight. On the few occasions that he had come here before, he usually arrived after dinner to hang out with a few friends. In the cool evening air, they shared beers and watched the brilliantly lit streetlamps and neon signs near and far. In Ah Mak's tipsy vision, they looked like fireworks that had frozen in the sky—a postcard version of Hong Kong's dazzling nights.

Suddenly, loud noises disrupted Ah Mak's daydream. In the distance, a struggle broke out. A man was slammed to the ground and arrested. Tear gas seemed to come in all directions. Just a few feet from him, a canister landed on a tree and burst into a bright red-orange flare. As he ran away from the action, Ah Mak inhaled some tear gas. He felt his throat swelling and pressure on his windpipe. He began to choke. He thought he was going to trip and fall. He feared he would get arrested.

Two young volunteer medics caught up with him and grabbed his arms on either side. "Hold your breath! Keep running," they shouted. Leaning on their support, he kept going. His eyes were stung by the toxic gas and tears streamed down his face. He couldn't see. He couldn't breathe. But he kept running.

Soon, the medics helped him into an alley. They sprayed asthma medication into his mouth, rinsed his eyes, and wiped down his face. He was gasping for air. His throat was still burning with excruciating pain. He wanted to vomit. When he looked up, he saw that just steps away were the bars and nightclubs he used to frequent. One night a few months ago, after having too many drinks, Ah Mak stumbled through these streets, held upright by his friends. Just like that drunken night, he was given gulps of water but kept spitting it back out.

The repeated rinsing eventually relieved the tightness in his throat. Sitting on the ground, he realized he was filthy and doused with saline and unknown chemicals. They were only a few blocks away from the protest route, but Ah Mak felt like he had ducked into another world. The streets were brilliantly lit as usual. Around him, tourists and shoppers walked undisturbed. A music shop nearby was playing an old Eason Chan track. Everything was hazy and unreal. Suddenly, a thought washed over Ah Mak: He was no longer a casual viewer at a theater. He had become part of the action.

Within a few weeks, Ah Mak transformed into a radical frontline protester. Perhaps it was his long-simmering repressed emotions bursting into action. Gone was the novice Ah Mak who was clumsy with a gas mask. He now showed up at protests armed with iron pipes from the depot and dressed in full protective gear, finished with a motorcycle helmet and heat-resistant gloves.

When tear gas canisters came flying, he whipped out his water bottle and coated the canisters with water before they touched the ground. Once, a canister landed at his feet without exploding. He picked it up. The heat of the metal shell seared through the fabric of his glove. Without flinching, he grasped it and raised it overhead. His upper body slightly leaning backward, he took aim and hurled it with all his might at a cluster of riot police.

Truth be told, Ah Mak was surprised by his own swift transformation. Once he decided to give up on his ideal mode of resistance, "Peaceful, Rational, and Nonviolence," his actions escalated quickly and his tolerance for brutality was dialed up. For the rest of the summer, he spent his weekends on the street, where tensions ran high. He extinguished fires and took hits from rubber bullets; he smashed shop windows displaying pro-government signs and threw Molotov cocktails at police vehicles.

Having become a fearsome force of destruction, he also feared the possible consequence of being destroyed. Once, beanbag rounds struck his gas mask, and its plastic shattered against his face, lacerating his lips and cheeks. He tasted blood in his mouth. Running around and dodging the police all day, Ah Mak felt like a gecko, solemnly bearing its pain, ready to sever its tail for survival.

Sometimes he moved alone. Sometimes he had the company of peers he had met on the frontlines. They often stayed out late till the last train. At the end of exhausting days, his friends and he bid goodbye to one another on metro platforms. As the train doors closed, sometimes they shouted, "Don't die!"

When he arrived home, Ah Mak flicked on the light, often pricking his hand behind the cabinet. He took a shower and soaked his gear. Sleepless, he turned and tossed in bed, reading up on the day's new developments in group chat. Come Monday, he reported to work as usual.

Somehow, he grew even quieter. At the depot, he rarely interacted with anyone. It was as if there were two dueling versions of Ah Mak. The more frenzied and reckless he was on the streets, the more detached he was in his daily life. Perhaps the resolute resistance fighter in him was siphoning away all the vitality of Ah Mak, the ordinary guy.

He had changed in many ways, but he hadn't become the man Chan Yuek had wanted him to be. It was easier to throw a Molotov cocktail at a car than to confront a coworker at the depot. He could navigate escape routes on the street but not the complex questions Chan Yuek asked. He was still the man who couldn't work up the courage to meet Chan Yuek's gaze, the man who couldn't say anything when his mother started to move out. He couldn't live up to or defy their expectations.

And then, they left him.

After Ah Mak's mother returned to the mainland, she sent him money every month. But it was his aunt who watched over him. She occasionally stopped by with her daughter Panda, bringing him household essentials. As his aunt peeled fruit, she urged him to keep an open mind and not to blame his mom. Ah Mak was taken aback. He never blamed anyone. He knew people sometimes didn't have a choice.

When Chan Yuek and he used to watch movies together, she relished the thrill of Tarantino flicks, where villains paying for their own misdeeds was an inevitability. He preferred films like *A Brighter Summer Day* and *Three Billboards Outside Ebbing, Missouri*. In these stories, some innocent people died, and some equally innocent individuals were made to take the fall. This kind of pain and powerlessness.

Ah Mak had never imagined himself capable of such rage, such hatred in real life. And it wasn't a film that he could pause or walk away from. All around him, he saw injuries and antagonism snowballing. They spurred him to go on. The world was burning, but it barely scratched the structures of power.

Once upon a time, Ah Mak watched and rewatched *V for Vendetta* and read the original graphic novel. He had believed that most people were like the film's protagonist, Evey: They were timid conformists, but with the right ideas, they would readily transform into rebels. He had imagined that the picture of these men picking up V masks, fearlessly charging at the military army and riot police, was what resistance looked like. He had thought that ideas were bulletproof.

Now, he knew, ideas didn't even shield anyone from tear gas or rubber bullets. In a superhero movie like *V for Vendetta*, every plot twist hinged on the practically bulletproof protagonist, V. Without his special powers, the people would never be able to triumphantly break through the military line. Instead, they would be massacred.

Demoralized by these thoughts, Ah Mak tried to refocus on his task at hand. He began dismantling a display screen in the rickety metro car. The glass was cracked and warped. The faint yellow light made his head hurt. He set the screen down and stepped outside for a break.

His left arm still hurt. A week ago, he was at a rally when things turned violent. A beanbag round injured it so badly that he temporarily went numb. Before he could react, the police advanced toward him and other protesters. They began running, only to be ambushed by another squad of officers around the corner, cutting them off from the crowd and closing in on them. Batons swung wildly, Ah Mak remembered. Protesters were pinned down, the officers' knees were on their throats, and their faces were beaten, swollen and bloodied beyond recognition.

Ah Mak ducked into an alley and managed to escape. He wanted to notify his peers' families and friends, but they never exchanged their real names. Back at the apartment, he cleaned up and bandaged his forearm and hand. Ready to rest, he went to his room. Feeling his way in the dark, he groped around in the gap behind the cabinet. The wound limited his mobility, and he couldn't reach the switch. His palm, swollen from weeks of chemical exposure and burns, scraped against the rough wooden back of the cabinet.

In that instant, he remembered Chan Yuek's reproachful look. Ah Mak grabbed his backpack and retrieved an iron pipe. He had been carrying it to protests. It was scarred with marks from all that smashing and clashing. Suddenly fueled by boiling rage, he felt ready to destroy the cabinet that had overstayed its welcome. Its impractical nuisance was taunting him. Finally, he acknowledged it. He resented his mother for placing it there without even consulting him. In the darkness, he raised the pipe with his good hand.

But he couldn't do it. There was another way. He gripped the edges of the cabinet with both hands. He channeled all his remaining strength to pull the furniture away from the wall. In this lurching movement, the contents inside toppled and tumbled onto the floor. And just like that, a space opened up behind the cabinet. Ah Mak poked his head in to check. Although the switch was still obstructed, the gap had become wider and there was now enough space for a hand to slip in and out with ease.

He turned the light on. All sorts of items had slipped behind the cabinet over the years, hiding in the gap without anyone knowing: a lone sock, a CD, a few postcards. There was also a scattering of pink crystal beads, glinting softly in the dust.

Life During Wartime

Chan Yuek's left eye was bloodshot, streaking red like a fish gill. The pain was so intense she could hardly open it. She dug her knuckle into her eyelid and rubbed vigorously, as though trying to squeeze out a piece of red filament to alleviate the discomfort. The more she rubbed, the more it swelled. The man by her side grabbed her hand. In her hazy mind and muddled vision, she almost mistook him for Ah Mak. He had been like this too. He liked to stop her from rubbing her eyes.

She murmured, "It hurts. It hurts so much I can't see a thing."

The man tried to soothe her. "It'll get better. It'll get better. Something must have gotten in there." He squeezed drops into her eye and gently pressed a warm towel on it. Leaning in, he gently blew into the irritated eye.

After a long while, the overlapping images slowly merged back into a single figure. Her vision cleared up. As if coming to from a trance, she realized the man by her side wasn't Ah Mak.

Of medium height, the man had skin so fair that it looked like he had never been exposed to the sun.

"Ho Sam, I'm scared," she said.

Was she having that feeling again? When something happened so abruptly that she wasn't quite able to register it physically or emotionally. It was like what happened during one of her first hospital visits as a child. A nurse called out her name, distracting her at the very instant when a long, thin needle poked under the skin of her upper arm. Before she knew to react, the needle was already gone. A tiny trace of blood oozed out in its aftermath.

As they left the hospital, her mother praised her for being so brave. She was treated to a Happy Meal and a visit to a toy store. But perhaps Chan Yuek had known even then, it wasn't that she was fearless; in fact, being stunned could appear a lot like calmness.

That night, lying in bed clutching her new toy, she couldn't resist rolling up her sleeve to examine the site of the puncture. Observing the faint red dot and the slightly tingling numbness in her arm, she came to comprehend—an opening had been made on her body, although it was very small.

This feeling returned from time to time in the years to come. In junior high, when her first confession of love was rejected, she kept a smile on her face throughout the day. The disappointment only caught on after she got home when she buried her face in a blanket and sobbed uncontrollably. A few years later, she picked up part-time work as a waitress, and when a male customer stalked her after her shift, she confronted him and drove him off with a stern, commanding voice. When she was at last alone in a bathroom stall, the feeling finally sank in. She couldn't stop trembling and hugged herself tight.

Several years after breaking up with Ah Mak, she would still lose sleep as she revisited their last few months together, regretting her prideful naivete. Having taken impatience for courage, she hurt a man she had loved and forced their relationship to a premature end.

In the days after they had fled from Tamar Park, Chan Yuek was often visited by a dream. In it, she saw Ah Mak, standing straight and tall, with his back turned toward her. That afternoon, when they ran along the waterfront in the direction of the International Finance Centre mall, they briefly paused near the Ferris wheel when she began coughing uncontrollably. As she caught her breath, she looked across the street and saw the customers and staff in a store on the second floor. By the store window, they crammed together, shoulder to shoulder, palms and faces pressed against the glass, straining to get a look at her and the other fleeing rallygoers from their elevated point of view.

Once they reached the relative safety of the IFC mall, Ah Mak told her he had to go and asked if she wanted to head to the metro together. Chan Yuek shook her head. The camera strap around her neck was coated with ashy tear gas residue, digging into her skin. Her hands and feet had been injured. Ah Mak relieved the camera from her neck and bought some first-aid items from a nearby drug store. On the sidewalk, he rinsed her wounds before disinfecting and bandaging them. Then he washed the camera strap, too, and gently wiped her neck clean. Now that she seemed more comfortable, he suggested again, "Let's get out of here."

For reasons she couldn't explain, Chan Yuek didn't want to go yet. She wanted to stick around perhaps to see what was going to happen to the people at the rally who hadn't managed to get away as fast as they had.

She watched Ah Mak walking toward the metro entrance. His back was straight, and he looked so tall. Her eyes followed him, but he didn't glance back, not even when he paused at an intersection, waiting for the light to change. She kept her gaze fixed on his back until he grew smaller and smaller before vanishing altogether.

In fact, Ah Mak had told her in advance that he'd need to leave early that day for his grandfather's birthday banquet. They hadn't expected the peaceful assembly to turn into a violent crackdown. She also knew, when danger struck, he had taken her hand and took her to a safe place. He had taken care of her immediate needs and urged her to leave with him. She knew, deep down, that leaving now was the rational choice. Yet, sorrow overwhelmed her. She didn't want to just go home as if this were just the end of another date.

Ah Mak wasn't in the wrong, she realized. But on those nights when she woke up in tears, haunted by the horrific memories from Tamar Park—the thuds of rubber bullets, the shrills from the terrified people, the smell of tear gas, the oppressive heat, along with the image of Ah Mak disappearing into the crowd—Chan Yuek concluded that this tangled knot of pain could only mean one thing: Ah Mak didn't love her enough. No one had loved her in the way she wanted.

By mid-August, the broad avenues of the city were like freshly pressed shirts, straight and hot. On the roadsides, metal manhole covers bloated from the heat. Pedestrians avoided treading on them for long. Perhaps they feared doing so might trigger some long-repressed echoes from the underground. Silently, they walked, half a beat slower than usual, as though they were stepping on invisible tails of their own shadows. It was hard to tell where the restless fatigue of the heat ended, and where the stifling dreariness for the movement began.

One early afternoon, yet another protest descended into violence. This time, it was in Causeway Bay, on the north side of Hong Kong Island. The shopping district that rivaled Oxford Street in London was transformed into a battleground. As the police and protesters played cat and mouse, the street was covered by objects left behind by their panicking owners: helmets, umbrellas, masks, bloodied bandages, and single shoes. The police had set up roadblocks in the area to trap their counterparts in a cage. Chan Yuek searched for an escape route on her phone.

Since the movement began, people had started social media groups for this purpose. In these groups, volunteers acted as virtual sentries, uploading real-time reports on traffic and police presence across the city. Chan Yuek exchanged intel with a few other female protesters she had met that day and they decided to head east toward Quarry Bay, where it would be easier to slip through the police blockade.

To avoid the roadblocks, the women negotiated the back alleys. Chan Yuek knew these streets by heart. About twenty minutes later, as shops turned into residential buildings, they arrived at the edge of Quarry Bay. One woman in the group suggested that they change out of their black clothing and protest gear first. The group went into an empty public restroom, leaving one person keeping watch outside. Standing by the sink, the women wiped away the sweat and saline water from their skin before stripping off their outfits and changing into clean dresses. They quickly rinsed their goggles and helmets under the faucets to dull the stench of tear gas.

They went through this routine with efficiency that came from practice. When they were almost done, a tall woman broke the silence by asking if anyone had a spare hair tie. She had lost hers earlier in the commotion of the escape. Chan Yuek loosened her ponytail and handed the woman a purple scrunchie with an oversized bow on it. She had no qualms about giving it away. She had picked it up from Ho Sam's nightstand. It must have been left behind by another female companion of his.

Chan Yuek carefully arranged her canvas tote: Her black clothes and protest gear were stuffed at the bottom; sitting atop of them were a makeup pouch, a bottle of green tea, and some wet wipes—she was just an ordinary young woman out shopping. Having finished her transformation, she left the bathroom on her own and walked two blocks before catching a double-decker bus. On board, she scanned the streets for police roadblocks and didn't see any. Finally able to relax, she climbed the stairs to the upper deck and settled into a window seat where she drifted into drowsiness.

It was a little past four in the afternoon, but the sunlight was still intense. Chan Yuek looked through the window and was surprised to find everything on the street in a blur.

As the bus went by, the shop signs appeared to be wavering, and the pedestrians looked like ghostly silhouettes. The world seemed tipsy. Or was it her? Chan Yuek put her hand over each eye, and realized the cause wasn't any kind of drunkenness. Her left contact lens must have fallen out.

About an hour later, the bus pulled into the dimly lit terminus. She was still groggy. When she got up, the entire upper deck was empty. Outside, the dusk was thickening, and a chill crept in. She felt as if the blurriness surrounding her were a grayish-blue flood threatening to sweep the bus station and swallow her whole.

From time to time, she often found herself in an odd state of dejection.

Last week, she spent some time at Ho Sam's place. After they had sex, she wanted to linger under the covers to bask in the tenderness. But Ho Sam got up and jumped into the shower, leaving her alone in bed. Looking for distraction, she turned on the TV to watch local news live updates. In one district, tear gas was fired; in another, dozens of young people were arrested. In a close-up shot, she saw that some of them looked so young they were practically children. Their faces were bloodied. Before being hauled into police vans, they shouted out their own names to the camera.

Chan Yuek knew they did so for practical reasons. Typically, after a protester was arrested, her family or lawyer wouldn't be notified until several hours later. By then, physical beatings or a forced confession might have already taken place. By shouting out their names, the young arrestees were trying to get timely help. But Chan Yuek felt they were also making some kind of declaration to the world.

Ho Sam came back to bed after toweling himself off. He kissed her on the cheek. When she didn't respond, he sat by her side and watched the news. A few minutes later, he wanted to change the channel and reached for the remote control. Chan Yuek, still naked under the sheets, tightened her grip on it, refusing to surrender. She fixed her eyes on the TV screen, unaware of a faint red kiss mark on her shoulder blade.

Ho Sam sighed and stepped out to the living room to grade his students' homework. Chan Yuek breathed out in relief, curled up, and hugged her knees in the bedroom. Tears silently slid down her cheeks. She held back sobbing. She had seen Ho Sam's gentle side. When he inadvertently made her cry, he apologized endlessly, and fussed over her with sweetness, as if she were the flesh of his own palm.

But that wasn't what she wanted.

However lovingly Ho Sam and Ah Mak once cared for her, in moments she needed them, they got up and left. All she wanted was for someone to stick around, to hold her, to keep her company in witnessing these changes washing through the city, onsite or on TV. Was this too much to ask for?

Chan Yuek's thoughts kept returning to that day at Tamar Park when her life was on the cusp of being turned upside down. It was her first time attending a peaceful rally. At twenty, her ideas of large-scale social movements had been vague. Sure, she remembered the Umbrella Movement from five years ago, when protesters occupied the financial heart of the city for months to fight for direct elections, or "One person, one vote," as the slogan went. But she was still in junior high and barely kept up with the news. She recalled a well-known photo, which ended up gracing the covers of several foreign magazines and newspapers. It showed a man in a surgical mask, holding up a pair of umbrellas, standing alone amid smoky air.

At the park, as she ran with Ah Mak, she thought of that photo again. The man in the still had impressed her as heroic, but only on that day, she came to know the viciousness of the smoke in the picture. She too had been tear-gassed.

Chan Yuek and Ah Mak joined the crowd moving across the park toward the waterfront promenade. There was only a narrow path flanked by meticulously planted flower beds. Incredibly, everyone slowed down and lined up in single file, waiting for their turn to pass through. Like Chan Yuek, most of them hadn't known what chaos looked like, and were unfamiliar with this new world, where disorder was to become routine. Years of civic education had instilled such a deep sense of propriety in these citizens that even in a moment like this, their instinct was to remain courteous, yielding to one another and unwilling to trample the plants.

"Why are we lining up? The cops are coming after us, and you're worried about stepping on the plants? Worried about public decency?" a man shouted in frustration as he stomped straight through the flower bed. Instantly, he opened a floodgate. People ran on the flower beds, snapping leaves, stalks, and buds and trampling them on the ground. Mud stuck on their shoes. As they ran, some of them muttered, "Ugh, so dirty!"

Soon, the people at the very front reached the end of the pathway. There, they discovered that this section of the waterfront had been cordoned off with metal fencing. A food festival had been scheduled for that weekend, and rows of stalls had already been set up. Again, they hesitated. As they debated whether to take a detour, the riot police fired several rounds of tear gas in their direction. Canisters exploded near their feet. And just like that, no one spoke of decorum anymore. Fleeing for their lives, they scrambled up the fence, pushing and pulling one another. The metal spikes tore through the fabric of their clothes and even their flesh. Chan Yuek was slashed in her thigh and arm as well. There was blood on the ground. The tear gas smoke seemed to follow them. Behind her, someone screamed, "Anyone have an asthma inhaler? Help!" Ah Mak told her not to breathe in. He soaked a kerchief with bottled water and pressed it over her mouth and nose.

A frantic, graceless, uncivilized flight had taken place in this modern city. Chan Yuek had never experienced anything like it before. It was like a disaster movie. By the time they were at the IFC mall, her heart was still pounding. All she wanted was to cling tightly to Ah Mak, and for him to hold her just as tightly.

In the months and years to come, Chan Yuek had often wondered, if that afternoon, had she managed to tell Ah Mak, "Please don't go," would everything have turned out differently? Later, would he say it back to her instead of quietly accepting the breakup?

Chan Yuek stumbled away from the bus stop. The evening temperature had dropped. A wind grazed her light dress. She sneezed. She decided to text Ho Sam and asked if he had gone out today and whether he was safe. After a while, her phone buzzed.

"All good here. I stayed home prepping for a class. You?"

"Prepping for what class?" She knew he was a teaching assistant at a school but not much beyond that.

"The director asked me to try teaching a summer class for junior high students. I'm working on a lesson plan."

"Oh, I won't bother you then. Let's catch a movie tomorrow?"

"Sure. Afterward, you should swing by to see Hanta. He misses you." Attached was a photo of his gray British shorthair. The cat was sleeping soundly on its back, exposing its belly.

She suspected this exchange must have been just one of many chat windows simultaneously flashing on Ho Sam's phone. That very cat photo had probably been sent to multiple women, along with the same line: Hanta misses you. To borrow a term her friend had used, Ho Sam was one of those "gentlemanly fuckboys"—no lies, no games, just indiscriminating flirtation and naked desire for those who were looking for the same.

They had met on a dating app about two weeks ago. Chan Yuek was new to the app, and Ho Sam was the first guy she ended up meeting with. He appeared mature for being just two years out of university. Chan Yuek was pleased that the dating profile pictures didn't lie: He was just as good-looking in person, with fair skin, large eyes, and a dimple that appeared on his left cheek when he smiled.

When their eyes met, a cliché flashed in her mind: his eyes looked like a deep sea.

When they tried to have a conversation, however, it didn't go so well. Though Ho Sam was outgoing and talkative, they shared hardly any common interests. Both had backgrounds in the humanities, but for Ho Sam, it was just a way to make a living. He cared about social systems and believed that in this age of technology, big data determined everything. He liked to say, "Being earnest is a sure way to get hurt." Chan Yuek, on the other hand, like every other artsy youth, was drawn to film, photography, and literary and philosophical theories. She longed for romance and world peace. She was still new to dating, and didn't yet understand that making conversation on first dates was like a game of catch, requiring intuition to match each other's rhythm and pace. By design, all that drifting from one topic to another was never intended to expose one's sincere feelings.

Chan Yuek was grateful when Ho Sam brought up his cat, a near-universal topic of interest among women. When Chan Yuek heard his cat's name was Hanta, she asked if it was a tribute to the reclusive narrator in Bohumil Hrabal's *Too Loud a Solitude.*

"Bohumil Who?" Ho Sam seemed embarrassed. He told Chan Yuek he inherited the name when he adopted the cat. He asked if it was a trendy *Chicken Soup for the Soul* kind of self-help title. "Isn't the title a little pretentious?" he joked lightly. "Too loud, *and* too much solitude!" He clearly had no idea how to deal with this artsy type and was just about to give up when she pivoted the conversation to current politics. This was before the even more dire developments that conditioned people to keep their guard up with strangers. Her breakup with Ah Mak was still fresh, and she desperately needed someone to discuss politics with. She asked him what he thought about the movement.

Ho Sam told her that on July 1, he was right outside the Legislative Council. It had only been three weeks since the Tamar Park crackdown, but the world had changed. In this new reality, a march of two million people was no longer a rarity. Another line was crossed when a martyr emerged. As shown on TV, a man in a yellow raincoat jumped off a building, protesting the government with the cost of his life. As the anger and sadness grew thicker and thicker, many people began to feel that more radical means were justified. By July 1, the anniversary of the British transferring Hong Kong sovereignty to China, a group of protesters decided to occupy the legislature. Ho Sam was there, he said, watching the protesters storming in the building.

"That doesn't really answer my question," Chan Yuek said. The way he put it left his involvement open to interpretation. Was he a mere bystander? A sympathizer? She pressed him further.

"I believe that's enough of an answer for you." Ho Sam let on his irritation. During this first meeting, Chan Yuek didn't yet know this about him: He usually avoided people whom he considered rigid and self-serious, especially the "idealistic students coddled within the walls of academia." In that moment, he just told her bluntly that in the real world, people were bound to disagree about things. There were endless reasons for contradictions and conflicts. Such tensions were the source of fascination and torment, and they could drive the earnest to the brink of madness.

Chan Yuek hated it when people spoke in riddles. In the case of Ho Sam, she gathered then, there was a cruel pragmatism in his way of seeing the world. He was probably a fuckboy too calculative for love. After they parted ways that day, she blocked him. She thought of Ah Mak again. She had wanted to get to know him better. His reluctance to articulate his feelings really frustrated her. She could never quite figure out what he was thinking. But perhaps she preferred his silence to Ho Sam's riddles.

She met Ah Mak at a film screening. They were both still students and shared similar tastes—everything progressed naturally. Over time, however, their differences became clear. She loved to express herself, whereas Ah Mak was reserved; she insisted on absolute rights and wrongs, whereas Ah Mak was often more comfortable with being noncommittal. More importantly, she believed in a larger-than-life power in verbal communication. Her education had impressed upon her that there was no problem that couldn't be solved through dialogue; that there was no subject in the world that couldn't be talked through and made sense of. But she failed to see how this vehement insistence could make her come across as overbearing. Sometimes, it drove people away.

After Ah Mak started working last year, his job was like a speedboat, taking him away from Chan Yuek, who was still safely moored in the sheltered waters of university life. Their schedules were no longer in sync; his tolerance for ambiguity increasingly clashed with her need for moral clarity. She grew increasingly restless, diagnosing his lukewarm responses and indecisive behavior as symptoms of someone already absorbed by the system. A system she intended to resist. Chan Yuek took Ah Mak's entering working life as a warning: after graduation, she must never become a cog in the machine.

On July 1, Chan Yuek was, in fact, also a bystander of sorts. She had followed the new developments at the Legislative Council closely on the livestream. Many journalists broadcasted from inside the building. After about a hundred protesters breached the Legislative Council Complex, it became clear that they hadn't agreed on their next steps. Inside the legislative chamber, as they debated whether to stay or to retreat, a young man climbed onto a table, took off his mask, and called out to the crowd.

"We have nothing left to lose. There's nowhere to retreat. If we pull back now, the certain fate for the student and movement leaders is being arrested. Civil society will suffer a destruction that it won't be able to bounce back from for the next ten years," he said. "Please stay. Let's occupy this place together. The more people in this chamber, the safer we all are."

"We'll stay with you!" some fellow protesters echoed his sentiment.

Yet, within a few hours, protesters began to depart the building like a receding tide. The police had left the premises after announcing that they would return at midnight. People were free to leave by then and anyone who chose to stay would be arrested. A handful of diehards remained, determined to hold out to the very end, using their bodies as the last line of defense.

On the livestream, a reporter talked to a petite teenage girl who had returned when she was almost out of the building. She decided to come back, she explained, to plead with those who insisted on staying.

Upon hearing this, the reporter could barely hold back her tears. In a trembling voice, she asked the teenager, "Why didn't you just get yourself out?"

Gasping for breath from the running back and forth, she said that she was terrified for her own safety—she was only fifteen—but she was even more afraid of what might happen to those who stayed behind. "If we choose to stay, we stay together; if we decide to leave, we have to leave together."

By midnight, the remaining protesters were either persuaded to leave or were forcibly carried out by several fellow protesters. A clip of the livestream was quickly shared by hundreds of thousands of people. Everyone praised it as a heroic rescue. That night, no one was arrested in the building. Chan Yuek found the solidarity deeply moving, but the thought of their dispersing into their individual lives made her want to scream. In the next two years, many of them were arrested based on footage and other evidence from that day.

She turned off the livestream. Loneliness overwhelmed her. Again, she replayed the memory of Ah Mak disappearing into the crowd.

A few days later, she met Ah Mak for dinner, and the conversation turned to the turbulent episodes at Tamar Park and at the Legislative Council. As they spoke, Chan Yuek watched Ah Mak patiently buttering his bread. It agitated her. These days, she felt disgusted by all the people acting like everything was normal: strolling with ease or cracking jokes stupidly. Fueled by this smoldering anger toward this abnormally normal world, she couldn't help but launch into another interrogation about Ah Mak's choice of taking a sick day. Ah Mak offered no additional explanation for himself, nor did he put up a defense on behalf of the world. He just lowered his head and focused on his soup.

After returning home, Chan Yuek cried her heart out. She was so pained by her powerlessness, her disappointment, and her loneliness. How could he fail to see that? Just after midnight, she picked up her phone and texted him. "Let's end things."

She stayed awake and watched as her message went from unread to read: Ah Mak had received her request but offered no words in return. No objection or agreement, just tacit acceptance. What a surprise. Chan Yuek let out a dry laugh. Even in breaking up, she was performing a one-woman show.

Mass demonstrations continued every weekend. One evening in late July, a crowd marched through the Sheung Wan area on the west side of the island, passing by the Beijing liaison office compound. Dozens of people stopped and gathered around there. Over the years, Chan Yuek had heard jaded comments that this towering building in Sheung Wan was the real political center of Hong Kong. Seeing it up close for the first time, Chan Yuek found it rather ordinary-looking.

An automated retractable metal gate protected the entrance. Inside, a few police officers and helmeted security guards stood in a row, projecting a sense of authority and order. Outside, some protesters showed their middle fingers and traded salty insults. Several people banged on the metal gate with their umbrellas. A man apparently came prepared and hurled eggs at it. Right next to the gate, a steel plaque read "Liaison Office of the Central People's Government in the Hong Kong Special Administrative Region." A spotlight shone on the plaque and illuminated the onslaught of eggs, whose yolks trickled down the metal surface.

Not far from the entrance, a teenager moved a metal barricade and leaned it against the wall. Adjusting the angle, he set up a makeshift ladder and began climbing it. Within two steps, the barricade was already teetering. It didn't have a stable footing. Chan Yuek and another protester simultaneously rushed over to steady the barricade, each bracing one side of it. The teenager kept going and took out a can of spray paint. Chan Yuek glanced at her collaborator. He wore black and was covered from head to toe. A black bandanna masked most of his face, exposing only a pair of dark, deep-looking eyes.

She thought of Ho Sam.

A minute later, the teenager finished his graffiti and climbed down to the ground. She let go of the barricade and looked up. A few crooked characters had been scrawled on the wall. "It was you who taught us that peaceful protest is useless." Chan Yuek's collaborator had already walked away.

Chan Yuek felt tired. She reached into her bag and fished out her phone. It was only six p.m. She clicked on the dating app and scrolled all the way to the chat at the bottom. She unblocked Ho Sam and asked what he was up to. Ho Sam replied quickly. To her relief, he didn't mock her for taking the initiative, nor did he ask where she'd been all this time. He acted like this was just a check-in from an old friend: "I'm in Wan Chai. You?"

"I'm nearby but heading home soon."

"Stay safe. Let me know when you get home," he wrote. Perhaps it was her exhaustion, but Chan Yuek wanted to cry. She wanted to look into the depths of his eyes again.

The following evening, Chan Yuek arrived at Ho Sam's place. She wore a floral dress and had put on strawberry-flavored lip gloss.

At first, they sat on the sofa in silence. Luckily, the cat came and curled up in her lap, giving her something other than Ho Sam's handsome face to focus on. As if suddenly remembering its existence, Ho Sam pointed at a sound system installed in the living room. His father had bought it for vinyl records. When he moved to the US and left it behind, Ho Sam appropriated it to listen to American and British rock bands. Chan Yuek didn't know much about that kind of music. She listened to indie bands from Hong Kong and Taiwan. A few from the mainland weren't bad, either.

He got up and put on a CD for her. *Fear of Music* by Talking Heads. It was a blend of late '70s and early '80s new wave with a touch of post-punk, he explained as he returned to the sofa. She didn't know the band or any of these terms. She didn't know how to talk about music. She started to wonder why she had come here. Hanta leapt off her lap, as if sensing her nervousness.

Then the music started playing. It was upbeat and a little trippy. After two songs, she became more relaxed. She gently moved her legs to the rhythm. Ho Sam asked, "Pretty great, right?"

"This is fun," she said, smiling and finally meeting his eyes. Ho Sam leaned in to kiss her. Chan Yuek didn't resist. She sank into the sofa, tugging at his belt as he hovered over her, warm breath against her neck. He deftly unbuttoned her dress. In the middle of making out, Ho Sam paused for a second. The track playing now was his favorite, he said. It was called "Life During Wartime."

Chan Yuek didn't think much of the title. She felt lightheaded, as if her brain were starved for oxygen. She was overtaken by an urge to hold Ho Sam and kiss him hard. She pulled his head down toward her, pressing his lips against hers. The bright, bouncy melody reverberated throughout the living room and receded into the background. Chan Yuek felt like she had become a character in a foreign film who danced while high on weed.

Later, when she looked up the song and listened to it again, she heard the lyrics for the first time.

No time for dancing, or lovey-dovey
I ain't got time for that now

Following that night, an ambiguous relationship developed between them. He said he liked her. She didn't know if she believed him. She kept going to his place and kept sleeping with him. He watched movies with her—not the art films she preferred, but the blockbusters playing in every theater. Strangely, over time, she found them quite enjoyable too.

The day after Chan Yuek texted Ho Sam from the bus stop, they watched one of those blockbusters on offer at a cinema near Ho Sam's place. During the movie, Chan Yuek's left eye grew itchy. She couldn't help rubbing it hard. By the time the movie ended, it was bloodshot. Ho Sam grabbed her hands to stop her from rubbing, and tried to soothe her. Chan Yuek was convinced it was the toxic residue from being tear-gassed the previous afternoon. Was she going to lose her vision? Ho Sam persuaded her to let it be for now and promised to take her to the hospital if it didn't resolve on its own.

Later that night, gradually, her vision became clear again. Relieved, she embraced Ho Sam and felt an object slip from her left eye. She caught it in midair. It was the contact lens she thought she had lost the day before. It was shriveled, all dried out.

It lay in her palm, like a stranded tiny boat.

Sai Mui, Baby Girl

Sai Mui hated being called "Sai Mui," *baby girl*. It made it seem like she was smaller than everyone else. But her big sister, Panda, had bounced into the world almost ten years before her. Panda was cute and outgoing, the kind of kid people couldn't resist. All the grown-ups in the family liked calling Panda "Ah Mui," *little girl*, gifting her red envelopes stuffed with money and pinching her cheeks. After so many years, the nickname stuck. So, when Panda's baby sister arrived in this world, there was no choice but to call her by the further diminutive, "Sai Mui."

Panda didn't care for such names. As the family had lunch one day, she said, "I'm already in my twenties, about to graduate from university, and people are still calling me 'Mui' this and 'Mui' that. They don't seem to see anything wrong with it, but I find it mortifying." Then, she turned to Sai Mui. "You better step up and advance from 'Sai Mui' to 'Ah Mui' so I can be spared my suffering."

Panda had barely finished speaking when Sai Mui was caught off guard by a tiny bone from the mackerel in her mouth. It was no longer than a bit of stubble, jabbed upright between her gum and teeth. She tried picking at it with her fingers, but that was of no use. Mom scolded her for having no manners and told her to finish what she was doing in the bathroom. In front of the mirror, Sai Mui pulled back her lips and finally plucked out the thin, stubborn fragment with two fingers. Her gum was slightly swollen.

Sai Mui knew the ache from a hard-to-reach fish bone stuck in her gum. Yet, she didn't know, in life, there were many tiny sharp pains just like this barely visible wound in her mouth. She was still too young to recognize the pattern of her emotions.

Sai Mui turned twelve this year and just started junior high. Sometimes, she told lies. One day during recess, for example, she was trying to slip past a group of gossiping boys on her way to the bathroom, and one of them suddenly shouted, "Hung Sze Ling—are you yellow or blue?" Yellow meant support for the protesters, and blue signified pro-police. Her family name, Hung, unfortunately, sounded like "red." The boys were teasing her again, "Hung Sze Ling isn't yellow or blue—she's *red!* Red Sze Ling! Red Sze Ling!" They burst into laughter.

Panda had told her that the first month of junior high was crucial, especially for Sai Mui, whose grades weren't great and therefore had been placed in an average school in the district.

Most of her classmates were either new immigrants or "anchor babies," products of birth tourism, and they were fluent in Mandarin, which they preferred to the local tongue of Cantonese. Sai Mui treaded carefully, aware that the popular topics in the classroom changed faster than seasonal trends in a fashion boutique. Fail to keep up, and you'd end up like last season's leftovers, lonely and forgotten in some corner.

Before the new school year, she had prepared a few conversation starters about mainland influencers and variety shows. But come September, the wind had shifted, and the talk of the classroom was centered on local news in Hong Kong: fire magic (Molotov cocktails), TG (tear gas), and the other TG (Telegram).

"Are you yellow or blue?" "Deep yellow or pale yellow?" At the start of the school year, these questions had become a kind of secret code among new classmates, a way of saying hello that sounded as casual as asking which sports team someone cheered for or which celebrity they were a fan of.

Some classmates had taken part in the protests and instantly became the center of attention in class, going on and on about everything they'd seen and heard. One boy even smuggled a gas mask into school. It was a gray, fan-shaped plastic cover with spongy pieces tucked on either side, like an oversized bra insert. Sai Mui didn't get too caught up in the hype. It was just like the time someone brought in limited-edition merch from a celebrity or a game, or when everyone got into Ghost's Saliva, a novel kind of glittery slime. That jellylike goop was super satisfying to squish. She bought a cup and brought it home, only to receive a side-eye from her big sister. The next day, she gave it away to her desk mate, Mei Yan.

Just because Sai Mui had learned to occasionally opt out of the fads didn't mean she became immune to teasing. When the boys aimed their stupid jokes at her, Sai Mui felt like a target in a shooting game with an apple balanced on her head. She told the boys that her family name had nothing to do with colors or her politics, and that she had always been a supporter of the movement. It didn't help. She found herself caught in the eternal paradox: Her earnest explanation only became fodder for another round of teasing. "You reacted like this because you were found out!" a boy said. Sai Mui suspected that she could never prove herself and that her classmates were looking at her differently now.

Sai Mui knew, the moment the boys talked to her, she was no longer just a girl on her way to the bathroom, but a defendant in a courtroom drama who had to step up to the witness stand for cross-examination. She needed to choose her words carefully, or else the classroom jury might hand down the dreaded verdict: social death. And she still had years ahead of her at the school. Whatever she was going to say had to be overwhelmingly convincing. She needed to force those boys who looked down on her to shut up.

"In fact, I've been to a protest," Sai Mui found herself saying.

It sounded like a plain statement, but the slight lift in her voice gave away a hint of pride. The moment the words slipped out, Sai

Mui felt a twinge of regret. Was that a lie? She hadn't exactly *participated* in a protest, but one weekend, she was out with Panda and Mom, and they did run into a group of demonstrators marching down the middle of the main road, shouting slogans. She saw that many people held up homemade banners and flags. When the wind blew, the signs fluttered as if part of a fire dragon dance at the Mid-Autumn Festival. Mom gripped her hand tightly as the densely packed tide of people surged past them. She wasn't afraid. It felt like a festive circus of people dressed in black had rolled into the city.

As soon as Sai Mui made this announcement, sure enough, a few of the girls gasped. One of the boys shot back, "For real? Did you see anyone throw fire magic? Did you get hit by TG? Did you run into any cops?"

The questions came at her as if a full mailbox was flung open in her face, everything spilling out at once. Before she had time to think, her vanity ballooned. Against her better judgment, she said, "Yeah, and I was pretty close to the action. Anything you wanna know, just ask!"

Sai Mui had a lot on her mind lately. For one, her sister, Panda, hadn't been home in more than two months. For a while, she had appreciated the luxury of having the room all to herself. But now, thanks to that impulsive, foolish lie, she became responsible for the bloodthirsty curiosity of her classmates. She had to find a chance to speak with her sister to gather details from the front lines. Of course, she would also need to come up with another lie to avoid disclosing the first to Panda.

The other issue that had weighed on her had to do with Mei Yan, her good friend since elementary school. Recently, Mei Yan tearfully complained that Sai Mui didn't understand her. That day during break, as soon as Mei Yan opened her lunch box, she let out a loud cry and ran off to the bathroom. Sai Mui rushed after her, asking what was wrong. Was the food not to her liking? Mei Yan's lunch was always homemade, while Sai Mui used the school meal plan. The menu of the day was a fish fillet sandwich and fries. Even though this was one of Sai Mui's most anticipated combos, if it could stop Mei Yan's tears, Sai Mui would trade lunch with her in a heartbeat.

Sai Mui caught up with Mei Yan in an empty stairway. Mei Yan said it had been a few rough months. Her parents believed the movement was undermining the rule of law; meanwhile, her boyfriend, who was already in high school, volunteered to be a medic during protests. She felt torn. Before Sai Mui could marvel at how grown-up Mei Yan's problem sounded, she went on about the tension at home. Her mom used to pack freshly cooked foods, such as sunny-side-up eggs and stir-fried choy sum greens, and deliver the bento box to school at noon. But today, her lunch box contained hastily reheated leftovers that had been sitting in the fridge for days. She took a bite of the soy sauce chicken and found it was still cold inside!

Mei Yan sobbed, "Mom doesn't love me anymore. She's treating me like this." Sai Mui took Mei Yan's hand and said, "No, no, don't think like that. I'm sure your mom still loves you." Mei Yan slipped from Sai Mui's grasp and glanced at her coldly. "Forget it. What would you know? Your whole family is yellow. You're all on the same side, supporting the protests. Must be nice."

Sai Mui didn't know how to respond to this unexpected accusation. Also, was the reality that nice? She recalled the weekend when Panda left home. Mom was out at a beauty appointment, and Sai Mui watched Panda packing her things in their room.

"So what if Mom said she was yellow? Who can't make an empty statement?" Panda was sitting on her overstuffed suitcase, struggling to zip it shut, but there were too many things crammed inside. "It's messed up when you can't follow up with actions. Mom hasn't even been to a protest." Sai Mui retreated and left the room, unable to make sense of what was happening.

Everything had been perfectly fine just that morning. They all joined her uncle's family for a dim sum breakfast. At the restaurant, a TV was playing news footage from a protest. Uncle was chewing on a har gow dumpling, speaking with his mouth full, cursing the police crackdowns. "Why are there so few adults showing up for these kids?" Wiping his mouth, he continued, "Our generation really had it easy, like swiping a credit card without thinking about payments. And now we are letting the young people take on our debt."

Aunt stopped eating, and her eyes grew red. Mom handed her a tissue, urging her to tune out a little bit to save herself some heartbreak. "Those cops have no conscience," Mom said, before letting out a sigh. "It's not news that the Communist Party is cruel. Now the kids are getting hurt—it's just too sad. But that's what the central government is like. You fight them, you can't win."

Sai Mui eyed a sesame ball. Worried it might be too greasy, she elbowed Panda, hinting at splitting it. Panda either didn't notice or didn't bother to respond. The network was replaying the news. The broadcaster's tone and perspective clearly leaned toward the establishment. Uncle was fuming and asked the manager to change the channel. "Why are they still airing this kind of channel at a time like this? We'll punish them with our wallets and stop coming here. Worst case, we'll switch to that place on the seventh floor." Mom put on a smile, allowing the flustered manager to slip away, and refilled Uncle's tea. "If you don't like it, don't watch it. No point in getting so worked up—why make yourself suffer?" she asked. "And the lotus-seed paste here is so well done. Pops loves its fragrance. We're here to eat as a family. Let's keep politics off the table."

Mom picked up her chopsticks and split a lotus-seed paste bun in half, placing a piece in Grandpa's bowl. "Pops, we have to watch your blood sugar. This is all you can have." While Mom was tending to Grandpa, Sai Mui dropped the unwanted half of her sesame ball into Mom's bowl. Deep in her own world of dim sum calculations, Sai Mui was oblivious to how tightly Panda pursed her lips.

Things got a little weird at breakfast, but that didn't bother Sai

Mui. The real highlight was going to happen afterward. Mom had promised to take Sai Mui shopping for back-to-school supplies, and she wanted a Snoopy notebook. Grown women flaunted their handbags; kids flaunted their stationery. That, too, was a kind of status symbol.

After the bill was settled, Mom got a phone call from her beautician, Auntie Ning. They had originally scheduled a facial treatment for the day before this dim sum gathering, but the spa had to cancel the appointment after protests shut down the trains and buses. Mom was a regular at Auntie Ning's spa in the Sheung Wan neighborhood, on the west side of Hong Kong Island. She trusted no one but Auntie Ning, who was quick and thorough with deep cleansing and extractions of acne and blackheads.

Mom turned to Panda. "The protest is in Kowloon today, right? Since nothing's happening on Hong Kong Island, Auntie Ning said she can take me right away." Then she turned to Sai Mui, "Is it okay for Ah Mui to take you shopping instead? Sorry, Sai Mui." She gave Sai Mui a hug and kissed her on the forehead. Slipping a large banknote into Panda's hand, Mom whispered in her ear, "Be careful when you go out this afternoon. Don't carry anything on you. As they say, the shot hits the bird that pokes its head out. Don't try to be a hero. If you see the cops coming, turn around and run. They aren't going to be humane. Don't worry about the others. Keep yourself safe first." Sai Mui tried to peek at the amount on the banknote, but as she leaned in, she ended up hearing every word. Panda gripped the money tight and didn't offer any response.

Mom didn't notice anything as she dashed out. "See you at dinner. Let me know what you feel like, and I'll make a reservation. *Mwah!*"

A quiet apartment awaited Mom that evening. Panda had packed two large suitcases and moved into her university dorm full-time. From that day on, through the entire summer and even after school started again, she never came back.

Lately, Sai Mui started to feel that Mom had changed.

Growing up, she was used to Mom's indiscriminate bright smile. She was always cheerful and personable, and repeated that saying, "A smiley face dissuades an angry fist." Panda must have inherited that temperament, but not Sai Mui. In school, when she learned to use similes, she had an exercise that read "The warm sun is like . . . ?" She filled in: "Mom." The teacher marked it wrong with a big red X and told her to correct it. But Sai Mui thought it was spot-on.

After Panda left, Mom still put on a smile, but she looked lost. Every night, Sai Mui and Mom sat together and watched TV. Whenever there were footsteps in the hallway, Mom immediately turned to stare at the front door, as if her gaze could penetrate a long distance and reach a faraway place. As if she could see her daughter's key slide into the lock. Each time, the footsteps faded, and Mom shifted her focus back to the screen.

When Mom went grocery shopping, she always got excited when she found imported fancy strawberries at the store. As soon as she returned home, she liked to soak them clean before sitting down at the table and using a toothpick to gently remove the seeds dotted across the crimson skin of each strawberry.

As much as Sai Mui had seen Mom doing this, she still found the sight surreal.

Panda had loved strawberries since she was little, but at some point, she developed a fear of clustered patterns: beehives, lotus-seed pods, pine cones—eventually, even the tiny sesame-like seeds on a strawberry's surface bothered her. It was a heavy blow for Panda, since they were her favorite fruit. And so, Mom came up with a solution: seedless strawberries.

She began perfecting this meticulous craft that was as delicate and precise as embroidery or carving. Strawberry flesh was tender, easy to become bruised or mushy. Press too hard, and the whole fruit would be smashed. Move too slowly, and the juices would ooze under prolonged pressure.

No one knew how their mom had honed her skill for this peculiar and demanding task, but from then on, Panda ate pristine and seedless strawberries. And in those moments, even Panda, usually so bold and brisk, would grow uncharacteristically tender and say, "It's delicious! Thank you for the effort, Mom!"

These days, Panda wasn't around, but Mom kept up with it and froze the seedless strawberries. "What if Ah Mui comes back wanting some strawberries, and finds none? She might get upset and run off again!" Mom said, only half joking.

"It's best to stock up," she murmured. "Maybe if she can eat them to her heart's content, she'll forget what has been bothering her, and won't leave."

Sometimes, Sai Mui caught Mom sitting at Panda's desk letting out a quiet sigh. Much of the desk had been cleared, leaving only a few toppled tubes of lip gloss and a bottle of toner. Usually, Panda worked a part-time job on weekends and got up before Sai Mui. Woken by the commotion, Sai Mui watched her older sister propping open one eye with two fingers, pinching a thin lens and pressing it right onto her eyeball. In the mirror's reflection, Panda's pupils looked large and sparkling like an adolescent character from shōjo manga. Spooked by the idea of placing a foreign object onto her eyeball, Sai Mui often yanked the blanket over her head. Only someone as brilliant and confident as Panda could pull that off.

Sai Mui knew that it was impossible for Mom to evenly divide her love between two daughters. And Panda was so smart, so independent, and so likable. In contrast, Sai Mui felt so ordinary. Her grades were average, everything about her was average.

Everyone always treated her like a little kid, while her extraordinary first-born sister always received preferential treatment, including with their sleeping arrangement: Panda occupied the lower bunk, and Sai Mui had to climb up to the top every night.

Sometimes, when she looked up from her bunk at the tiny bugs swirling around the light bulb, she thought of herself. Circling round and round Mom like those annoying insects around the bulb.

Panda used to annoy her to death. She had wished that one day her older sister would disappear and take with her the loud phone calls with her friends, the lamp she never turned off late into the night, and the constant teasing that made Sai Mui out to be a bratty little kid. Then maybe, just maybe, everyone would see that Sai Mui was becoming a proper grown-up. If one day her sister left for good, Sai Mui used to imagine, she would be able to claim the lower bunk and monopolize all the care and love from Mom.

As much as Sai Mui indulged in such fantasies, part of her also knew—even though she didn't want to acknowledge it—that the absence of Panda might mean even more loneliness instead of more closeness with Mom or Dad. Just like on Grandpa's seventieth birthday back in mid-June.

Weeks ahead of the occasion, Mom started informing everyone that their presence at the birthday banquet was required. This included the family members who didn't live on Hong Kong Island: Great-uncle from Tsing Lung Tau, Great-aunt from Ap Lei Chau, even Mom's younger sister who had married off to the mainland. Mom also made sure that cousin Ah Mak, who was always a little distant, understood the mandatory nature of the event.

When Sai Mui got out of school that day, Dad picked her up and drove to the restaurant. It was quiet in the car, and he turned on the radio. "The Legislative Council had originally scheduled to resume the second reading of the Anti-Extradition Law Amendment Bill Movement today. . . . Around four p.m., police near Tim Mei Avenue by the Legislative Council deployed tear gas. . . ." Dad abruptly switched the channel to a station playing soft, lilting classical music. Meanwhile, Sai Mui stared blankly out the window at the light rain streaking across the glass, fine and dense as animal fur. When traffic crawled to a halt, the rain seemed to grow heavier, drops pounding at the windows. Sai Mui imagined the car to be a snail with a cracked shell dragging its body forward, leaving a murky trail behind it.

She wanted to ask Dad, why did he change the station? But as if to preempt her question, he started talking about the orchestral music on the radio, then asked how her violin lessons were going. Sai Mui replied vaguely. She didn't feel like reminding Dad that she only tried violin back in second grade, and she had since switched to trumpet. What difference did it make to him? She knew he wasn't really paying attention.

In his question, "violin" could've just as easily been replaced with "Chinese classic dictation," "math exam," "bok choy," or "radishes." It was as random as the kind of conversations that took place when Sai Mui stood in a long line outside the girls' bathroom. If standing next to her was a classmate whom she didn't know very well, it was common courtesy for one of them to initiate small talk to kill the awkward silence. It was best to ask a question, so the other person could respond to it and come up with a new one, a kind of polite duty, passed back and forth until it was their turn to get into the bathroom.

Sai Mui had plenty of opportunities to practice this. But why did this conversation with Dad remind her of the bathroom line? Admittedly, she wasn't particularly close with Dad. Thanks to his work shifts, she barely saw him. Before she left for school, she sometimes caught a glimpse of him sleeping through the crack of the master bedroom door. But did that explain everything? Was she just like some classmate he happened to run into while waiting in line for the bathroom?

Thinking this way, she didn't care to ask why Dad changed the channel anymore. What difference did it make? She already learned what was going on near Tamar Park that afternoon from classmates who secretly used cell phones.

Sai Mui was exhausted from thinking about these difficult questions. She looked outside the window. The sky was dusty gray. Was it because of the rain or the smoke from the tear gas mentioned in the news?

That night, more than thirty guests filled three large round tables. Mom wore a sequined dress. She held on to Grandpa's arm and greeted relatives and friends. She gifted him a golden "peach of longevity," which made him so happy that he kept grinning with his mouth gaped open like a shirt missing a button. Sai Mui chewed on her yi mein egg noodle and surveyed the banquet hall. The fabric-padded red walls were decorated with square banners with the character "longevity" on them. The lazy Susan reflected glints of gold from the spoons and chopstick rests. Mom's dress shimmered as she twirled between tables. Sai Mui wanted to ask Panda, wasn't Mom just like a radiant sun?

Sai Mui turned her head, then remembered Panda hadn't come.

Mom stopped by several times to ask if Ah Mui had arrived yet. Each time, Sai Mui shook her head. She had tried calling Panda, but it went unanswered. Mom soldiered on with her smile. She patted Sai Mui on the head, telling her not to be bothered by it. But Sai Mui could see Mom's disappointment from the crease between her brows. Her usually quiet cousin Ah Mak was here. He seemed a little awkward with his mother. Grandpa's children and grandchildren were seated at a twelve-seat round table, and only one seat remained empty. In front of it, a burgundy napkin sat atop a round porcelain plate. Sai Mui had an odd feeling of emptiness. It was like when she lost her final baby tooth last year. She felt the hollow space in her upper mouth whenever her tongue happened to brush against the absent tooth.

After Panda moved out, Mom obsessively brainstormed ideas to persuade her to come back. When she recalled Panda's complaint about her failing to support the movement with her own actions, she figured she should do something about that.

She scoured online forums for businesses that openly backed the movement. With Sai Mui in tow, she visited them one by one: coffee shops, home-goods retailers, stationery stores, fashion boutiques. . . . Sai Mui didn't understand—how did buying a pair of shiny leather shoes or enjoying a delicate slice of cake in air-conditioned comfort prove anyone's commitment to the cause?

"This is contributing to what they call a 'yellow economic circle.' Without a democracy or votes that count, we can still speak with our wallets. As the saying goes, 'Brothers climb mountains together, and they each have different things to offer.' Some people lead the protests with physical effort; others stay back and offer financial support. Look at us—just a woman and a kid. What would we be doing on the front lines? But by supporting these like-minded businesses through our spending, they can use the profits to help those young people on the streets. Word is, some business owners even hire protesters who'd been arrested to help them make a living." Sai Mui thought Mom's explanation seemed logical.

A week before school started, Mom took Sai Mui to another "yellow" establishment. The restaurant was pretty out of the way. They were on a bus for a long time before transferring to a minibus. When they got off the minibus, they found themselves on a dirt road flanked by a field of weeds. Mom double-checked their location via Google Maps to make sure they'd gotten off at the right stop. The app guided them through a residential area with laundry lines, and they finally arrived at a narrow alley.

Even from a distance, they saw the swarm of people lining up on the sidewalk, crowded together like a beehive, packed so tightly that pedestrians had to step into the traffic to get around them. A couple snapped photos of the black bauhinia and bleeding eyeball stickers on the window, symbols of resistance against the government. Near the entrance, there were kids writing messages on a wall covered in sticky notes.

Sai Mui knew this was called a Lennon Wall. She had helped Panda reorganize one of these in the tunnel near their building. They meticulously glued the curled corners of posters back to the wall.

At first, they didn't know what they were doing. They had picked up a few glue pens from a stationery shop, which turned out to be a hassle. The pens ran dry after just a couple uses. Panda and Sai Mui had to shake the pens so vigorously that Sai Mui felt her wrists were about to pop out of their sockets. Sometimes, the pressure was off, and the glue came out unevenly, clumping in one spot. They had to smear it around with their fingers, which became grossly sticky.

Later, they ran into some pros in the tunnel who taught them to buy canned glue, thin it with water to make a paste, then apply it with a paintbrush, like painting a wall. That was a game changer. It produced twice the result with half the effort. Sai Mui was intrigued by this novel technique and loved maneuvering the brush. She liked watching the thin white liquid glide along the grid-patterned grooves of the tunnel wall, pooling into a single stream before dripping onto the ground, like a bathroom towel that hadn't been wrung dry.

At the popular "yellow" restaurant, a waitress seated Mom and

Sai Mui in a booth. "Good thing we made a reservation, or we'd be waiting till the end of time," Mom said cheerfully. "We've got to support the 'yellow economic circle.' Comrades helping comrades! I'm done eating at those pro-government chains. I used to think that at my age, habits are the hardest thing to break, but how would I know if I didn't try? Here I am supporting small businesses every day, and it doesn't cost me any extra. It's all about determination, really."

Hearing the word "determination," Sai Mui thought it was a good thing her sister wasn't here today. Otherwise, she'd probably have grabbed her bag and stormed off again, just like she did last time outside the beauty salon.

They ordered risotto and a beef burger. The kitchen was clearly overwhelmed by the number of customers. Nearly half an hour passed before their food arrived. During this time, Mom chattered away like a firing cannon about a group chat she'd recently joined where members exchanged tips on supporting "yellow" businesses. "Turns out even hair salons are divided into yellow or blue—who knew? Hey, what do you think—is Auntie Ning yellow or blue? Actually, never mind. I don't care what her politics are. It's hard enough to find someone with her skills. But some people are saying the information in the group chat isn't reliable anymore. I heard that infiltrators are sneaking in."

Even though her stomach was growling with hunger, Sai Mui did her best to keep smiling through all this long-winded talk, nodding attentively and chiming in now and then with "Oh, I see!"

"Huh, is that so?" and "*Mm-hmmm*, got it." She hoped Mom would pat her on the head and call her a thoughtful kid. Maybe she would even promise to blow-dry her hair after her shower tonight.

Sai Mui pictured herself sitting at Mom's vanity, watching in the mirror as Mom stood behind her. Holding the blow-dryer in one hand and a comb in another, Mom's movements were soft and gentle. A faint rose scent wafted from her hair, the smell of Mom's shampoo. Then she met Sai Mui's gaze in the mirror and said, "We really are mother and daughter. Look how much you resemble me." This idea had been etched into her mind ever since she spent the night at Mei Yan's place last year and saw Mei Yan's mom blow-drying her daughter's hair.

When their food arrived, Mom took out her phone, fussed over the table setting, and adjusted the camera angle. She brushed aside Sai Mui's hands to keep them out of the frame. Then, as if in a frenzy, she snapped a series of photos with her made-in-China smartphone. Sai Mui heard *click click* one after another and lost count. This was yet another of her sister's complaints about their mom. "She doesn't even know how to put her phone on silent. Always blasting videos on the bus or out on the street. I can't take it anymore," Sai Mui recalled Panda saying.

Sai Mui cut her burger into small pieces and took a bite. The patty was thin and dry, crumbling in her mouth. It felt like she was chewing tissue. The cheese slice was still cold, and the lettuce was limp. She thought of the American-style restaurant her sister had taken her to a month ago, down in the basement of New Town

Plaza. That burger had been tender and juicy, the cheese melted perfectly on top of the patty, just the right amount of savory fat. As soon as she caught herself in this thought, Sai Mui interrupted the memory and told herself this place was good too. A "yellow" restaurant was always superior to a fast-food chain.

Mom's risotto didn't seem any better. The rice was all mushy, as if it was oversoaked with water, and the sauce looked pathetically thin, reminding Sai Mui a little of the white glue she and her sister used for Lennon Wall posters. "We got fooled. How can people form such a long line for food this bad? It's nonsense." Setting down her spoon, Mom dabbed her mouth with a napkin. "I'm still all for supporting a business with a conscience, but when Ah Mui comes back, we won't take her here."

She was still like this, thinking that Panda would come back, as if everything would go back to normal, as if the world would soon return to the way it used to be.

A few days ago, Panda took Sai Mui out for afternoon tea. It wasn't the first time the sisters met up alone. Since moving out, Panda sometimes realized that she had left something at home. Not wanting to see her parents, she often asked Sai Mui to play messenger. In return, she treated her little sister to a meal. At the tea parlor, the sisters' chat inevitably turned to Mom. "She has always believed that everything is perfectly fine. Sure, it's fine for her. She lives in a comfortable bubble, completely sealed off from the outside world. Why would she care if anyone else lives or dies?" Panda spoke coldly as a waitress served her an iced lemon tea.

"That's because Mommy's an optimist." Sai Mui jumped to Mom's defense. "And isn't it nice for the whole family to be together? Please come back. She's been talking about buying your favorite egg-custard mooncakes for the Mid-Autumn Festival next month," Sai Mui pleaded.

"I'm not going back. And tell her to stop sending Ah Mak to try to talk me into it. The same goes for you. It's a waste of time."

As if to change the subject, Sai Mui handed her sister a plastic bag. Panda rummaged through it to make sure everything she requested was in there. Then she pulled out a Snoopy pencil case. "Why did you bring this? I told you I don't want it."

Sai Mui had always loved Snoopy. A few years ago, she spotted a Snoopy pencil case at a store and wanted it badly. Panda glanced at it and remarked, "Oh, it *is* nice-looking." Mom saw that both sisters liked it and said that if they placed into the top ten on their next exams, she would buy one for each of them. Sai Mui nodded enthusiastically, sealing the deal. Panda was nonchalant. "It's okay. I'm not really that into it," she said. Sai Mui gave her an elbow jab.

Because of that promise, Sai Mui skipped playtime to review her schoolwork. Meanwhile, Panda leisurely tried out different kinds of makeup products and various colored contact lenses. Sai Mui secretly looked down on her for it: Panda never seemed to put in any real effort. She was always so laid-back, so indifferent. Whatever was given to her, her response was always, "Okay," "Sure," "No problem." It was as though she had no goal to work toward.

In the end, it was Panda who got the pencil case. And Sai Mui? Even though she had pushed herself hard, she still received middling scores. Even more annoying to Sai Mui was that Panda really wasn't that keen on the pencil case. She coolly cited the saying, "A person of noble character doesn't take what others truly desire." Without removing the case from its wrapping, Panda offered it to her little sister.

Sai Mui flatly refused, bristling with indignation. "It was given to you—it's *yours*. Did *I* get grades that good? Did *I* spend every day putting on makeup, curling my lashes, acting like I didn't care while secretly studying nonstop? You're such a fraud!"

Panda looked completely puzzled. "Why would I study hard just for a pencil case? Why am I a fraud?" Instead of addressing Sai Mui's accusations, Panda said, "Suit yourself," and tore off the packaging out of spite. She left it on the desk they shared.

This stung Sai Mui like a betrayal. She tried so hard but still couldn't make herself deserving of it, while Panda got it without even lifting a finger, only to cast it away like it meant nothing. A swell of humiliation and resentment rose in her chest. It had always been like this.

Panda didn't even think about the pencil case when she left home a few weeks ago. But Sai Mui did. "I thought you were planning to come back for it later," she said, wiping the thin layer of dust from the surface. Snoopy's eyes and nose had faded from sitting on the desk over the years. If it had belonged to Sai Mui, she never would have let it end up like this.

"No. As I told you, this is yours. I never wanted it that much. God knows why you got all worked up about it and left it on the desk all this time. Just take it." Panda poked at the lemon in her tea with a long spoon.

"Oh." Sai Mui didn't resist because her mind was whirling with competing thoughts. She knew she should focus on her undeclared purpose for this meeting. This was the perfect chance to ask her sister about the protests, she thought. The more extreme, the more dramatic, the better. She wanted details of blood, bullets, fire, people fleeing for their lives. She couldn't wait to dole them out at school, bit by bit. She would never spill everything all at once. That would be a waste. Like a good TV drama writer, she would dispense the story skillfully to keep her audience hooked. But instead, she asked, "Why won't you come home?"

"I can't stand the way Mom is—forget it, you're still young. You wouldn't understand even if I explained it to you."

Mei Yan had said the same thing. "Forget it, you wouldn't understand. What would you know? Your whole family's yellow anyway. Must be nice." Sai Mui had felt deeply wronged. With Mei Yan, she hadn't been able to defend herself, as though she were the one who had done something wrong. What was it she wouldn't understand? Then explain it to her, tell her, make her understand!

She was even more mystified with Panda. In other families, when there was a falling out, it was usually because of clashing politics. But Mom had never once scolded Panda. She always said she supported the young people, and had taken action to patronize "yellow" businesses. Why was Panda still so hostile? Even more perplexing was the fact that even though Panda was always upset with Mom, Mom still poured all her love into Panda, letting her squander it, right in front of Sai Mui's eyes.

Sai Mui's anger flared. She couldn't stand the sight of Panda leisurely sipping her beverage across the table. She wasn't audacious enough to knock over the glass of lemon tea, so she yanked out Panda's straw and flung it onto the floor. To a surprised Panda, she muttered sullenly, "You don't know how lucky you are. Mom loves you so much, and you don't even care. You have no idea how upset she was when you ran off outside the beauty salon. What could be so unforgivable? What can't be made right?" The more Sai Mui spoke, the sadder she became. She broke into tears.

A month after Panda left, Mom finally managed to convince her to meet up.

"You've been exposed to so much tear gas lately, your pores must be clogged with toxins. It's bad for your skin. Come get a proper facial. Auntie Ning will be pleased to see you," Mom told Panda in a text message.

Although customers called her "auntie," Ning On was only in her thirties. She ran the modest salon on her own and earned a reputation for her meticulous and honest service. She was always thorough with the cleaning and gentle with the massage. Unlike her competitors, she never pushed her customers to buy products. Mom and Panda had been frequenting her salon for years.

After a pause, Panda agreed to the invitation.

Mom was over the moon. She brought Sai Mui along. She said they'd all go out for a feast afterward and Sai Mui could order anything she wanted. When Sai Mui sat in the common area of the salon and waited for Mom and Panda, she swung her legs, giddy with anticipation. She considered whether they should go for pizza or sushi. Mom looked so nice that day in her pearly white lace blouse and royal blue cropped pants with the designer handbag Dad had bought her. And Panda seemed more at ease than before. She may not have said much to Mom, but she hadn't rejected the suggestion of having lunch together, either. Sai Mui started to believe that her older sister might really come home—if not today, then maybe sometime soon.

However, when the facials were underway, the scheduled public rally elsewhere on the island was cut short by the police, who declared it an unlawful assembly. In response, people began organizing their own impromptu marches across various districts, including one that popped up in Sheung Wan.

And so, when they stepped out of the beauty salon, they greeted a stream of protesters head-on. Some of them placed barriers on the road to prevent police vehicles from advancing. A few young people in black were using wrenches to loosen the bolts on metal fences dividing the car lanes and pedestrians' way. As soon as a section came free, people carried it to the middle of the road as an impromptu roadblock. Along the side of the road, a few others propped open umbrellas to shield their faces from passersby or potential cameras.

Mom, Panda, and Sai Mui quietly observed from a side street for a moment, then Panda said, "Let's go. Just standing here doesn't do anything, and we can't help anyhow." So they walked down a side street toward a nearby sushi restaurant. When they reached the address, they found the business was closed for the day.

They headed back to the main road. Around a corner, they came across a teenage girl changing clothes in an alley alone. She looked to be about the same age as Sai Mui. She had just put on a black shirt and black protective sleeves; her gas mask and goggles hung around her neck. Upon finding herself suddenly face-to-face with strangers, she froze. Her body stiffened like a cat cornered against a wall, back arched in alarm.

Panda must have understood her panic at once. She nudged Sai Mui and tugged at Mom's blouse. "Stop staring at her. She's clearly startled." She hurried them down the alley.

Mom suddenly seemed to remember something and dashed back toward the girl. Before Panda or Sai Mui could react, they heard Mom's voice. She had already approached the teenager, who was in the middle of fastening her mask. "Add oil, keep going! You're doing the right thing! I support you all!" Sai Mui, trailing behind Panda, could make out their mom shouting a few more slogans.

The teenager was taken aback by this sudden attempt at engagement. After all, she was sheltering in the privacy of an alley to put on her disguise. She quickly snatched up the long umbrella from the ground and bolted toward the far end of the street without even zipping up her backpack.

To Sai Mui, though, what happened next was incomprehensible. Panda's face suddenly darkened. She tossed the bag she'd been carrying to the ground. Its contents—face masks, skincare products, and health supplements Mom had bought her—spilled out. She was gasping with rage. Sai Mui had never seen her big sister like this: all serious, jaw clenched. For a second, she thought Panda might actually start screaming or take a swing at Mom. Anticipating an irreversible rupture, Sai Mui braced herself, ready to run up and grab Panda around the waist to stop her. Just then, Panda opened her mouth, each word stretched tight and squeezed through her teeth: "I—swear—I'm—never—going—home," she said. She turned around and ran off, disappearing down the alley.

Remembering all this tension, Sai Mui went on sobbing for almost ten minutes. She cried as if the grief she had carried for weeks were bursting out all at once. Panda took the seat next to Sai Mui and pulled her into a hug. She gently wiped away Sai Mui's tears and cooed softly, "Let's stop crying so much, okay? You're about to start junior high. Be a big girl."

Sai Mui whimpered, her eyes red and swollen. Everyone kept

telling her she knew nothing. But she knew all about Mom's quirks and she knew everything about Panda's temper. Why did things have to be this way? Even if Mom never joined a protest, even if she only gave support in words, she was still their mom. Just like how, despite the time that had passed and the unpleasant things that transpired over the pencil case, she still longed for it. It was still Snoopy on it! What could be so unforgivable? Why couldn't she make her family whole again?

Okay, she may not have understood everything. Her wishes in life were simple. She wanted Mom to hold her tight, to blow-dry her hair, to dote on her the way Mei Yan's mom treated Mei Yan, the way Mom was to Panda.

And Panda, her bunk-bed roommate, her gourmet guide, her classroom social adviser, her big sister. She always held the key to the very things Sai Mui fought so hard for, only to toss it aside like it meant nothing to her. At this very moment, Sai Mui would feel like she owned the world if Panda could just nod and agree to come home with her. But instead, Panda said, "Sai Mui, baby girl. Someday you'll see. It breaks my heart too, not being able to say yes to Mom's gestures of kindness." Panda's smile seemed clouded. "But what is the cost of always accepting business as usual?"

Terrain of Skin and Flesh

For Ning On, summer break was usually the busiest time of year. With school out, female students flocked to her salon for treatments. Brightening, dark spot treatment, hair removal. . . . They saw every mark on their bodies as a flaw and an invitation for improvement. They put their faith in the sleek, modern machines, hoping to achieve a bodily upgrade before school started. But this summer, where had all those young women gone?

Ning On's salon was located in a modest shopping mall. One Saturday, she locked up a few hours earlier than usual, greeted the security guard, and pushed open the glass door of the mall. Outside, separated from Ning On by metal barricades, protesters were marching down the main road. As soon as she took off her mask, she spotted Little Professor in the crowd.

She was struck by how easily recognizable he was. He was tall and broad-shouldered, and wore a black mask, no hat, and a black T-shirt with a yellow oval Batman logo printed across his chest. Maybe this was deliberate, but the T-shirt was clearly too small, clinging tightly to his sculpted chest and abs. She knew how much he loved feigning nonchalance while showing off his muscles. She really had zero interest in them. She thought this behavior was like a love-deprived little boy flaunting an expensive remote-control toy car.

Little Professor walked leisurely along the procession, a Guy Fawkes mask dangling from his backpack. At protests, a leader often guided the crowd in chanting slogans. When he or she called out a first line, the crowd often finished the rest of the slogan in unison. Like a priest leading a prayer, the lead chanter always appeared focused, devout, and even fanatical. At that moment, Little Professor was leading his section, crying out, "Liberate Hong Kong!" "There are no 'rioters'!" "Disband the police!" The crowd repeated each slogan before rotating to the next line. Even though his voice was coming through a face mask, it was so loud and forceful that it almost covered the chants from the group just ahead of them. He seemed to feed off the rhythm of this interaction with the crowd, shouting harder and harder. Eventually, he tugged his mask down. His body trembled slightly with excitement and tension. This sight was something she knew all too well. His body—so strong and so vulnerable—quivered the same way when they had sex.

Ning On didn't go over to catch him, nor did she join the march. As the crowd passed by, she observed the faces. They were obscured by masks, but she could still tell that most of them were in their teens and early twenties. They seemed so full of drive, charging ahead without hesitation. Suddenly, Ning On keenly felt she was not young anymore.

The nearby shops had also shuttered early. The sidewalk was nearly deserted. Once the crowd was gone, only she remained, alone, by the row of barricades. She tossed her mask into a trash can and walked toward the bus stop, her head lowered. She wanted to shower and change into fresh clothes as soon as she got home.

It was nearly four when she arrived at her apartment. As usual, her daughter, Ning Yuet, wasn't there. On the living room floor lay a crumpled face mask, a single glove, and several snipped zip ties strewn haphazardly near the front door. Ning Yuet had clearly rushed out without tidying up first, like an infant leaving a trail of breadcrumbs. Ning On picked up the loose objects, suddenly exhausted. She decided to put showering off for now. Instead, she washed her face and switched on the TV.

It was already September and school had resumed. The boundary between the movement and everyday routines was dissolving. Demonstrations were no longer limited to the weekend. This afternoon, people were clashing with the police throughout the city's districts. The news channel cycled through these sites at regular intervals: one minute it focused on Hong Kong Island;

the next, it moved north across the harbor to Kowloon; then, it went farther north to the New Territories bordering Shenzhen.

Ning On muted the TV. She didn't know which district her daughter had gone to. She hadn't asked. The message from Ning Yuet read: "I'm going to a classmate's place to do homework. I'll be home a little later." Ning On knew her daughter probably said so to save her from worrying all night, so she didn't call out the white lie. She had been caught in a web of good intentions. One day she was cleaning up when she accidentally discovered a gas mask in the girl's backpack. Ever since then, every weekend Ning Yuet spent "going to a classmate's place to do homework" left Ning On on edge.

She could never tell if her daughter was out on the streets, or if she was really doing homework in the safety of a classmate's home.

Sometimes, amid this torment, she managed to prepare a meal of three dishes and a soup, so that when Ning Yuet came home, they could eat together as if nothing were wrong. Other times, such as today, the strain of apprehension drained her. She had been working since early morning, and fatigue set in as she kept an eye on the TV. Half an hour went by. The broadcast was still showing various civilian-police confrontations. The footage played in silence, looping over and over like the demo reels in an electronics store. It was surprisingly hypnotizing. Ning On lay down on the sofa and drifted off to sleep.

The sound of running water from the bathroom roused her from her slumber. She looked around the room. On the dining table, two take-out bowls of crossing-the-bridge rice noodles had been set out along with a side dish of century egg with chili peppers. Feeling relieved, Ning On realized she was quite hungry, so she dug in without waiting for her daughter. Immediately, she was comforted by the spicy broth. The noodle soup was their favorite.

As she enjoyed the food, a faintly acidic smell drew her attention to Ning Yuet's forest green backpack on the floor. There was a dark blotch on it. The stain was brown and had dried through. She couldn't tell whether it was sauce or something else. She didn't dwell on it.

Her phone vibrated on the table. She glanced at it and popped a piece of century egg into her mouth. It was too late when she realized that she had bitten down on the head of a chili pepper. Her face flushed from the heat, and she broke into a coughing fit.

The sound of running water stopped. Ning Yuet emerged in a light pajama set. Towel-drying her hair with one hand, she poured her mother a glass of water with the other. Ning On gave her a quick once-over, inspecting from head to toe for any injuries. There were none that she could see. She downed the water. The burn in her mouth calmed temporarily.

They ate their rice noodles in silence. Ning On wanted to remind her daughter to dry her hair first—and that she shouldn't scroll through her phone while eating, that it could lead to indigestion. But Ning Yuet barely touched her food, clutching her chopsticks mid-motion while tapping away at her phone. She was so absorbed that she didn't even notice when the towel slipped from her neck onto the floor. While clearing the table, Ning On saw that most of the noodles in her daughter's bowl remained untouched. She couldn't bring herself to throw them out, so she covered the bowl and placed it in the fridge.

After Ning On washed the dishes, her daughter was still sitting there glued to her phone. Ning On fetched a blow-dryer and began drying her daughter's hair. It used to be carefully maintained and cascaded down her back, as glossy as a raven's feathers. Since a few months ago, Ning Yuet had started keeping it short, just grazing her neck, and rarely used hair products anymore. It felt stiff and prickly to the touch.

Caressing her hair, Ning On felt a rush of emotions. The girl before her had once been carried inside her. An existence as intimate as a tiny growth of her own flesh. In what felt like the blink of an eye, that same child now was decidedly her own person. They could be eating the same food, yet the teenager was unwilling to share a single thought with her. Ning Yuet's hair was still damp, but she couldn't sit still any longer. Without saying anything, she shook her head, stood up, and darted to her room. She switched on her computer and closed the door behind her.

Those fine strands of hair had slipped so swiftly from Ning On's palm, as if they'd already gone far beyond her reach. She unplugged the blow-dryer, untangled the cable, and put it away.

Sitting back down at the table, Ning On clicked open the message from half an hour ago. "I'm free now. Still want to meet?"

As soon as Little Professor and Ning On entered the hotel room, he wrapped his arms around her from behind, kissing her hair at the nape of her neck. He drew his nose close, inhaling the faint fragrance of her skin, then exhaled softly. It sent goose bumps rippling across her flesh. He said he missed her; that he'd been thinking about her. Ning On couldn't tell if those were just sweet nothings. She ceased thinking. The tip of his tongue was grazing her ear now, teasing it with dampness. She always got queasy when he did this. Her body shuddered in a wave of tremors. Just as she was about to turn around and kiss him hungrily, she caught a whiff of a light but acrid smell emanating from him. It made her wince.

Then it dawned on her: It was the same smell that had radiated from her daughter's backpack. The thought made her stiffen with fear. She didn't want to know where the smell came from.

Little Professor must have observed this mood shift. He looked at her, sorry as a scolded pet. "I already rinsed off once. Is it still too strong?" He launched into a long-winded explanation. "I couldn't help it. There weren't many of us today. Now, everyone has grown afraid of getting rounded up, no one dares to—ow!" Ning On bit his shoulder, cutting him off with seductive provocation.

She didn't want to hear more. Not wanting to know what her daughter had been up to was the reason she came here. He, however, never seemed to get tired of sharing, but it was always the same stuff: dodging bullets, evading arrest, racing like it was a matter of life or death. Blah blah blah blah. He always recounted everything in vivid detail, letting on his survivor's guilt. It was laced with a smug sense of superiority.

She didn't care in the slightest.

In the wide world outside, a hail of tear gas and rubber bullets rained down. Inside the elegant confinement of this room, she just wanted to concentrate on making love, pure and simple. She was so tired. She wanted to disappear into a strong, muscular body. Why did everyone have to express themselves? Why the rush to open their mouths, repeating their scripts over and over?

Of course, Ning On locked these thoughts tight in her throat. She clenched her legs firmly around his solid, lean waist. Lost in the animalistic frenzy, she moaned in scattered bursts. She submerged herself in the moment. She feared that sharp, biting complaints might slip past her lips as soon as she let up. No, she was just ignorant and uncomplicated Ning On. At least, that's what he seemed to believe. That's what everyone—her clients, her daughter, her ex-husband—expected her to be.

Perhaps she believed it too. Better to be ignorant. Ignorant people were the happiest.

Ning On was thirty-five and divorced. She saved up to open her beauty salon on her own. Her daughter had just started high school. These were things she never told her clients. Sharing personal details with them was a bit of a gamble, like tossing rainbow-colored rings in a game. If a ring landed just right, you gained a reward. But when it missed, it knocked things over, creating a mess. Ning On knew sharing details of her life or views might appeal to some customers and help her lock in a loyal clientele. However, it might also rub some individuals the wrong way, and then she would not only lose out on business but also risk becoming fodder for gossip. The last thing she needed was the kind of politely packaged advice steeped in condescension. Hence, she became a quiet listener.

Her tiny shop front was divided into two private rooms. When things got busy, she'd finish extracting blackheads for a client in one room, then rush to the other for a laser hair-removal session. When it was inevitable, she cut some corners to make do, but people didn't stop coming. It was largely thanks to her quiet bedside manner, or so she believed. Some of her clients had vented that when going for a haircut, a massage, a facial, or some other services that entailed one-on-one interaction, what they dreaded most was a chatterbox who needed to fill the air with endless babble. Even with a highly skilled practitioner, if he or she didn't know how to read the room, the hours of service could feel like pure torture, paying good money just to suffer. Some of them asked intrusive questions about personal matters; others ranted about social issues, acting like know-it-alls.

In the last few weeks, Ning On saw a number of long-lost clients returning to her salon again. Apparently, as politics became heated, they couldn't stand the opposing views expressed by their regular aestheticians. Protest supporters and opponents alike came to her shop, drawn by her lack of a public stance.

"I've missed your salon, Ning On. Much more relaxing when I'm not bothered by any annoying comments." Clients fawned over her silence, but usually went on with their own drawn-out monologues. Some of them poured out their arguments; others merely rambled. Ning On had heard fragmented words in every shape and form imaginable. Amid all these, Ning On focused on her work, applying pressure to the flesh beneath her hands, or guiding a machine across skin. She offered no response. Only her ears half-tilted, picking up the endless stream of stories.

Some bodies were plump like ripe, glistening fruit; others were scrawny like parched earth. But that was on the outside. Beneath each surface lay an immense ball of tangled thread. Once the tip of the thread was tugged from one's lips, the talking would start to unwind, and go on and on and on. The spool inside a body spinning fast. The more words it churned out, the greater the desire to go on talking.

Perhaps it was not her body or her personality that kept Little Professor coming back to her, she thought. He was so full of himself and so starved for affection. He needed a quiet, obedient listener in these chaotic times. And she played the part well.

The customer was king. Many people had been saying that capital was the lifeline of this city, so resistance didn't necessarily have to mean blood and sweat. Consumption, too, could be weaponized to express allegiance or mete out punishment, a way of establishing an economic circle based on political priorities. The public scrutinized every business—the decor, the staff's remarks—to figure out their stance on the movement, sorting them into categories for support or boycott. This raging tide swept away the practical considerations for service, quality, and price. The primary standard for evaluation became *Do you share my politics?*

Ning On had heard as much when she recently joined a few salon owners for tea. "I've got so much business, I can barely keep up," said Aesthetician A. One day during a protest, a few young people were hit by water cannons and cried out in pain on the street corner near her shop. Upon hearing their voices, Aesthetician A picked up a handful of towels in her salon and rushed over to help. Within a few days, requests for bookings flooded in via phone, email, and text messages. Only then did she realize that those young people had posted their experience online and expressed gratitude to her while naming her business. The post made the rounds, spurring customers her way.

"Is it that easy? Maybe I'll make a little extra by having my son hype me up online," Aesthetician B scoffed. "Might as well say I ran out and got hit by tear gas . . . wouldn't exactly be a lie, either. This area is always getting hit. A hundred-something rounds in one night is nothing. Plenty of times, I sat at home and choked on the fumes. It stung like hell."

"It's not right to lie," chimed in a third woman, Aesthetician C. "She really did hand out those towels. What have we done to deserve being hyped up? Besides, taking a stand is risky. Who knows when the other side might come looking for trouble? Damned if you do, damned if you don't. Both sides are pretty scary. I came down from the mainland to do business here precisely because I liked that Hong Kong didn't mess with this kind of thing. Now, it's gone to the extreme. Even beauty has to be political." Many business owners and workers in the industry were from the mainland, and C had been the first among those at the tea gathering to move to Hong Kong. She ran a hair salon in Sham Shui Po, and after closing time, a few fellow mainlanders would gather there to chat over tea.

"You don't say," Aesthetician A said. "Just a few days ago, an older woman working at a department store rushed a few customers at the sample counter before closing, saying, 'Hurry up, I need to get off work. Those thugs will come to riot again soon, and once the roads are blocked, I won't be able to get home.' One of the shoppers posted it online. That led to lots of complaints to the store, and the company announced she was suspended, effective immediately. It's so scary—with just one sentence, they can take away your job. They think they're buying not only the products but also how you're allowed to think."

Ning On was familiar with the incident. Little Professor had played a video for her. The woman in the department store incident was delivering a public apology. He introduced it as a victory of mass mobilization, the first step in overturning capitalism. On the screen, the woman sat blank-faced before the camera, holding a sheet of paper, reading its content mechanically. She stumbled through the lines, pausing a lot. At the end, she bowed her head in apology, pleading for forgiveness. It was like a public punishment.

As Little Professor watched, he critiqued her performance: she seemed insincere; she bowed while remaining seated; she obviously hadn't practiced the script enough; the whole thing was so perfunctory.

Ning On felt like puking. The world had gone mad.

People like Little Professor seemed to expect the pain and anger of everyone to be calibrated into a single, precise aim and fired at a common enemy. Instead, this hate festered like spores of mold, scattering in fine specks, multiplying, floating aimlessly, seeping into everyone's system.

By the time she woke up, it was already noon the next day. The TV was playing a live news broadcast, the volume turned down to a whispery hiss. A protest was probably about to begin. The journalist on the scene reported the crowd size, traffic conditions, and the police deployments. Little Professor was on the phone, keeping his eyes on the news. "I'll skip today. You didn't show up yesterday. Hardly anyone was there. It's impossible to operate with so few people. The folks in the middle and back were all scared, bailing faster and faster. The kids up front, on the other hand, were too reckless, provoking the police line without thinking ahead about how to get away. They were just draining our resources. I'm not going. This is becoming impossible."

He spoke a little longer on the phone. Before hanging up, he said, "If you do go, remember to swap out your SIM card. Don't waste your time going to Victoria Park. At this point it's just helping these organizers pad the turnout. For what? So they could jerk off to vanity numbers? Do you still buy into that pan-dem crap? There's no democracy in Hong Kong because too many idiots still can't tell if we are having a social movement or a revolution. Are they still dreaming that just by showing up a few times they would be able to force Beijing to hand us real universal suffrage? Fucking morons."

Ning On's body was all soft. Her throat felt dry and sore. Her bones ached like they were coming apart. All she wanted was to sink back into sleep. She didn't want to hear any more of his grand theories. But Little Professor came over and urged her to get up. "You awake? Lounging in bed all day will just make you more tired. I told the front desk that we are checking out a little later. We can have lunch together first." She saw two plates of food on the table.

Classic Little Professor. When he lectured you on the downside of one thing, he was in fact pushing you into doing another. "Lounging in bed will make you tired" really meant "Get up already and eat with me." "Do you know how many calories are in a can of beer?" meant "Watch your weight."

"You're wrong" meant "I'm right."

EVERYDAY MOVEMENT

Since the beginning of the year, twice a week, Ning On stayed out late. On these days, she usually smoked a cigarette after closing up shop and heading to the fitness center for yoga.

When she finished a class package, it was already August. By then, even on weekdays, protests and clashes were happening everywhere in the city. Tear gas was deployed as unpredictably as a lottery drawing. No one ever knew which day or what time it might descend on their own neighborhood. The center was conveniently located between her work and home, and yoga had been a welcome reprieve, so she went to buy another package. Maybe it was the economy, and there was a new promotion posted at the front desk: Pay a little extra and get full access to the gym facilities. Like getting a bundle of free scallions with your groceries. She thought it was a good deal, and swiped her card on the spot.

It wasn't until she walked into the gym that she realized it was a battlefield. It was packed with fit bodies in athletic tank tops, mostly brawny men, straddling and scaling machines of varying heights and mechanical logic. Men were lifting weights, doing pull-ups, pushing heavy loads with their thighs. Their faces were all contorted. Their teeth clenched, as if they were enduring immense pain but weren't allowed to make a sound.

There was a quiet undercurrent of competition among these sportsmen. She saw a young man squatting thirty kilograms.

Next, another man did thirty-five. When he left, the first man immediately came back to challenge himself with forty. He clearly struggled with this abrupt ten-kilogram jump. He bit hard on his lip and gasped. His two spotless, bunny-like front teeth peeked out, lending him an air of boyish defiance.

Ning On had some middle-aged female clients who took up sports to stay in shape. They believed that exercises like bodybuilding and dancing were the most honest pursuits. If you put in the effort, you'd receive payback, unlike such fickle things as romance, investments, or politics. Once she started hooking up with Little Professor, he claimed absolute authority over all matters relevant to the body. He micromanaged her health, diet, and workout, tolerating no questions. This was nearly dictatorial, but Ning On never argued.

Maybe that was the last bit of territory he could defend. She didn't have the heart to tear it down.

In reality, Ning On had only planned on using the rowing machine to work on her abs and waist. On her first day, she sat down and gripped the handle at both ends. Bending her knees, she pressed her feet against the plate. There were cables connected to the handle. Her body moved at the same rhythm as the cable recoiled, leaning forward and back, contracting and extending in clean, deliberate motions. In no time, she had sweat on her forehead, and her heart was pounding. She wasn't young anymore. She may have looked young—taking good care of her appearance was a requirement of her job. People often had a hard time figuring out her age. She knew, however, her physicality was undeniably deteriorating. She was also growing jaded.

The wilder you were in your youth, the faster you aged. Everything had to be repaid. Earlier this year, Ning On shared a meal with her ex-husband. He said that twenty-five was a dividing line for women. Past that point, they ballooned up and retained water, their skin sagged and their flesh turned flabby. Just the thought of it made him lose his appetite, he said. He soon moved to Shenzhen. His WeChat timeline was updated daily with photos of him and various pretty young women enjoying different cuisines. He looked so slim she couldn't tell whether it was the result of overzealous photoshopping, or if he had actually lost weight. She barely recognized him.

"Miss, your posture's wrong." A voice disrupted her thoughts. She then noticed the approaching figure. It was the rabbit-toothed young man who'd just been trying to outdo the other man.

Ning On loathed being intruded upon, but professional courtesy compelled her to step aside and let the young man demonstrate his point. He launched into an enthusiastic explanation on how to distribute force across the back muscles, core, and arms. In one go, he outlined where she should feel the tension and which muscle group she should target. It was actually clear and easy to follow. "You got it?" he asked at the end.

He probably enjoyed the thrill of guiding and advising others. The glint in his eyes reminded Ning On of a manicure client. She sat calmly getting her crystal nails done amid the raucous protest and rumbling traffic outside. With such loftiness, she said, "Sure, their intentions are good, but they're being too reckless. That's how young people are. They go ahead with all the destruction without any strategy. Smashing up shops? There goes the public support." The client went on, "I heard the other day that some troublemakers tore down a Lennon Wall and beat up protesters in a tunnel. Let me tell you, those kids who got beaten didn't fight back. Now that's real calmness and reason, the mark of true leadership. That creates a sense of moral appeal. You understand?" Ning On nodded lightly and thought to herself, thank God for the mask on my face.

Just as the young man yielded the machine back to Ning On, a trainer walked by and teased him. "Hey, Little Prof, playing trainer again? Why don't you just get certified and switch careers for real?" The young man clearly didn't appreciate this and went on lecturing her about health trends, from the keto diet to the 16:8 intermittent fasting method. Ning On still didn't interrupt him. She knew these things already. In her line of work, one needed a few expert-sounding tidbits in her back pocket to impart to clients. Surprisingly, she rather enjoyed watching him preach so earnestly. Those two prominent, boyish rabbit teeth peeked out every now and then. He clearly wanted attention and approval badly. She didn't bother correcting the few errors in his information.

When she was leaving, he popped by again and told her that lately he had been taking a course in fitness training. Helping others was a way to help oneself, he proposed. Could they exchange numbers? If she ever had any questions, he'd be happy to help. "Keep in touch," he said, after saving her number on his phone.

He spoke in a polite manner and came across as a decent guy. Ning On assumed that "keep in touch" meant grabbing a drink or a bite and having a chat. It began with that, but they somehow ended up at a hotel. The first time, she could blame it on the booze. Fine, admittedly she'd been eyeing that firm chest of his at the gym. The morning after, he confessed that he still "technically" had a girlfriend. The relationship was on its last legs but they never officially broke up. She felt guilty and didn't want the drama, so she stopped texting him.

In the following days, the protests kept escalating. Sometimes, when the roads were blocked, there was no business. With nothing else to do, Ning On joined the security guard at the mall entrance, watching the marchers pass by. Many of the kids looked about the same age as Ning Yuet. A lot of her fellow aestheticians were mothers too. When they brought up their children, it was always "Of course it's too dangerous out there," or "If he dares to take it to the streets, I'll kill him." Some even bragged about their methods of stopping their children: changing the locks, throwing out their gear while they slept, cutting off their allowances. . . .

Ning Yuet kept coming home late, and sometimes even stayed out till the next day, but Ning On never asked. She wanted to stay ignorant and happy.

A week later, Little Professor messaged her again. Ning On realized she missed those two cute rabbit teeth. They skipped the tedious formalities and tentative cautiousness and fell back into each other's arms in no time.

He told her that "Little Professor" was a nickname, one tinged with mockery. He wasn't actually a professor, or a lecturer. He wasn't even a PhD or master's candidate. He studied social sciences in college and used to be a theory nerd. He spoke in an old-fashioned way and loved to lecture, lending him a professorial air. His classmates teasingly called him Little Professor, assuming he would find a bright future in academia. He believed it too. After being called Little Professor for a few years, he practically forgot his actual name.

Unfortunately, however, he failed the postgraduate entrance exams several years in a row. Out of pity for his perseverance, professors in the department used their research funds to hire him as an assistant. He compiled data, handled paperwork, answered department calls, and drafted project proposals. To put it frankly, it was little more than grunt work. Two or three years went by quickly.

Little Professor didn't mind. On the contrary, he made use of his position to organize a reading group and became close with the students. The reading group grew into a tight-knit after-school club. They debated ideas, talked about their aspirations, drank by the campus lake, shared late-night snacks. When they got tired, they quietly snuck into a member's dorm room, nearly ten of them piling onto the floor, shoulder-to-shoulder, unbothered by being cramped. The students, just a few years younger, all looked up to him. They came to him about everything: love, school assignments, jobs, interpersonal problems. He truly lived up to his nickname.

When the department overhauled its curriculum, and the university announced plans to open a campus in China, debates flared. Little Professor and his cohort made posters and banners with big characters on them overnight. The next day, they hung the banners from the rooftop of the administration building. White paint had splattered all over Little Professor and a female student. They couldn't wash it off their clothes, but it didn't matter. He was exhilarated by being part of a group in action. Or more precisely, he was exhilarated by leading them to act.

They looked at him like sheep following their shepherd dog. He bathed in their trust and admiration. He thought he could watch over his flock forever.

Perhaps that's why, nowadays, he enjoyed leading chants in protests. He also loved posting field observations on social media, teaching others how to assess situations. He tracked his Likes and Shares as if they were stock prices. He was thrilled as the numbers climbed, convinced his insights were serving the greater good. When he read comments full of praise and gratitude, he felt as if he was among his flock again.

The banner incident made the news. The department administrators reviewed the CCTV footage and identified him. It nearly cost him his job. He kept his chin up. The student movements of the '60s and '70s had burned bright on fearlessness, he told people around him, and the same should hold true now. He was willing to risk it all.

His old professor worked hard to smooth things over, and warned him: Once you graduated, you had crossed a threshold. You were no longer a student. "I know you have a bond with these students, but they will move on from this campus and head to their respective futures very soon," the old professor said. "And you need to think about yours." These words were like a needle. One prick, and it let the air out of Little Professor's fantasy balloon.

When the undergraduates moved up to their junior and senior years, they got busy with internships, exchange programs, thesis writing, and job hunting. Meanwhile, new students were enrolled every year. This revolving door of friendship was like the sun rising and setting. Over the years, he kept building relationships, only to see them fading in a couple of years. It wore him down. His old professor's warning began to feel like a prophecy. Graduating meant crossing a threshold, and upon leaping over it, most of his former best friends never looked back. Only he stayed in the same spot.

Once, he texted the group chat and tried to gather a few former students to organize an academic event. No one replied. A few days later, one young man spoke up in the chat. "I do miss our university days from time to time. It's wonderful that the university is the setting of your life and that you have time for this kind of thing. But out here, society is complicated. It takes everything we've got just to keep going. Sorry, Little Professor."

In the end, only one person stepped up to help him organize the event. It was the woman who'd ended up covered in white paint when they made the banners. From then on, she kept showing up: helping him invite freshmen to book clubs; attending public talks with him. Just as he felt let down by everyone, he noticed her constant trailing behind him.

They started dating. The sweet intimacy temporarily released Little Professor from the feeling of dejection. Six months later, however, she, along with a few other former students, breezed straight into the graduate program he'd long dreamed of. At first, he tried to laugh it off, telling himself that these kids were opportunistic with their research topics, pandering to trends of the academic mainstream and were void of personal perspectives; that their theoretical frameworks were outdated, appealing only to the old fossils in the department. . . . He tried to put a name to this restless indignation. Over time, it brewed into resentment. It poisoned everything.

Little Professor gave up on his little club and shifted his focus to his tedious administrative work. When the department secured new funding, he was promoted from junior research assistant to project manager. The pay improved, but he drifted further from a career in research. This anxiety grew in him, and he grumbled to his girlfriend that he was stuck with tasks like typing official memos and emails when he was born for penning profound scholarship. His job was grinding time into dust with minutiae.

He had wanted his girlfriend to comfort him, to take pity on his wasted talent. Screw the world. If he could see his ideal self reflected in her eyes, that would have been enough. But instead of soothing him, she wanted to give him the truth. "You know that's not how things are," she said. Little Professor feared her sharpness. He had lost his last sheep.

When Ning On first woke up, she checked her phone. There were no new messages from her daughter. Before leaving home last night, she had stood outside Ning Yuet's room and told her she was going out. Her daughter didn't open the door. A mix of noises came from her room. After a long pause, her daughter said, "Okay, got it." She didn't ask what Ning Yuet was up to. Ning Yuet wasn't curious about her reason for heading out at night, either. They weren't the kind of mother and daughter who told each other about their day and had heart-to-hearts at bedtime. She wasn't the kind of mother who made bento lunches for school or took her daughter on shopping trips. Ning On was still young and needed her space; Ning Yuet was growing up fast and needed hers too. Trust had drawn just the right amount of distance between them.

When Ning Yuet was small, she used to act up for attention, and Ning On had always given in. But after her daughter started junior high, things shifted. Sometimes Ning On came home late or not until the morning after. She left money or a prepared meal behind. When Ning Yuet said she was spending the night at a friend's, Ning On never checked. Like players standing on opposite sides of a court, separated by a net, they shared an unspoken understanding, each holding to her own small territory without intruding on the other, yet managing to keep things going. This didn't mean they didn't love each other. Now, however, Ning On found herself caught in that loose net of Ning Yuet's white lies, unsure what to do with the secret on the other side. She wanted to preserve this balance, this trust. But she also wanted to make sure her daughter was staying safe.

When Little Professor saw the troubled expression on Ning On's face, he assumed she was distressed about the state of the world and tormented by everything unfolding around them. He pitied her, this quiet, exploited, and ignorant member of the working class. She was spending her life in an industry devoted to women reshaping their bodies and appearances according to the patriarchal gaze. How tragic!

He also thought of those intellectuals who churned out thousands and thousands of pretentious words—statements, manifestos, op-eds—advocating for "engagement with the people," "community building," and "educating the public." After stepping out of their faculty housing, they probably didn't even know where to buy toilet paper. Last month, he helped organize an interdisciplinary symposium at the university. After the event ended, he joined the professors for dinner at a nearby restaurant. One female scholar proudly declared, "I'd never go to an old neighborhood like Sham Shui Po on my own. I hear those back alleys are full of junkies and criminals."

He was different, he thought, from those professors who sat comfortably in offices and research labs, occupying themselves with theorizing. They were basically dehumanized academic machines. Unlike them, he knew the smell of the streets. His sweat had soaked the asphalt roads. He had rinsed the burning, itchy wounds of the injured. What's more, he had led the chants for the people. "Liberate Hong Kong!" "Revolution of our times!" Each time, the crowd echoed his voice before falling into a patient silence, waiting for him to call out the next slogan. Little Professor liked to repeat each slogan three times, quickening with each round, building a sharp, rhythmic momentum. It was him. It was his voice leading the crowd.

He was the one truly standing with the people. And with Ning On, he practiced what he preached by literally putting his body on the line. He chuckled at this thought but then became self-conscious of it. If he said this out loud, it might offend some feminist activists or leftist scholars.

Little Professor took Ning On's phone away, telling her to finish eating first. "Remember what I said? You might not be able to make the world better, but you can make yourself a better person. The body is the capital of revolution. You have to stay healthy to outlive the regime." He loved spouting off these slick lines. When he posted some of them on social media, they always racked up Likes and Shares. In a city steeped in despair, the meek needed faith and those good with words needed followers. Together, they cultivated a kind of spiritual opium, feeding one another in turn.

Ning On pushed down her irritation and finished the fruit bowl. There was no point in letting it go to waste. She wasn't the one paying for the room or the meal. When there was a protest or a rally, Little Professor and his friends always booked a hotel room nearby to use as a safe house. They used it to store gear or, if it came to that, as a retreat where they could hide from danger. Rumor had it that the cops sometimes conducted door-to-door searches in guesthouses, hotels, and inns near the protest sites and uncovered stashes of supplies left in those rooms by protesters. Recently, Little Professor's friends no longer dared to stay overnight, afraid of cops barging in on them. But he continued to use the hotel rooms. He liked to be able to shower and change just steps away from the protest and spend the night to relish and digest the excitement.

Occasionally, he invited her to join him there.

Aside from his self-assured grandstanding and endless gripes about everyone around him, Ning On found few things to nitpick about Little Professor as a fuck buddy. He was well-built, with strong arms. He was eager to please and kept her satisfied.

Sometimes he was tender, sometimes feral. She enjoyed it all. Each time, he left her feeling limp as if she were melting into the bed. Occasionally, she felt uneasy, fearing that she had turned into some greedy witch draining every drop of vitality from a strapping young man. Okay, speaking of greed, she had one more wish. If only someone could sew his mouth shut, or edit out all his long-winded speeches during mealtimes.

Ning On told herself, she was only in it for the sex like an ultimate modern woman. But from time to time, she thought about the half-healed wound on his left calf. It looked like a terrain mapped on human flesh.

After they checked out of the hotel, Little Professor asked if she wanted to see a movie. Sometimes it happened this way: after, before, or in between sex, they grabbed a meal, wandered the streets, or watched a film. It was usually his idea, like he was her guide showing her the world.

She had shown him part of her world once. At her insistence, he had visited her shop for a skin-care treatment. Maybe it was because of her profession, but she couldn't stand being intimate with someone who didn't take good care of his skin. It made things less pleasurable for her. She would never admit it. Perhaps her insistence to offer him a facial also had something to do with that ragged wound on his calf. She didn't know the story behind it, and he wouldn't let her find out. She suspected it must have hurt like hell.

As soon as Little Professor settled into the spa treatment, steam wafted over his face. As if on cue, he began telling her that the concept of beauty was a capitalist tool used to exploit and oppress women. But even he couldn't deny that it felt so good to pamper his face, especially after having trapped it for so long beneath protective gear against chemical irritants.

His skin was dry, dotted with clusters of blemishes. Ning On extracted them one by one with the tip of a needlelike tool. Now, for once, he was quiet. As she squeezed, lanced, and drained the tiny pimples on his nose, forehead, and cheeks, his eyes watered from the pinches, his face contorted into a pitiful expression. Slightly amused by it, Ning On slowed down and savored this wicked thrill. She wouldn't mind prolonging this moment and keep him lying quietly on this little treatment bed.

Sometimes she replayed that pimple-clearing session in her mind when he talked too much. She did it again that day. After watching the movie, Little Professor went on and on about the novel it was based on and took her to an independent bookstore nearby to show her the title. Being in a bright, crowded place with him made her wonder, what did they look like to others? Siblings? Friends? Colleagues? The more time they spent together in public, the more paranoid she became. She feared running into a client, or one of her daughter's classmates. She wouldn't know how to introduce him. Or, if they ran into someone he knew, how would he introduce her?

Ning On didn't want to know. But perhaps this implied that she already knew the answer but wasn't willing to face it.

In the bookstore, there was a poster promoting a protest concert, set to take place in an open lot across from a district police station. Local indie bands and singers were slated to perform, and the concert title was unapologetically dry. It directly borrowed the name of a pro-democracy anthem: "Democracy Will Triumph and Return."

Little Professor sneered at it. "Thirty years ago, during the Tiananmen protests, people sang democracy anthems for China—where did that get them?" he asked. "Some people are so ridiculous. They still buy into that 'Brothers climb mountains together, and they each have different things to offer' crap. It's the same bunch of armchair generals, most of them hippies, leftards, and cynics, blabbing empty slogans with zero action for the last thirty years. They've been dragging us backward. That's how we ended up here." He was irrepressible and went on. "You know what else? Some young intellectuals just started a reading group, proclaiming that books can save their country—what a joke. If they ever come out of their dens and show up at the front line, they'll see if books can stop bullets."

She noticed that Little Professor distanced himself from "the young intellectuals." She had learned of this emerging cultural collective from a TV segment. She thought this tirade was even more cynical than his usual self-righteous posturing, but Ning On had come to know his feelings better. She had seen his anger, his jealousy, his humiliation, and his helplessness. These emotions ran wild, but Ning On learned they were like the patches of flare-ups on his skin. She had seen that behind each of them, there was an untreated injury eating at him. She wanted to reach out and stroke his freshly washed hair. It was like the fur of a pet.

In the beginning, they met once a week at a fixed time. They always had dinner first before checking into a hotel. Ning On liked it that way. It made it easier to plan around her work. Her days were often a whirlwind of scheduled sessions as well as client bookings and cancellations. She was old-fashioned and still used a thick notebook-style planner to track everything. Its pages were covered in cross-outs, scribbles, and smudged ink. Only she could decipher the notes. It was according to her own sense of order, something she'd built and insisted on, like a private sanctuary. It was not for anyone else to understand or interfere with.

But during the final weekend of August, Little Professor messaged her out of the blue. He asked her to meet, refusing to take no for an answer. She checked the address. It was a hotel in a conflict zone. She looked up the route: public transport had shut down, police had cordoned off the streets. At a time like this, she knew, cab drivers were likely unwilling to take passengers that way. Ning Yuet was out late again and hadn't responded to her messages. Ning On hated this collapse of order. She hated all these factors beyond her control. She was about to turn him down when he sent a flurry of messages saying he needed her to come and that he was going to wait until she showed up. It seemed that he had no one else to turn to. He had pleaded so softly, pitiful as a child, like when Ning Yuet used to ask if she could sleep beside her. Ning On could never resist such requests and cradled her daughter's head against her chest, comforting her with the warmth of her body.

Ning On lost the strength to say no. After she arrived, he curled into her embrace and whimpered softly as he gently suckled her breast, begging her to kiss him, to wrap her arms around his neck. She ran her fingers through his hair. He was much taller than her, but he felt so small, so delicate. His eyes were misted and his palms were trembling. He asked her to hold his hands tight and not to let go. They clung to each other tightly, as if nothing remained on Earth except the two of them. They were both desperate and only anchored to this life by each other's warm bodies.

When he finally fell asleep, he was visited by nightmares. Clearly terrified, he was drenched in sweat. He shouted, "Run! Run!" It woke Ning On up. She tried to soothe him. "It's okay, it's okay now. *Shh*, you're safe. It's all right." He drifted back to sleep, his brows furrowed tightly, the corners of his eyes damp. He clutched her hand again. Ning On had trouble going back to sleep. She propped herself up and watched him. Gently, she let her fingertips glide over the broad, solid surface of his skin like a tiny boat surfing an ocean.

When it came to imperfections on the skin, Ning On thought she understood them better than anyone: she used a needlelike tool to extract blackheads; lasers to treat spots and marks and for overall brightening. Her clients came to her, lay on her tiny treatment bed to endure various tortures. In those intimate rooms, men and women alike teared up, eyes red, crying out in pain, begging for mercy, as if stripped of their dignity. These days, she knew, outside her salon, outside the little mall they were in, on streets all over the city, men and women had watery eyes too. They were subjected to a different kind of pain. When white smoke filled the streets, tears welled up in their red, irritated eyes.

And then, there was the laser machine. When it was switched on, it made *pop pop* sounds like an electrical bug killer. For a facial treatment, she usually moved the device in sweeping motions, back and forth along the chin, jawline, and all the way up to the forehead. Sometimes she focused on spots, zapping pigmentation, blemishes, and pores. From time to time, she felt she could smell scorched skin.

Maybe she'd use it on Little Professor one day. She looked at his perfectly toned and tanned left calf. There were several jagged dark brown scabs. Some of them were curved like a hook or a stroke. Others were merely a dot. They all clustered together in a tight little group. One was particularly large, in an irregular arc shape. Its purple-black center was surrounded by blotches of varying shades and textures, raised or sunken at places. Tiny beads of blood had seeped out and dried into tiny specks. Along the edges, fresh pink flesh had begun to grow, forming a dull white border where it met the scab. They appeared like a dried-up patch of terrain stitched onto his body, ghastly to look at. The largest among them had stiffened as if it were an unyielding, parched island. She and her laser machine couldn't touch this territory until the scabs were fully healed and had become scars.

She tucked the blanket around him. She knew, in the morning, he would be spilling sarcasm and indignation once more. If his preaching got on her nerves again, she imagined, she would abruptly and unceremoniously reach up and ruffle his hair. Caught off guard, Little Professor might be stunned into peaceful calmness. He might lower his head slightly, letting her caress his hair. She would once again confirm its pleasing texture.

This reminded her. Perhaps on her way home she would pick up a new hair product for her daughter.

PART TWO

Panda

The sky hung dark as if shrouded in dense smoke.

Ah Lei couldn't tell where this fogginess came from. Perhaps it was the misty air of summer giving way to fall? Or, was it the remnants of tear gas fired on this street the other day? She imagined the exhaust trapped between buildings on either side with no crevice to escape.

And what was this itchy sting on her neck? Was it a reaction to the chemicals in the tear gas? Or was it from the coarse strap of her heavy bag? It had dug into the flesh of her neck and shoulders day in and day out. A rash was spreading in patches.

Panda never wasted time pondering useless things like the various probable causes of a fog or an itch. She would have told Ah Lei, "Of course it's because of the tear gas!" Lately, Panda traced many things to tear gas. Just a few days ago, she told Ah Lei that tear gas had killed a cat. It was true, she said. She had seen it in a YouTube video. One night, the tear gas smoke was so thick outside, a Hong Kong woman in her sixties who lived in a street-facing apartment shut all the windows and blasted the AC. The next morning, she found her ten-year-old cat dying on the floor near her bed. She rushed it to the vet's office, but it was too late. "The vet didn't dare say it was the gas. He just said the cat was too old. Natural causes! Who are they trying to fool? Definitely the tear gas," Panda said.

In the last few hours, Ah Lei kept herself busy cleaning up Ah Mak's room. She searched for flyers, books, protest gear—anything that was evidence of what he had been up to. As she did so, she cursed the fog, scratched the itch, and tried not to think about the eyewitness photo of Ah Mak getting handcuffed.

This afternoon, Ah Mak and Ah Lei went to a protest in Kowloon. On their way there, they chatted about plans for the Mid-Autumn Festival, which was just a few days away. Strictly speaking, this kind of outing couldn't really be considered a date, but in the few weeks since they started going out, they spent a lot of time in the street.

The couple had developed a protocol. Since Ah Mak always ended up at the front of the crowd, every half hour, they met up at a designated spot so they could check in on each other and decide whether to stay or leave. In the late afternoon that day, however, things turned chaotic. The cops caught everyone off guard by advancing on them without prior warning. The demonstrators scattered in a panic.

Ah Lei called and texted Ah Mak. He didn't respond. Not sure what to do, she went to Ah Mak's apartment with the faint hope that maybe he had gone home and was waiting for her there.

He was not.

She opened Telegram and frantically searched large groups for "Kowloon District, 6:30 p.m." for updates. She sent Panda a direct message: "I lost contact with Ah Mak at the protest." For months, people she knew had frantically and discreetly looked for their friends or family who disappeared while attending protests. Today, she became one of these frantic people. Only now did she realize how lucky they were to skate by unscathed in the last three months.

Then, in a Telegram group where eyewitnesses submitted photos from the site of the arrests, she saw the photo of Ah Mak. Her fear was confirmed. She messaged a few more well-connected friends, and some of these volunteer groups and lawyers. Through a string of referrals, a woman working in arrest support called her. She introduced herself as Sister Ka and was an alumna of Ah Lei's university. She instructed Ah Lei to hurry and clear out anything linked to the movement in Ah Mak's apartment. She promised to get on the case right away and call Ah Lei as soon as she managed to locate Ah Mak.

Ah Lei collected every piece of potentially incriminating evidence she could find: tools, pamphlets, books. All these things that had been closest to their bodies, closest to their hearts this summer were now hot potatoes to be off-loaded. She spread them to different dumpsters in the area. As soon as she got back, Sister

Ka called. "Ah Mak has been moved a few times. Most likely he was sent to Sham Shui Po Police Station," she said.

It was after eleven, but Ah Lei had to go there. However, she needed to call Panda first. She looked for "Panda" in the contact list on her phone but couldn't find the entry. The roommates barely talked on the phone. They were either in the dorm together or kept in touch via direct messages.

Then she remembered: It wasn't saved under "Panda," but under her real name, "Hung Yi." Hung Yi had been "Panda" since junior high. For reasons unknown to Ah Lei, her classmates teased Hung Yi, calling her "Endangered Species" and "National Treasure," joking that she should celebrate her birthday at Ocean Park, laughing about sending her off to Sichuan with Ying Ying to learn how to mate.

Back then, Ying Ying and Le Le were household celebrities and especially popular among schoolchildren. They were two pandas gifted by the Chinese government to Ocean Park in 2007. This generous gesture was to commemorate the tenth anniversary of the return of Hong Kong—or, as Hung Yi no doubt would roll her eyes and mutter, "the transfer of sovereignty." The pair of precious beasts lived in Hong Kong for years without producing any offspring, causing concerns for zookeepers in Hong Kong and up north. The public felt invested too. It was as if they were hoping for a neighbor's middle-aged daughter to receive a marriage proposal, or a long-unemployed nephew to finally land a job. The enthused citizens waited and cheered on two animals entirely unrelated to them, willing them to bring new life into the world. To blossom and bear fruit. To birth noble heirs. To carry on the family line. What a joy it would be!

For this reason, Ying Ying had been sent back to Sichuan—the homestead of pandas—for fertility experiments. Nevertheless, for a local teenager named Hung Yi, the nickname "Panda" stuck.

The memory brought a brief smile to Ah Lei's face. She dialed Panda's number.

One evening in August 2008, when the phone rang, Hung Yi's family was in front of the TV. Their eyes were glued to the opening ceremony of the Beijing Olympics. The domestic helper picked up the phone. She bent over and addressed Mom in a hushed voice: "Ma'am, there has been an incident with your sister."

An hour later, Mom and twelve-year-old Hung Yi arrived at the Sham Shu Po Police Station to pick up Auntie Lan and Ah Mak. Hung Yi took a good look at the police station on her way out. The building spanned the junction of Yen Chow Street and Lai Chi Kok Road. It was low, wide, and long, more like a battleship than a police station, she thought.

Having grown up in one of the new towns, she'd always imagined government buildings as modern, towering skyscrapers, but wasn't this building in front of her just like one of those old

European museums she'd seen on travel shows? A columned portico with half-moon-shaped arcades. Low, closely spaced railings were installed just outside the windows. If this was in the afternoon, and you put a few tables and chairs there, it would be a perfect setting for a leisurely snack of French toast, soaking in the sun.

Mom tapped her head and shot her a look. Taking the cue, Hung Yi fished out two squashed buns from her pocket and offered them to her aunt and cousin. Auntie Lan and Mom were born from the same womb, so naturally, they were equally well-versed in the ways of the world. Auntie Lan accepted the bun with a smile. "Ah Mui is so thoughtful," she praised Hung Yi. She thanked her profusely and apologized for the trouble. Mom cut in, feigning annoyance. "What're you talking about? Don't be so formal with us."

Ah Mak leaned against a column. He was only three years older, but Hung Yi had always found him a little intimidating. When she offered him the other bun, he rejected it. "I'm not hungry," he said. She held the squashed bun in midair, frozen in an awkward pose, unsure whether to keep insisting out of politeness or take the hint and pull back. Around her cousin Ah Mak, her usual sharp tongue never quite worked.

Every Sunday, Mom took her to visit Auntie Lan. The sisters usually retreated into a tiny room, sliding the folding door shut. They gossiped in their native Hakka, unintelligible to the kids. At such times, Ah Mak always cleared off the cluttered sofa, brushing away questionable dust and crumbs before gesturing for her to sit down. Their weekly ritual was to watch a TV program called *Sunday Theatre*. All afternoon, the cousins sat in solemn silence, as though they were attending a church service.

It was always the same few Hong Kong movies playing in rotation. Either cop-and-gangster shootouts or incongruous slapstick comedies. Either *Bang bang bang!* or *Wah wah wah!* Nevertheless, they watched them over and over again, picking up a bunch of swear words and slang. Hung Yi started to notice some common tropes. For example, whenever a gun went off, a flock of white doves took flight. Also, shootouts always happened in shopping malls or on busy streets; knife fights, on the other hand, tended to occur at late-night alleys, under Yau Tsim Mong district's massive neon signs, where the redness of the lights and the redness of the blood blurred into one.

Back then, she was mesmerized by the vivid plotlines. It wasn't until much later, when Ah Mak took a film course, that he told her those white doves, shootouts, and neon signs were all symbols. Scholars loved studying these, calling them the characteristics of the city.

Hung Yi's favorites were the Stephen Chow and Ng Man-tat comedies. Even though she had watched the reruns enough to know every line by heart, she still giggled at all the jokes. Ah Mak, however, just sat there stone-faced, forcing her to swallow her laughter in embarrassment.

Out on the streets past one in the morning, she awkwardly

offered him that squished bun, marking another failed attempt at winning him over.

In the past two weeks, she had spent most of her days on the sofa with Ah Mou, the family dog. Ah Mou was also twelve. They were both bored and waiting. Ah Mou waited for the moment Mom or Dad opened the door so he could welcome them back by wagging his tail. Hung Yi waited for a phone call.

That May, an 8.0 magnitude earthquake hit the mountainous heartland of Sichuan Province. The death toll eventually rose to nearly seventy thousand. For weeks on end, the disaster and its aftermath took over the news. At Hung Yi's school, students were asked to each write an essay titled "In Memory of the Wenchuan Earthquake." Their submissions were entered into a citywide competition. Hung Yi had always been a top student. Usually, she didn't need to work too hard to score the highest in her class. Perhaps because of this, when she occasionally failed to do so, it grated her.

She was determined to win the competition. In the ten days before the assignment was due, she consumed every piece of content she could find on the subject. And she had plenty of sources. Several TV stations sent reporters to cover the rescue-and-recovery efforts on the ground. Cameramen followed firefighters as they struggled through the rubble and debris in search of survivors. There was also footage of a villager frantically digging through the mud and gravel with his bare hands, screaming and sobbing as he tried to recover his loved ones. Neighbors and relatives pulled him away from where his house used to be. He collapsed and wailed. Not far from him, a few survivors who had just been rescued were wrapped in shawls. They sat stoically.

Hung Yi studied these clips and tried to place herself at the scene. It wasn't just about learning what happened but also about the emotions she could feel from it. She realized it wasn't difficult to overload oneself with feelings: a young mother used her own body to shield her infant from the impact; rescue workers kept a trapped man conscious by chatting with him for hours before he was rescued. He died on the way to the hospital. Hung Yi sniffled and cried over these news stories. In the end, she was satisfied with the essay she submitted. Her teachers often said good writing was usually filled with emotions resonating with real-life experiences.

Back in elementary school, a teacher had once told Mom that Hung Yi seemed to "understand things a little differently from the others." For instance, in a Chinese writing exercise, students were told to make a sentence with these components: "leads to / diligence / laziness / success / leads to / failure."

The correct answer was: "Diligence leads to success; laziness leads to failure."

But Hung Yi's answer was: "Success leads to laziness; failure leads to diligence."

When the sheet was returned to her, she saw a big red X

slashed across her paper. Baffled, she ran up to the teacher's desk and asked what was wrong with her answer. She earnestly laid out her reasoning: "If someone keeps succeeding, they naturally become complacent and start slacking off. Just like in 'The Tortoise and the Hare'; the hare kept coming in first, so it underestimated its opponent and lost to the tortoise. On the other hand, failure makes people work harder. Like Edison—he ran more than eight thousand experiments before he finally invented the light bulb. How is this wrong?"

The teacher seemed mildly amused by her argument but wasn't sure what to tell her except to not be so pessimistic. She wasn't convinced. The teacher was losing patience. "Anyway, let's stop talking nonsense. Your answer is different from the standard one, so it's wrong. Understand? Besides, you already have the highest grade in the class. Why make a fuss over a fraction of a point?" Her classmates nearby quickly joined in, jeering at her for not knowing when to quit, for scoring so high and still nitpicking. Wasn't she just rubbing salt in the wounds of those who scored lower? Did she think she was really all that just because she got good grades?

After school she told Mom about it, only to become more upset when Mom tried to comfort her by suggesting that she should be happy with being "good enough." "Don't be so hard on yourself," Mom said. Everyone was missing the point. This feeling of being misunderstood sent young Hung Yi into an unknown sadness. Revisiting the memory of that day, Hung Yi mused that the teacher's warning against pessimism and Mom's advice on flexibility had likely backfired. She grew to defend her points of view even more.

A couple of weeks before the Olympics opening ceremony, Hung Yi's best friend, Ah Sze, mentioned receiving a phone call. The host of the writing competition informed her that her essay had made it to the final round and would be included in an upcoming anthology. She was also invited to a press conference where the winner would be announced. Ah Sze and Hung Yi read each other's submissions. Hung Yi privately thought Ah Sze's writing was filled with lofty declarations and flashy words. Her own piece was obviously superior. After all, she had cried real tears in the process. Also, her grades had always been far better than Ah Sze's. If Ah Sze had become a finalist, it was only natural to expect that she'd receive a call too.

In the following days, Ah Sze kept asking if she got her call. At first, Hung Yi took this impatience to be an endearing wish that they could both receive prizes and be in the anthology together. But soon she found it annoying, and tinged with a hint of boastfulness. Among girls their age, they became aware of an undercurrent forming beneath their previously innocent friendships. For years they'd been all smiles and lovey-dovey. Suddenly, they started to hear an edge in their friends' innocuous-sounding comments.

Even more anxiously, Hung Yi waited for the phone to ring. Mom teased that she was turning into Ah Mou. Jittery as a puppy, she hovered by the phone. She refused to drink water in case she needed to pee and missed the call. She kept her eyes locked on the base unit, waiting for the green light to flash so she could snatch up the receiver and answer.

"Hello?" Having recently lost a few baby teeth, her words came out slightly lisped. On the night of the Olympics opening ceremony, when the helper picked up the phone, Hung Yi had imagined a warm and official voice on the other end, saying, "Apologies for the late call, but we are glad to inform you. . . ."

The writing competition business not only made things weird with Ah Sze, but also drew Hung Yi's own emotions into question. These were more difficult questions outside the framework of the essay. Questions that Hung Yi didn't have standard answers for. Sinking into someone else's sorrow was so easy—should she guard her own heart? If she did all this as part of her schoolwork, were these feelings even real?

Was her sorrow contrived and manufactured for the sake of a prize?

She wanted to defend her intentions: The thought that many, many kids her age had been sitting in class one minute and were dead the next had undeniably made her sad. But what kind of grief was this? Was it like her fear of losing Ah Mou as the dog approached old age? Was it like when a beloved character got killed off in a TV show? Or, was it like what Dad said, the victims were compatriots and they were bound to her by blood?

To prove that her intentions were pure, one weekend, Hung Yi woke up early to join a fundraising drive. It was a raffle organized by the local community center. She was the youngest and shortest among the volunteers, but her fervor impressed all others. She carried raffle tickets in her hand and a clear box on her back. Running through the neighborhood, she called out, "Please help with the Sichuan earthquake relief! Save our compatriots."

When she returned to the center, she handed the clear box back to a staffer. The nice-looking auntie turned it upside down and colorful banknotes rained onto the desk. The auntie praised her, "What a gutsy girl. Maybe you'll one day make a living with a microphone in hand!"

The community center auntie wasn't far off. Eleven summers later, Hung Yi was out in the bustling streets again, leafletting, postering, setting up encampments. She ran around day and night, lugging speakers and megaphones with her. "Withdraw the evil law! Stand up against the extradition bill!" Hung Yi shouted herself hoarse. Would the auntie praise her courage this time?

As the bus approached Sham Shui Po, Panda had a feeling of déjà vu. It was as if she were twelve again, arriving at this neighborhood late at night, fearing that her cousin Ah Mak might be in trouble. Walking toward the police station, she could now see the low-slung building in the distance. It looked just like what she remembered.

"Why don't we pick up some food before meeting up with Ah

Lei?" A man's voice brought Panda back to the present moment. "Having some food in the stomach will help everyone feel better," he said. It was Ah Ming, Panda's new boyfriend. She had first seen him at a protest, tossing Molotov cocktails like it was the end-times. Was that what had attracted her? She was certainly charmed, later, when she saw the radical turning all soft and kind at a dinner gathering, thoughtfully ordering food for the table and refilling friends' water glasses. They stopped to order at a street food cart and watched the preparation.

They were still new in this relationship, learning each other's tolerance for spice and preference for drinks and swapping childhood memories. On their ride here, Panda told Ah Ming about her patriotic fundraising effort as a child. Ah Ming said he had a patriotic story too. "I was once a flag bearer in elementary school," he shared. "From flag bearer to flame thrower?" Panda chuckled. Ah Ming smiled and went on. Every National Day, his school organized a flag-raising ceremony, and the Civic Education teacher picked three students to do the honor in front of the whole school. "We all wanted to be chosen and behaved so well in civics class. My friends were very jealous when I got picked," he said.

"Did the experience live up to your expectations?" Panda asked teasingly.

"The air was muggy and stifling that day," Ah Ming said. "I watched the flag moving to the top, but without any wind, it hung limp without even showing all five stars on it." He feigned sadness.

"Poor you! Your opportunity of heroism turned into a public display of lousiness." She laughed and patted him on the back.

When they carried the take-out food and turned onto Yen Chow Street, they saw the block was teeming with family, friends, and supporters of the arrestees. People were busy talking on the phone, texting updates, or explaining the situation to those who just got there. Panda spotted Ah Lei sitting under a streetlamp, curled up like a cat in cold weather. Without making a sound, she snuck up and pressed warm tea and a bowl of fish and lettuce soup against Ah Lei's cheek.

Panda was used to seeing Ah Lei being gloomy, but she was still taken aback by how down she looked. "It seems like we're always eating whenever we're together," Ah Lei said as she lifted the lid off the bowl. Steam rose. "Remember the time we had burgers with Ah Mak? That was my first meal with him. I knew you were trying to set us up."

"I wasn't! But you ended up dating anyway," Panda said, trying to lighten the mood. She sat down by Ah Lei's side. Ah Lei's eyes were rimmed red. She looked up to the sky, as if trying to get her tears to flow back. "It's the steam. The bowl's so hot," she said. "You know, he doesn't have many friends. Even I don't know him that well yet." Panda set Ah Lei's bowl aside and pulled her into a hug. "It's okay, it's okay. He has us. And we're here now. We'll get to see him soon," Panda said, stroking Ah Lei's hair.

The dense buildings cropped the dark sky into a square. Streetlights flared bright. It was a sleepless night for people all around them. Contradicting speculations of the arrestees' fates circulated. One version said they weren't going to be charged, another said they were all going to face riot charges. Trying to piece these together frayed their nerves. Panda changed the subject. "Did you know I actually picked up Ah Mak here a long time ago?"

When the phone rang that evening, Hung Yi and her parents were enjoying the opening ceremony of the Beijing Olympics.

The show was spectacular. At one point, numerous performers stood side by side in staggered rows, creating a vast sweep of whiteness. They held bamboo slips and chanted scripts. Another group moved nimbly on the stage and became formations of Chinese characters. Soon, they turned into the Great Wall and then cascades of peach-pink blossoms. Each sequence was accompanied by perfectly coordinated music, lighting, and special effects. Mom and Dad were stunned and kept saying things like, "This is insane!" and "How do they do that?"

Hung Yi slapped her arm hard, trying to dispel the tiny bumps that had risen on her skin. She suspected it wasn't just about being moved or being excited by the visuals. Usually, she only got goosebumps at unsettling sights, especially clusters on beehives, lotus-seed pods, and strawberries. Just thinking about it made her scalp tingle.

When the show cut to commercial break, they could finally sit back. "If I'm being honest, I have mixed feelings about this," Mom said. "So many people died just a few months ago, and now the whole country puts on a big show of celebration. Sure, it's amazing to look at, but I feel a little iffy about it."

Dad came out of the kitchen, carrying freshly brewed mulberry-mistletoe tea. "Isn't it precisely when people are heartbroken that they need something uplifting? We can't live in grief forever," he said. "Besides, this may not sound nice, but it's not like our country is lacking in population. Am I right?" The broadcast resumed. Mom turned back to the show without engaging with Dad's comment.

Hung Yi snuggled with Ah Mou and thought about what Dad had just said. His words were meant to be uplifting and positive, but they left a knot in her chest.

On TV, aerial shots showed magnificent scenes made up of groups of synchronized performers. Yet in that vast sea of color, Hung Yi couldn't make out a single person.

Later that night, when Hung Yi followed Mom to the police station, she witnessed a spectacle of another kind.

Auntie Lan's left eye was half shut and swollen like an egg, her face blotched with patches of purple and blue. Her hair was a mess. Her clothes were torn. She was screaming and pointing her finger at her husband. "He hit me! He hit a woman! Why aren't you locking him up? Please help me!" An officer ordered her to stop shouting and sit down.

Ah Mak's dad was calm. "I never laid a finger on her. This is all an act."

Ah Mak sat next to his mom and didn't say anything.

Mom was anxious and had brought in a lawyer. But it looked like the police weren't going to press charges. After taking statements from both sides, they asked Auntie Lan whether she wanted to file a formal complaint. The same Auntie Lan who'd been so frantic fell quiet for a moment. She conferred briefly with Hung Yi's mom and the lawyer. She said no.

On the ride home, Auntie Lan dozed off in the passenger seat. Hung Yi fiddled with the button on the door, making the window go up and down. "Stop." Mom said just the one word. Hung Yi complied and left the window open at the top. Wind whistled through the crack, carrying the heat from the streets.

Next to her in the back seat was Ah Mak. Without looking at her, he said in a low voice, "Do you believe my dad hit my mom?"

Even before the visit to Sham Shui Po Police Station, Mom had always told Hung Yi to be nice to Auntie Lan. "She's a gentle soul and has endured a lot. Fate hasn't been kind to her. We owe her that much," Mom said. For as long as Hung Yi remembered, every weekend, she followed Mom up the six flights of stairs to Auntie Lan's. Each time, Mom lugged bags from the grocer's and the butcher's up the narrow, winding stairwell, and never tired of reminding her, "You must listen to Auntie Lan. You can give me attitude all you want, but you can never be disrespectful to her. We owe her that, okay?"

Hung Yi nodded. She wasn't really sure who constituted "we": the entire family? Or just Mom and her? And what exactly did they owe her? Why couldn't they just pay her back? What she knew was what she saw. Around Auntie Lan, Mom always put away her usual flamboyant personality and played the part of a deferential little sister.

Auntie Lan's family rented a unit in a postwar tenement building in Sham Shui Po. Like with most old tong lau buildings, the rent was cheap, but there was no elevator.

Enduring the stairs was apparently one of the things they owed Auntie Lan. The building looked skinny from the outside, but it was like a spiraling tower from the inside. Its steep stairs seemed to never end. Hung Yi navigated dead cockroaches, toppled liquor bottles, and suspicious, foul-smelling puddles. Occasionally, old men in rubber slippers and saggy undershirts emerged from a unit with a MASSAGE sign on it. Hung Yi tried to get out of their way.

By the time they arrived at Auntie Lan's door, they were gasping for air. Mom forbade Hung Yi from ringing the doorbell. Instead, she knocked on the door herself once they both stopped panting. Once or twice, Hung Yi had pressed the buzzer before Mom could stop her. Auntie Lan opened the door quickly and immediately began apologizing for making them huff and puff.

"Poor little Ah Mui. Having to come all this way every week, sweating buckets. I'm sorry."

Auntie Lan was quick to say "I'm sorry." She said it when people bumped into her on the street, before ordering food, and even more frequently around her own family.

"Happy birthday, Ah Mui. Your uncle's busy today and can't make it to your party. I'm sorry."

"This old building is stinky and has roaches. I'm not sure if you can get used to it. I'm sorry."

"You spent money on fish and meat again. I'm sorry."

Until Auntie Lan and Ah Mak moved in with Hung Yi's family, she had always thought Auntie Lan was simply exceptionally polite.

Mom sighed when she spoke of Auntie Lan's past. Auntie Lan had dropped out of elementary school to work in a garment factory. She was good-looking, no doubt about it, but perhaps she was too picky, so she didn't marry until after turning twenty-eight. A friend played matchmaker and introduced her to Ah Mak's dad. They got married pretty quickly and had Ah Mak three years later.

Mom couldn't stand Ah Mak's dad. She found his mustache an eyesore and said it made him look like a sleazy informer. Fortunately, they didn't have to see him that often. After 1997, he went to work on the mainland and rarely came home. To be fair, he did wire living expenses on time. Auntie Lan never lacked for anything.

Mom was seven years younger than Auntie Lan, but they married around the same time. Supposedly, Mom met Dad while studying for her diploma. She worked for a year or two after graduation, and they tied the knot once Dad passed the civil service exam.

On June 28, 1997, Hung Yi was born. Relatives joked that she "popped out" just in time, sneaking in a few breaths of British air before the July 1 handover.

Mom gave birth in a private hospital after more than ten hours of labor. She had clutched Dad's hand, screaming her lungs out. Her fingernails dug into his skin. She swore she would never have another child. Dad repeated, "No more, no more," promising to get a vasectomy.

Hung Yi was born with a big head and weighed three kilos. A photo time-stamped from three p.m. that day showed Mom lying in bed. She was pale but smiling. Her hair was tangled in unsightly clumps. She carried a pink lump of flesh, whose face was all scrunched up. When Hung Yi was shown this first ever photo of herself, she refused to believe the barely human creature was her.

Three days after Hung Yi's birth, the sovereignty transfer ceremony took place. Inside a grand hall, the ceremony began. The Union Jack and colonial Hong Kong's lion-and-dragon flag flew high. President Jiang Zemin of the People's Republic of China and Britain's Prince Charles each delivered a speech. Then, just before midnight, the blue flags were lowered to "God Save the Queen," marking the official end of more than a century of British colonial rule.

At midnight, the Five-Star Red Flag and the new Bauhinia regional flag were raised. The Hong Kong Special Administrative Region was officially established. A long-lost child was welcomed back to its motherland with a promise of fifty years of self-governing. The live broadcast played in the empty hospital lobby while Mom and baby Hung Yi slept soundly in the maternity ward.

As Hung Yi grew up, Auntie Lan liked to jokingly complain, "Ah Mui, fate has been so good to you. You have a clever mom who knew to apply for a British National Overseas passport on your behalf. Having an education makes all the difference. Your poor cousin Ah Mak wasn't as lucky. He has nothing because he got into the wrong womb. He got stuck with a mother like me."

After they left the police station, Auntie Lan and Ah Mak moved in. Auntie Lan took Hung Yi's room, Dad slept on the sofa, Hung Yi shared the main bedroom with her mom, and Ah Mak spread out a mat on the floor. Auntie Lan and Ah Mak had stayed here several times before, after Auntie Lan showed up in the middle of the night in tears. But on those occasions, she never stayed more than a few days. When her anger cooled, she went back to the tong lau apartment in Sham Shui Po.

This time, however, months went by. The temporary sleeping arrangement seemed to become permanent.

Mom and Auntie Lan were often out all day, returning only in the late afternoon. Mom was developing a temper. At night, once she closed the master bedroom door, she lashed out over trivial matters, such as Hung Yi's failure to wear indoor slippers, not drying her hair properly, or letting her nails grow out too much. Hung Yi felt so wronged, but there was nowhere for her to be alone. At night, she sometimes bit the corner of her blanket and cried silent tears.

Perhaps Mom had imagined that no one heard what she said behind closed doors. But everyone knew. Afterward, in the morning, Auntie Lan always discreetly slipped Hung Yi milk candies, saying, "Ah Mui, I'm so sorry." Even Ah Mak noticed her red, puffy eyes as they walked to school. He told her to press a boiled egg on them.

Hung Yi felt embarrassed. Why bother closing the bedroom door if everyone could hear everything? After witnessing Auntie Lan's meltdown at the police station, the two families' troubles seemed to have all bled together. Hung Yi thought of the bun she'd offered Ah Mak that night. Would Ah Mak have preferred it if she didn't offer the bun, or if she wasn't even there at all? More importantly, why was Mom becoming so volatile? What on earth was happening during the day? When she asked, Mom told her it wasn't anything she should be bothered with and instructed her not to ask Auntie Lan such unnecessary questions.

Normally, when she got home from school, she kicked off her socks haphazardly in the living room, and didn't even bother changing out of her school uniform before sprawling out on the sofa. She liked to snack on a Popsicle while watching cartoons. But now, Ah Mak was always hanging around, and when Auntie Lan and Mom were home, they sat around the living room chatting as if they had been separated at birth and had a lifetime's worth of stories to catch up on.

How do they find so much to talk about? Once in a while, Hung Yi talked on the phone with Ah Sze for an hour. The receiver got so hot it made her ear sweat and her face burn, and they ran out of things to say to each other. But such was not the case for Mom and Auntie Lan. From past weekends in the tong lau unit to her family's living room, they gabbed day and night, until Mom finally grew tired enough to turn off the lights.

They mixed Cantonese words with Hakka, their native tongue from their mainland hometown. Sometimes Hung Yi managed to catch a few Cantonese phrases: "up there," "ancestral home," "village entrance," "salted chicken," "old neighbors." Sometimes they got really excited, and their Hakka sped up. From the tone, Hung Yi could make out their irritation and resentment. Such verbal storms dissipated as suddenly as they appeared.

Soon, the topic shifted, and the rhythm of their conversation lightened. Auntie Lan occasionally even burst into bright, ringing laughter.

Hung Yi had always thought of Auntie Lan as a generous person. Even though she frequently said sorry for the old tong lau building, for Ah Mak being so quiet, for her husband's absence at family meals, she was never shy when fighting to pick up the bill at restaurants. She also lavished Hung Yi with gifts.

Since they moved in, Auntie Lan doubled down on this generosity. When they went out for dim sum, as soon as everyone sat down, she asked the floor manager for a menu and began ticking on the order sheets: har gow, siu mai, sesame balls, deep-fried wontons in sweet and sour sauce, glutinous rice dumplings. Soon, the table was crowded with oily and crispy dishes. Mom couldn't stop Auntie Lan, so she just glared at Hung Yi, urging her to eat up as if any waste would be on her. Hung Yi loved all these dishes, but having too much made her feel sick. She glanced at Ah Mak, who sat next to her, thinking surely these were his favorites. But he ate even slower than her, nibbling on a single tofu skin roll for forever.

She leaned toward him and whispered, "You can eat whatever you want, you know? Don't be shy!" Ah Mak heard her, but instead of lifting his chopsticks, he quietly took the order sheet, made a few quick marks, and slipped it to her under the table. "Tell my mom you want these. Remember, *you* want them." She skimmed the sheet: chicken feet, beef tripe, steamed chicken rolls. Not a single fried item.

When everything was served, the dishes took up half the table. Much of it had to be packaged to take home. That night, Mom added one more item to her list of criticisms. "From now on, when you're out shopping or eating with Auntie Lan, you're not allowed to ask for or show interest in anything."

Hung Yi should have known that Auntie Lan wasn't just staying for a few days when she brought three full boxes of clothes, along with a fold-out, multitiered portable vanity packed with makeup, serums, and other skincare products. In contrast, Ah Mak only had a small suitcase. Hung Yi had imagined it had model kits, comic books, or even a stash of adult magazines he couldn't show in public, but when Ah Mak unpacked in the living room, she saw there were just a few sets of clothes and a movie poster. Ah Mak unfurled it. Hung Yi recognized it was from *King of Comedy*, a film they'd watched together. The poster wasn't an original, probably just a film still he found online and inkjet-printed on paper. The colors were already beginning to blur.

In the poster, Cecilia Cheung wore heavy makeup and leaned against a tree. Stephen Chow stood beside her, one hand on his hip, the other lifting her chin with a finger. They looked into each other's eyes. Behind the tree was the sea.

"Okay if I put this up?" he asked her.

Hung Yi didn't care for the poster. Being funny was one thing; appearing tasteful was another. Even though she enjoyed laughing at the film's poop-pee-fart school of jokes, she had no desire to put something like that up as decoration. That would be tacky.

But she didn't want to reject this request outright. "Do you have one up at your place too?" No, he said. Hung Yi exhaled in relief. "My mom didn't allow it," he added.

This immediately brought Hung Yi to his side. She was familiar with the "Mom won't allow" problem. According to Mom, Hung Yi wasn't allowed to eat ice cream on the sofa, or to sit with her legs wide open, or to accept gifts from Auntie Lan. A solidarity between kids swayed Hung Yi's thinking. "I say let's do it! Put it up!" she said.

Ah Mak's eyes widened. He quickly tore off a few strips of tape and stuck them to the four corners, as if rushing to get it done before she changed her mind.

"My mom said she's picking us up after school tomorrow." Ah Mak offered this piece of information as he smoothed down the top corners. "If she suggests taking you to a clothing store, I advise you not to go. She'll insist on buying you something." Hung Yi blinked, letting on an air of innocence. "How do you know? Maybe she'll buy you something too."

The tape on the top right corner was crooked and creased, so Ah Mak scratched it lightly with his fingernail, then smoothed it out and pressed it flat. "No. Don't you get it? She wants to buy you clothes and ask you to immediately change into them. It's all for your mom to see. Even better if you could twirl around, sweetly profess your love for 'Auntie Lan.'"

In September, the new school year started. One evening, when Auntie Lan and Mom began to prepare dinner, Hung Yi announced that she was going to interview them. Her homework was to talk to a family member and write a short essay. Mom spread out old newspapers on the dining table. On top, Auntie Lan placed a bowl of minced cured meat, a bowl of shredded daikon, and a large basin filled with rice flour. Auntie Lan was showing Mom how to make "loh pet ban." Hung Yi didn't understand the Hakka word, so Mom explained that they were just like cha gwo, the steamed glutinous rice treats. Then, Auntie Lan went to boil some ingredients in the kitchen, and Mom added water to the flour. Hung Yi began her interview.

"My family is Hakka from Pingshan, Shenzhen. I had one older brother and three older sisters. In the late sixties, Pops first brought my brother and two of my sisters to Hong Kong, hugging a beach ball to cross the water. Half a year later, my pregnant Mama, who had no choice but to come, brought my third sister—your Auntie Lan—down by boat," Mom said as she stirred the water-flour mixture. "At first, things were rough. The family had to live apart. My mom gave birth to me in a squatter settlement in Ma Chai Hang. After the big fire broke out there in eighty-one we finally got assigned public housing, and we all lived together for the first time."

Hung Yi did the math: one older brother, three older sisters?

That didn't add up. She only had one uncle and two aunties. Where did this extra sister come from? She was about to ask when Auntie Lan walked over with another plate. "What, talking about me? Your mom had no idea how things were like for us up there. It's better down here. Ah Mui, your mom was born as lucky as you. She came into the world after the family made it to Hong Kong. Unlike poor Second Sister who clung to that beach ball, thinking she was finally going to have a good life. She didn't manage to swim over. Who knows if she ended up as shark food."

"Second Sister . . ." Mom began, but Auntie Lan cut her off and changed the topic. "Let's not talk about that anymore. Ah Ying, look, this is how you make 'ban ma.' You boil some small pieces of dough, and press them flat. Once they cool, you knead them into the raw flour. It makes the glutinous outer layer extra sticky." She poured blobs that looked like tofu pudding from the plate into the large basin, mixing them with the rest of the flour, and started kneading.

Mom leaned toward Hung Yi and asked softly, "Do you have to do the interview right now? It's a zoo in here, and we're too busy trying to get everything done. Why don't we wait till the dumplings are steaming, then we can go back to the room and chat?"

Hung Yi jotted down a few notes, thinking, but it's not like Mom's busy right now—isn't Auntie Lan the one doing all the work? Auntie Lan chimed in, "It's all under control. And we are never too busy to help Ah Mui with her homework. If we get this done now, she'll have time to walk the dog with Ah Mak later. Ask away! It's not like there are things that can't be said right here, right?"

Upon hearing this, Mom seemed deflated. Hung Yi thought she looked pathetic, but she was holding a grudge against Mom for all the berating in recent weeks, so she pressed on. "What's the most memorable experience from your childhood?"

Mom took over kneading the dough in the basin and thought about it. "There are so many. Going to the neighborhood shop to buy Popping Candy, hiding under a classmate's bed to watch TV, squatting at a street-side comic book stand reading comics." Auntie Lan stir-fried the cured meat, shredded daikon, dried shrimp, scallions, and garlic, and instructed Mom, "Make sure you knead it evenly! Otherwise, the wrappers will tear."

"I just need the most memorable one so I can turn it into an essay. Choose one with vivid details." Hung Yi was getting a little impatient.

"Oh, I have one," Auntie Lan jumped in. "When she was little, back in the squatter settlement, we kept a tiny yellow finch. At the time, the family only got to spend time together on weekends. Your grandpa felt bad that the three of us—Grandma, your mom, and me—only had one another to rely on, so he tried to make it up to us. Ah Ying and I begged him to buy us a yellow finch. He took us to the bird market and we picked one out. I still remember carrying that bamboo cage. We were over the moon. Your mom was so tiny and insisted on carrying 'the birdie.' But the cage was too big for her, so we carried it together."

When Auntie Lan told the story, her hands didn't stop for a second. She tore off a chunk of dough, flattened it and pressed it into the shape of a small bowl, then added the filling. "Pops used to take us to a teahouse and hung the birdcage by the window. We loved watching the little bird hop around. In fact, we kids weren't into teahouses. Your mom especially hated them and thought they were too old-fashioned. They were full of randos who were loud and filthy. Some of them coughed up phlegm into a spittoon. Pops had no idea we hated it. He always ordered us tons of dim sum—basket after basket of char siu buns, lotus-seed paste buns, steamed chicken rolls, beef balls. The table wasn't big enough. Ha ha, sound familiar? But we hardly touched the food. We were too focused on fussing over the little yellow bird in the cage. He got mad and claimed that if we didn't focus on eating, the bird in the bamboo cage would turn into chicken rolls in the bamboo steamer. Ah Ying was scared into tears." Auntie Lan was so amused by her storytelling, she burst into laughter.

Hung Yi was bored. She couldn't see why this silly anecdote had Auntie Lan so animated, her eyes practically lit up. Mom kept her head down, stuffing each dumpling with so much filling that she couldn't close them properly. Wanting to wrap up her interview as soon as possible, Hung Yi cut in bluntly, turning to Mom. "So the most memorable thing from your childhood is Grandpa buying you a bird?"

"Ah, no, no." Auntie Lan waved her hand. "Look at me—always going off on a tangent. Okay, okay, I'll let your mom take it from here. I'd better go rescue these poor dumplings." She picked up an oddly shaped dumpling Mom just made.

Mom took a sip of water and glanced at Auntie Lan, who paid her no attention. "We named the little thing Tweety, after a popular cartoon character at the time. Pops said once something had a name, it carried weight and needed to be properly cared for. When school let out early and Mama and your Auntie Lan were both at work, I liked to stick my hand in the cage to play with the bird, and it hopped around. I could never tell if it liked me or hated me."

One night, a fire broke out in Ma Chai Hang. It grew wild, Mom recalled, "like a red curtain" falling over the entire settlement. They woke up choking on smoke. They fumbled for one another in the dark. Mom had wanted to grab their washbasin and clothes, but Auntie Lan shouted at her to hurry. They escaped and stumbled onto the main road. It was pitch dark and very hot. That was when Mom remembered Tweety. They had left Tweety behind. Only eight at the time, she was too young to grasp the scale of the disaster. She threw a tantrum, wailing and screaming for her pet bird. Agitated, Auntie Lan smacked her across the face, then turned around and ran back into the settlement before anyone could stop her.

Auntie Lan paused her busy hands and looked at Mom.

"Ah! That's why you're so nice to Auntie Lan, because she saved your little yellow finch!" Hung Yi blurted out.

Neither Mom nor Auntie Lan said anything. They each returned to their tasks.

EVERYDAY MOVEMENT

After dinner, Hung Yi and Ah Mak took Ah Mou out for a walk. Lately, the responsibility of taking care of the dog had fallen onto the cousins. Well, to be precise, Ah Mak had taken on the responsibility of babysitting both the dog and Hung Yi. She had seen Mom slipping Ah Mak small amounts of money, telling him to keep an eye on her. Thankfully, most of the time, Ah Mak just took her to a fast-food joint after class, where they ate burgers and did homework. Sometimes Hung Yi told him about her day.

They walked the dog along the bike path near home. Ah Mak held the leash, and Hung Yi held a water bottle and some old newspaper. In this new town, urban planning was hardly consistent. At the beginning of the walk, they passed rows of houses. But soon, the scenery turned into a wilderness of overgrown weeds. On a wired-mesh fence, signs advertised development plans for the land. Occasionally, they ran into a stray dog, who jumped into a barking match with Ah Mou.

Hung Yi told Ah Mak that the head teacher told the whole class about Ah Sze entering the final round of the competition. "He even encouraged us to all go watch the award ceremony," Hung Yi said. "No one actually wants to go, but if you don't, you'll look unsupportive of your friend or overall antisocial. So now everyone said they're going. Ugh!"

"You don't want to go because you never got that call, right?" Ah Mak asked.

She wanted to deny it, but what was the point? He had seen her hovering near the telephone all summer. "I obviously wrote better than she did. My feelings were genuine. I definitely cared more about the earthquake. I even went around selling raffle tickets," she said.

Ah Mou walked over to a tree and lifted a hind leg.

Ah Mak seemed to regret having asked his young cousin such a sharp question. "Yes, yes, and you sold a ton. I know. The auntie at the community center even praised you."

"Yeah, and I bet while I was out selling tickets, Ah Sze was at home playing video games." Hung Yi twisted open the bottle and poured water over the spot where Ah Mou had peed to wash away the smell.

"You really want to know what I think?" Ah Mak asked.

"No, let's talk about something else," Hung Yi said.

Ah Mou seemed to be getting tired. When they first set out, the dog was tugging the leash to go ahead. Now, as they chatted, Ah Mou was lagging behind.

"Remember the other day I was late picking you up from school? My dad had showed up at school looking for me." Ah Mak reached into his pocket. "He gave me this." He opened his hand and revealed a gray-and-white slider mobile phone.

"Is this the legendary Nokia 5300? The phone that takes photos, plays music, and shoots videos?!" Hung Yi snatched the phone and inspected it. "I've never seen the real thing. Wait, how do you not have a single song on here?"

"He asked if I wanted to go with him."

She experimented with the camera and snapped a photo of Ah Mou sprawled on the ground, too lazy to keep going. She didn't grasp what it all meant. "Go where with him?" she asked.

"You have no idea what our moms have been up to these days, do you?" Ah Mak answered her with a question. She shook her head no. "Ah, of course, they wouldn't have told you. You have to focus on school, on your important upcoming junior high entrance exams," Ah Mak said. She couldn't tell if his tone was mocking.

"My mom wants a divorce. And she is trying to apply for public housing for the two of us. But she can't do these on her own. She doesn't know any English. She's barely literate. So your mom was helping her with all the forms and meetings."

That was a lot of information. Hung Yi tried to process everything. Wasn't divorce something that only happened in TV dramas? What was going to happen to their tong lau apartment? Would she ever see the dark, musty stairwell again?

"Have you ever wondered why your mom's always so nice to mine? Doesn't it feel more than just sisterly love?" Ah Mak went on.

"Does Auntie Lan have something on my mom?" Hung Yi blurted out.

"Not exactly. Have you heard about the Ma Chai Hang fire?"

"Yes, Auntie Lan saved Tweety!" Hung Yi was glad she knew something after all.

But that was apparently only half of the story.

"When I was very little, I used to bathe with my mom. I saw her body." He glanced at his younger cousin and spared her the worst details. Kissed by fire, Auntie Lan's skin was all discolored and jagged with ugly lumps and uneven layers of patches. She had often said to Ah Mak that if it weren't for this body, she would never have married his dad.

Hung Yi wasn't sure if she heard everything right. She felt like she had questions, but didn't have the words.

Ah Mak went on. "Perhaps your mom is there for my mom, every day, in some government building, holding their number in line and waiting for their turn to meet with an officer or a social worker; tirelessly filing the paperwork for an emergency case; claiming that my dad committed domestic violence. . . ." Hung Yi had never heard Ah Mak say so many words at once. He seemed almost out of breath as he finished the last thought. "Your mom is doing all these things without any complaint because she believes she ruined my mom's life and that it would take a lifetime to pay back."

Indifferent to their exchange, Ah Mou squatted and pooped. Ah Mak pulled the newspaper from under Hung Yi's arm, crouched down, and scooped up the pile.

By the time Ah Ming woke Panda and Ah Lei up, daylight had broken. They had fallen asleep by the roadside as Panda told Ah

Lei about her summer of 2008. Nearby, at the intersection where Yen Chow Street and Pei Ho Street met, hawkers were setting up their stalls. Trucks delivered load after load of vegetables, fruits, seafood, and meat. As though they were lifting sedan chairs, workers hauled in roast geese dripping honey glaze. Others carried butchered pigs that were split open at the belly.

Ah Ming told them support lawyers had arrived. Given the large number of arrests, he explained, the prosecution apparently wasn't ready to bring charges. Ah Mak would likely be granted bail, but he wouldn't be released before the police finished a complicated set of administrative processes. He wasn't allowed to receive visitors right now, so they should all go home to rest and regroup later.

Feeling a little more reassured, Panda and Ah Lei parted ways with Ah Ming and returned to their dorm. They each showered and settled into their twin beds. Ah Lei was about to doze off when Panda asked, "Do you want to hear what happened next?"

"What do you mean?" Ah Lei said. She was wrapped in a warm blanket and feeling cozy.

"What happened to Ah Mak and Auntie Lan, and my writing competition. I haven't finished the story yet," Panda said.

Ah Lei was silent for a moment. Then, already half asleep, she said slowly, "Go ahead. I'll pretend it's a lullaby."

The prize ceremony took place in a bookstore in late September. Near the back of the store, staffers had moved aside shelves of stationery and craft supplies to make room for a modest podium and three rows of chairs. A shopkeeper handed out the program printouts and directed guests—award winners, parents, and students—toward the designated area. On the wall behind the podium, a red-and-black banner read BODY TO BODY, HEART TO HEART—WENCHUAN EARTHQUAKE ESSAY CONTEST AWARD CEREMONY AND ANTHOLOGY RELEASE.

When Hung Yi and Ah Mak arrived, the seats were sparsely occupied. Not a single one of her classmates who vowed to show support was there. Only the front row was full. Among the kids and parents seated there, she spotted Ah Sze with her parents. Hung Yi sized up Ah Sze from behind. She had on the same black evening dress she'd worn for her piano solo at last year's school music festival. The bodice was embroidered with rose lace. It still looked so glamorous.

Just outside the ceremony area, a few children ran around the shelves. Occasionally, some adults came searching for products. They eyeballed the banner and walked away. By the podium, a staffer tested the microphone, which didn't seem to be working.

Hung Yi wouldn't admit what she had expected, but the scale and spectacle clearly fell far short. She would never tell Ah Mak what she had pictured: a venue as spacious as a theater where guests had to be guided to their seats by ushers. Maybe the host would even roll out a red carpet and the finalists' arrival would trigger camera flashes.

She didn't need to. He looked nonchalant as usual, but he had seen the care she put into her appearance that day. She was wearing a white satin dress, with a bow at the waist.

Even as the ceremony began, she hadn't completely given up hope. Surely there was some explanation to account for the extraordinary fact that she hadn't been notified that she was a finalist. Maybe her name was printed on a list posted somewhere for everyone to see, or in an envelope in the emcee's pocket. On that imaginary list, two characters, "Hung Yi," ranked high above Ah Sze's name.

Truth be told, Hung Yi didn't even like her name. The two syllables sounded curt, and she was constantly mistaken for a boy. Worse was her nickname, "Ah Mui," and the indignities associated with it: adults messing with her hair, pinching her cheeks, and offering in return a few candies or pocket change for her piggy bank. For a twelve-year-old, nothing was worse than being treated like a child. But she wanted to will her name into existence on some list. She was ready to see Ah Sze's stunned face. Oh, what a wonderful surprise, she would tell Ah Sze! My goodness, what would she even say when they presented an award to her? It wasn't like she had a speech prepared. Hung Yi would feign surprise and humility.

None of these fantasies came to pass. In their dorm room, Panda's face flushed when she remembered how naively, how ardently she had waited for the phone call. Why was she telling Ah Lei this old anecdote? "You remember how crazed we were back then, with all these certificates, awards, and diplomas," she sheepishly said. Ah Lei didn't respond. "To us, these were the proof of human worthiness," Panda went on.

Just a few years later, more and more previously unheard of prizes proliferated. Hung Yi came to understand what the writing competition really was: one of those sketchy companies that came up with grand-sounding awards catering to the hyper-competitive, credential-driven mentality of parents and their school-age children. For a piece of such honor, all the fees for registration and publication were just a small price. At reunions, Ah Sze's prize had become a laughingstock. "Can you believe it? Her parents bought her a place on the short list," a former classmate once whispered with a snicker.

Back in 2008, Hung Yi would have been so relieved to know the competition she had lost was a scam. But this revelation didn't explain all the boisterous feelings she had experienced that day: confusion, sorrow, envy, and indignation.

After an opening remark, a short documentary was projected onto a screen. It began with a montage. First, the central government dispatched troops and firefighters to Sichuan. Overnight, the heroic rescue teams rushed in. "Time meant the difference between life or death—they searched day and night for their fellow citizens buried beneath the rubble," a solemn voice-over said. Then the film focused on one particular case: A severely dehydrated young girl had been trapped under rubble for days before rescue workers found her. They used a tube to feed her glucose before deploying jacks and excavators to bore a passage. The team risked their own lives, the voice-over explained. If the floor above collapsed, they would have been buried along with her. Hung Yi tissued off her tears.

The girl was finally saved. "It turned out to be her birthday!" the voice-over exclaimed. Life triumphed over death! Suddenly, more than a hundred soldiers started singing "Happy Birthday" to the little girl. The film ended with a national leader standing atop the highest point of the rubble, rallying the crowd, "No hardship can defeat the heroic people of China!" Hung Yi felt profoundly touched by the thought that human life could contain such pure love and selfless devotion. What a proud people! What an extraordinary nation they shared! After the credits rolled, the emcee led everyone to stand in a moment of silence to mourn all who had suffered in the disaster. The audience bowed their heads. Some clasped their hands in prayer.

Then Hung Yi heard a noise from the last row.

She looked behind her and saw two women sitting with their backs to the podium, clearly only there to rest their feet. Oblivious to the larger-than-life drama of crisis and salvation behind them, they chatted and laughed. Their postures slouched and their legs crossed.

Hung Yi seethed at this travesty. Her righteous anger was approaching hatred. How inappropriate to behave so frivolously in a moment like this! If only she could make them regret it, she caught herself thinking.

The cousins sat through the ceremony and headed home together. Hung Yi had too many feelings in her chest. Most of them would take her years to unpack. But distinctively she was aware of her gratitude for Ah Mak's presence. This gratitude renewed over the years whenever they argued. She knew he must have picked up a number of embarrassing details from that occasion. He never filed them away to be used against her.

A few months later, after countless sessions of intervention and mediation, a social worker finally fast-tracked Auntie Lan's case under emergency provisions for domestic abuse. As a result, Auntie Lan and Ah Mak were soon allocated a public housing unit in the Kwai Tsing District, an industrial area. Their new home had been built relatively recently, complete with a community hall, sports court, and a park. A small shopping mall was a short walk away. More importantly, it had an elevator.

After graduating from elementary school, Hung Yi gained admission to an English-language junior high school just as she had hoped. She didn't publicize it around her classmates, knowing that Ah Sze didn't get in.

To celebrate, Mom and Dad treated Ah Mak, Hung Yi, and Auntie Lan to a trip to Ocean Park. Hung Yi had planned on riding all the roller coasters, but the others weren't fans of too much excitement. Instead, they toured the animal arenas to see jellyfish, sharks, and pandas.

Since Ah Mak had moved into their public housing apartment, she had been too busy with exam preparations to visit. They hadn't seen each other for a while. As Hung Yi tried to think of something to talk about, all the other visitors were getting close to the exhibit window to ogle at the panda enclosure. Its ground was grassy and populated with neatly grown trees and well-manicured shrubs. Ah Mak suddenly said, "Look, it's out!" A panda emerged from the enclosure, prompting a chorus of cries from the tourists—all kinds of accented Mandarin and Cantonese jumbled together to praise the cuteness of the beast. The crowd tried to figure out which of the panda celebrities they were seeing. An information board gave detailed instructions for the visitors to identify individual pandas by their facial features. But the panda was too far away for anyone to make out its face.

The crowd marveled at the national treasure's every move. It climbed down some steps and picked up a stalk of bamboo. After chewing it for a little bit, the panda dropped it onto the ground and turned its rear end toward the visitors. For a long time, it sat there without moving, as though it were resting. The visitors clamored for more action. At first, they called out to the panda. "Look here! Get up!" they shouted. Then some of them tapped on the glass.

Hung Yi had never seen a living giant panda before. She had only seen them on TV or in pictures. The animals were often introduced in educational materials as "an endangered species unique to China, and mostly found in Sichuan." Hung Yi read on a sign, "Hong Kong's four pandas were special gifts from the motherland—two in 1999 and another two from last year—all in celebration of the city's return. Since Hong Kong is a concrete jungle unfit to grow bamboo, all of the pandas' feed must be transported from Guangdong." Even though these pandas live in Hong Kong, she thought, they were literally still closely connected to China.

Photos and videos always depicted pandas to be funny, cuddly creatures. But now, seeing one in real life, Hung Yi thought they were overrated. She didn't feel any joy or excitement toward it.

All of a sudden, the panda got up. As the crowd looked on, it planted its four limbs and lifted its stubby tail ever so slightly. Its belly twitched, then, from beneath that short tail, a steady string of stool dropped to the ground.

The crowd began cursing. Some asked for a refund of the hefty park admission fee.

Unbothered, the panda climbed into a hidden crevice behind a rock wall and presumably went back to sleep.

"That was pretty smart," Hung Yi said. "The panda knew how to drive away the nosy tourists."

"Have you heard that some giant pandas in zoos are just people in costumes?" Ah Mak brought up the urban legend. Rumor had it that the first two pandas to arrive in Hong Kong didn't get along. Whenever they saw each other, they went at it. So if anyone ever spotted them at the same time, the legend went, one of them was actually an employee in a panda suit. These actors liked to crouch in a corner, pretending to nap so no one noticed the zipper on their chest.

Hung Yi was so shocked to hear this she turned back to have another look at the panda. “It’s just a joke. Lighten up,” Ah Mak said.

The next day, Hung Yi began junior high. At the start of the first period, the teacher asked each student to stand up and introduce themselves in English. Her new classmates seemed confident and funny. Hung Yi was a bundle of nerves. When it was her turn, she sprang to her feet. She told herself to lighten up and heard herself saying, “Good morning, everyone. My name is Hung Yi. You may call me Panda.”

PART THREE

The Final Class

It was a Monday night, and Ho Sam sat in bed watching Chan Yuek fall asleep. The weather had turned brisk with the arrival of October. He tucked the blanket around her. Earlier, when they were having sex, he caught a fleeting expression of pain on her face. Thinking of it, he reached for her hand. He had assumed that he knew how to decode all her side comments and little gestures by now. While it turned out that wasn't yet the case, it was certainly true that Ho Sam felt bonded to this headstrong young woman.

Lately, he noticed Chan Yuek had been running faster and faster. They had been going to rallies together for a couple months now, but for the most part, they blended into the crowd and often stayed in the back to support the injured. But ever since Chan Yuek recognized one of the arrestees via a group chat, she was spurred into rushing closer and closer to the front and was overall more involved in the action. She put out small fires and doused unexploded tear gas canisters with water. Ho Sam always followed her closely and tried to match her energy, but he was puzzled.

"If I don't run faster, I'll never catch up," she explained.

"Catch up to what?" he asked.

Chan Yuek told Ho Sam the arrested man was her ex-boyfriend, Ah Mak. The one she had accused of not taking enough of a stance. Was she feeling guilty? Did she have lingering feelings for him? Ho Sam couldn't figure out the answers to these questions, either, and he didn't want to ask. He gently squeezed her hand and slipped out of bed, making sure not to wake her. He tiptoed to the living room and sat down at his desk to grade his students' essays.

In September, Ho Sam began teaching a junior high five-week writing course. Every week, he gave the class a writing assignment. The prompts, he knew, were not particularly inspiring. But he was okay with it, knowing his students would reciprocate with their safe, predictable writing. The lack of passion was mutual. However, there was one exception. A petite girl, Ning Yuet, always chose ambitious subjects and expanded well beyond the required length of eight hundred characters. The topic he assigned last week was "Scenes on the Bus." Ho Sam wasn't surprised when he saw Ning Yuet had turned in another long essay.

> *. . . A squad of police officers boarded the bus, shouting at everyone to freeze. They demanded passengers produce their*

IDs, as though everyone present were heinous criminals. A baby began to cry, only to be scared into silence by an officer's menacing glare and brandished baton. A teenager in a black shirt had his backpack violently snatched; the officers dumped every last item onto the floor in an insulting manner. They discovered a utility knife inside his pencil case and used it as grounds for arrest . . .

Ho Sam pressed his temples to focus. He found Ning Yuet's papers hard to read. On top of the difficult subjects, she always submitted messy, handwritten drafts on grid paper. Her pen strokes leapt from one character to the next, sprawling across five, six pages of four hundred–character grid sheets.

. . . A few passengers stepped forward, trying to stop the officers from taking the teen away. The police immediately blasted their faces with pepper spray . . .

Ning Yuet's stories never strayed outside of three categories: condemning the violence of the regime; extending sympathy to the heroic protesters; concluding that justice would inevitably triumph over evil. No matter how dark the previous passages were, Ning Yuet always ended the essay with a strangely upbeat statement like a sun cap over a raincoat.

In the first class, Ho Sam told students to write about "Empty Seats." Most students wrote about dead grandparents or courtesy seats on public transportation. Not Ning Yuet. She wrote about a classmate who used to take the seat next to her.

> *He had been absent for a long time. Everyone just assumed he got sick. Well, yes, something did happen to his body. When he was arrested during a street protest, the police put him in a chokehold and beat him with batons. He had multiple fractures in his body. When I visited him in the hospital, his wrists were bound to the bedrail with metal handcuffs. How cruel! How could they treat a teenager like this?*

That essay also ended with "One day we will have democracy!" Perhaps, Ho Sam thought, it was a prayer in the disguise of a statement.

Ho Sam spent his first couple of years after graduation working at a bookstore and then a publishing house. He tried to write a novel, but it drained him. Wrestling all day with ideas and world-building on the page was a terrible way to live, he decided. A new outlook was established: He wanted an inauthentic, comfortable existence. Eventually, he landed a job as a teaching assistant at this school. He didn't have much passion for teaching, but it was, overall, a comfortable way to make a living.

When he was new, he was a little nervous. After all, schools were places that prized rules, order, and discipline above all else. Everyone put on a professional front during work hours: shirts pressed crisp, ties knotted tight. At first, he was stationed in the administrative office. The office used an open floor plan, and thanks to the public-facing information area fronted with a large pane of glass, the space was like a giant fish tank. Anyone passing by could see what everybody was up to. Ho Sam handled odd jobs, such as photocopying worksheets, sorting mail, and replying to emails. He was also put in charge of a few extracurricular activities. One Saturday morning, for example, he took students to a Red Cross first-aid training at seven. He endured these unwanted tasks as small inconveniences for an overall comfortable life.

He was the youngest among the administrators. There were about ten of them in that office: the secretary, the accountants, and clerks. They were all over forty. Their conversations revolved around TV shows and cooking. Ho Sam kept overhearing things like "Tonight I'm making chicken feet stew with peanuts" or "Watercress is in season now. Throw in some duck gizzard. It will make such a nourishing soup." Boring people never get tired of talking about boring things, Ho Sam thought.

The next year, Ho Sam was promoted to teach Chinese literature to junior high students. He was given a desk in the teachers' office but had to share it with another new hire, Lee. Lee seemed to be a sunny person. He had always wanted to become a teacher, he liked to tell people, and his dream had come true when he returned to his alma mater. Sometimes Ho Sam saw him playing basketball with the students. He looked like their older brother.

He must be one of those sincere, passionate types, Ho Sam thought. They made him uneasy. Just like Chan Yuet did on their first date. They seemed to live with a kind of conviction that Ho Sam didn't understand. They treated everything in life as a race with a clear beginning and a red ribbon at the finish line. They seemed to approach all goals as achievable. It was only a matter of time and effort. He normally wouldn't bother arguing with them—otherwise, they'd go full missionary on him.

To Ho Sam, life was an endlessly whirling wheel, repeating similar casts of characters and turns of events, spinning the living into dizzying despair. Therefore, he saw sincerity as a dangerous trait. It made people spend all their energy aiming for an unreachable apex on the ever-turning wheel. They kept trying until they became burned out.

Previously, Ho Sam thought breakfast—to be more precise, sitting down at a table to eat a full meal in the morning—was a waste of time. He always sacrificed this ritual for sleeping a little longer and grabbed a bun on the go, chewing it as he waited for the bus. But ever since Chan Yuek moved in, many things in his life began changing.

Chan Yuek had made a point of cooking breakfast each morning. On this Tuesday morning, she got up early as usual. She put on her fuzzy slippers, which were remarkably quiet when she walked around the flat. She shut the bedroom door before turning on the morning TV news and opened a can of cat food for Hanta. Then, she started making toast and scrambled eggs. She had some extra time and juiced a few apples too.

When the food was ready, Ho Sam had already finished washing up. They ate together and talked about current affairs from near and far. Ho Sam came to rely on these conversations to keep him sane. A morning dose of sobriety got him through a day of colleagues' mindless yapping. (The latest obsession at the office was hairy crabs and the "best recipes" to prepare them.)

"A teaching assistant from my department is going to run for district council," Chan Yuek said before taking a bite of her toast. Citywide elections took place every four years, and the next one was scheduled for late November.

Ho Sam wasn't particularly enthusiastic. He thought the entrenched powerholders were like territorial old snakes who fended off any new animals coming to their caves. Typically, pro-establishment camp politicians had a stronghold over district council seats. They courted local residents through personal and business connections, highlighting policies that would yield minor life improvements, such as increasing the number of recycling bins or building new rain shields at bus stops. Ahead of each election, they launched flashy projects, handed out gift boxes to residents, and organized day trips for local seniors, enticing voters with small favors. They categorically avoided talks about "democracy."

The young generation was generally disenchanted with the process. In recent years, many of them refused to vote at all. This year, however, things might be different. The movement had lit a fire inside the caves of local politics, rekindling people's hopes for elections and social change.

It was also Chan Yuek's first election after she became eligible to vote. She was excited about her university's homegrown candidate. "He's only in his early thirties. He has a good public image, and a lot of classmates and alumni have come out in support. Everyone calls him 'Little Professor.' He pledged to host community reading groups, vegetarian days, and build gender-inclusive bathrooms." Having finished eating the canned food, Hanta leapt onto the table, tufts of his tail fur drifting down onto Ho Sam's scrambled eggs. "He talked about creating pet-friendly public spaces too! We could take Hanta outside to play," Chan Yuek added.

Ho Sam took a sip of apple juice to stop his jaded feelings from spilling out of his mouth. Apart from not having much faith in the meaning of elections, he suspected that openly advocating for these progressive policies wasn't the best way to win over the constituents. He didn't voice any of these thoughts, however. "I didn't know Hanta longed to be outside," he said.

He wasn't holding back due to some kind of condescending

sympathy for Chan Yuek. He was drawn to her will to build a beautiful life and a bright future. He considered her visions to be radical, perhaps extremist in their optimism, but still, he was drawn to them, or to her. His vantage point was much closer to the ground: The present was crumbling down and he didn't know how to hold things together. Perhaps she was holding it together for him. After all, it was her who radicalized his morning routine. "In tumultuous times, we need a life with a clear sense of order all the more," she said. He ate quickly because he had a new duty at the school starting this morning.

When Ho Sam arrived at the teachers' office, his colleagues were talking about an incident from the previous week. At a protest, the police were using live ammunition and shot a high school student from their district. The bullet lodged a mere three centimeters from his heart. The latest news from the hospital said the student was going to survive.

"How close is three centimeters exactly?" the biology teacher said as he steeped Earl Grey in a glass teapot. "Imagine the diameter of a coin."

"That kid is beyond fortunate to be alive. Surviving a close call like that, he's bound to have some serious luck coming his way. If I were his mom, I'd go buy a Mark Six lotto ticket tonight." Director Choi had no filter. But since he was retiring next year, everyone was just putting up with him until then.

"My class is filled with students who are eager to stir up trouble out there. I tell them: Right now, your role is to be a student.

If you want to fight to have a say, this isn't the way. When you're nobody, who's going to listen to you? Don't you see the cops going straight for the kids during arrests? It's because they have no power and no influence. Crushing them is like squashing an ant. Zero consequences. You should focus on getting into university first. One day, you become professionals and gain some social standing, and who is going to mess with you then?" Mr. Chan chimed in as he inspected the stocks on his phone.

Despite Mr. Chan's views, the near-fatal shooting sparked an intense reaction from students across the district. They handed out flyers and masks, put up posters, and marched around their respective campuses. There was even a rumor of an upcoming multischool protest. At Ho Sam's school, teachers were worried that the situation might spiral out of control. During a meeting on Monday, a faculty member asked, "If we let things brew, aren't we basically harboring a new generation of ideologically driven fanatics like the Red Guards during the Cultural Revolution?"

After the meeting, the principal's office announced the campus should be a neutral space and banned any form of political expression. Starting Tuesday, Ho Sam and another teacher were assigned to stand at the school gate each morning to inspect students' belongings. Any posters or protest gear were to be confiscated. Students wearing black masks would be ordered to remove them before entry.

Ho Sam got to the school gate in time to screen the earliest arriving students. He opened a trash bag for the masks. Students looked incredulous as they approached him to dispose of them. He thought of what Chan Yuek had said about her experience at Tamar Park. Until tear gas canisters were actually fired into the crowd, no one believed it would happen.

For these students, the previously unthinkable had become reality: A fellow student was shot, and now there was a blanket ban of political expression on campus. Indignant, they felt betrayed by their government and their school. Ho Sam didn't feel he stood on either side of this betrayal, but as he held out the trash bag, he realized by maintaining his passive status, he was siding with the adults.

Lately, Ho Sam had often felt torn. His normal instinct was to recoil from overtly earnest people. People who were quick to assign moral values to ambiguous realities; people who were loud in professing their virtuous opinions. In fact, he had lived his life as a master of evading earnestness. The trick was to perch on a ground far away from the definitive moralities and automatically deflect any sincerity onslaught with a joke or a shrug.

This week, however, he came to the realization that he wasn't exactly the opposite of being earnest. For one thing, he still went to protests. And this morning, he found Chan Yuek's talks about Little Professor's aspirational proposals a lot more bearable than his colleagues' comments along the lines of "right now, your role is to be students" or their obsessions over watercress or hairy crabs.

He felt torn when enforcing the school's new policy. He wasn't sure if he should show sympathy to the students. He wanted to lend them moral support—there was nothing wrong with speaking up for a student wounded by police brutality. But would his gesture of encouragement embolden the students into dangerous confrontations with the school or the police?

He recalled an argument with Chan Yuek. It was a midsummer weekend. Many protesters gathered to march across Hong Kong Island to commemorate the fifth anniversary of the Umbrella Movement. When the crowd passed by the police headquarters in Wan Chai, hundreds of protesters surrounded the building, blocking off sections of Harcourt Road to its north and Queensway to its south. It shut down much of the traffic on the island. The police tried to clear the space with tear gas.

Supporters of the protest surged into this area from its western end, forming a human chain. They stopped near the junction of Tamar Street and Queensway about five hundred meters from the standoff. When Ho Sam and Chan Yuek arrived, they could see tear gas smoke in the distance. Some trees were apparently hit by canisters and caught fire. A few protesters threw Molotov cocktails at road barriers on the avenue to delay police advancement.

A man who had carried a telescope with him acted as a lookout. He positioned himself on a nearby footbridge and periodically shouted updates on how many meters the police had advanced or how many more emergency police vans had arrived. With each report, the spectators receded westward and dwindled in number.

Chan Yuek and Ho Sam heard a commotion break out behind them. Turning around, they saw a squad of half a dozen protesters in motorcycle helmets, masks, and gloves advancing against the direction of the dispersing crowd. Armed with fiber shields, batons, and umbrellas, they wore long-sleeved shirts and pants strapped with elbow and knee pads. Steadily, they marched toward the standoff to provide backup.

Stunned by this development, people moved aside to make way for this valiant squad to pass through. It was like Moses parting the Red Sea if the Red Sea were made of cheerleaders. They were met with applause and shouts of encouragement.

"They know what'll happen if they walk over there, right? How can they still do it?" Chan Yuek was in disbelief.

Ho Sam paused to parse this ambiguous comment—with the unspecificity of "they" and "do it," the sentence could mean one of two things. Either the crowd knew what would happen to the squad once they reached the police line. How could they still cheer them on? Or, the squad must know what would happen to themselves in time. Then how did they manage to still go on? The former placed blame on the bystanders; the latter expressed her guilty admiration for the squad. He suspected she meant the former.

"What are we supposed to do? Run up to them, drop to our knees, and beg them not to march at their own peril? Ask if they realize they could end up beaten and arrested? Ask if they really thought it through before coming out here?" Ho Sam knew he shouldn't speak like this, but he couldn't hold back.

Admittedly, when the squad appeared, he was swept up in elated admiration. But quickly he became wary of this rush. He thought it was irresponsible to indulge in the impulse of making heroes—martyrs even—out of mere mortals. But Chan Yuek, whose righteous indignation was typically quick to boil, had said it first. He hated that she was on her high horse again, so instead of agreeing with her, he lashed out.

"Why don't you charge ahead in their place? Do you dare?"

He heard his mean defensiveness and regretted it immediately. He wished that Chan Yuek would shove him or clap back. It would make things easier for him. But instead, she conceded.

"You're right. I don't have that kind of courage," she said. But that wasn't what he had meant to suggest at all.

Sometime after the argument, Chan Yuek told Ho Sam that she had been dreaming of a black duffel bag. There was something inside squirming and whimpering like a baby. She unzipped the bag and a pair of clear, innocent eyes looked up at her. It was the little black dog from her childhood.

Chan Yuek recalled the summer she spent in the countryside when she was eight. Every day, she played in her grandmother's yard. The family kept some chickens, and fed a black dog who used to be a stray. Whenever Chan Yuek scattered a handful of rice, the chickens gathered around her to peck at it. This motion always attracted the dog to charge at them, making the chickens scramble to get away, flapping their wings.

One afternoon, she was playing with the animals in the yard when she heard an argument between her mother and her grandmother. Their voices were sharp and shrill. Flies buzzed around chicken droppings. Her legs were covered in mosquito bites. The dog's warm tongue licked the itchy spots.

Suddenly, her mother burst out the front door, startling the chickens into flight. Flustered family members followed her out of the house, hurling insults. Paying no attention to them, she hauled Chan Yuek onto the motorbike, mounted the bike herself, and secured the dog between her feet. She jammed the key into the ignition and took off. Chan Yuek wrapped her arms around her mother's waist. The bike sped like the wind, and Chan Yuek felt like she could fly to the end of the world. When they finally stopped to fill the gas tank, Chan Yuek's mother asked if she wanted to go to Hong Kong. She nodded hard.

For years, Chan Yuek's father had lived and worked in Hong Kong. After many failed attempts, an immigration petition for his wife and daughter to join him was finally approved. Chan Yuek's mother had a job in Shenzhen and leaned on her family in the countryside to care for Chan Yuek. When she broke the news to her family, they weren't pleased. Disagreements escalated to a fight, leading to her storming out.

They waited in Shenzhen for another few months while the paperwork was finalized. When the day came, Chan Yuek's mother sedated the little dog and put it inside a black duffle bag. She carried it like hand luggage when they crossed into Hong Kong.

Chan Yuek's father had rented a tiny flat to accommodate all three of them. Their landlord forbade keeping pets in his building, so the dog was the family secret. But it wasn't long before a neighbor found out and reported them. If they wanted to stay, the landlord said when he dropped by one evening, they had to give up the dog. Chan Yuek clung to the dog. Her parents didn't say anything.

The next morning, when Chan Yuek woke up, the dog was gone. Her mother was cutting up fruit. "I took it out for a walk this morning. Suddenly it ran really fast. I couldn't catch it," she said.

This was a sad but convenient solution. Chan Yuek's mother took responsibility to make the decision and even created a cover story so her husband and daughter didn't need to feel implicated. The family got to stay in the apartment. But in the years to follow, her husband never forgave her. From then on, he couldn't see his wife beyond her callousness of abandoning the puppy, and warned Chan Yuek never to become like her. The rift between her parents scarred Chan Yuek's young heart. Over time, the hurt and guilt hardened into an anchor of her being.

In her dream, she tried to lift the little dog out of the bag. But the animal began to fall backward, and the inside of the bag turned out to be vast like a bottomless sea. Reaching for the dog, Chan Yuek was nearly dragged into that abyss.

When Chan Yuek woke up, her mother's voice echoed. *Living is a battle. Sometimes, for what truly matters, you can't afford to be kind. Look at your dad—what did he ever achieve in life?*

She wasn't strong enough, she told Ho Sam. Neither was she kind enough. She remained powerless in dream and in life.

In the last few months, things had turned upside down. People on both sides—pro-government and pro-movement—launched doxing campaigns and urged individuals on their side to collect the speech and actions of those around them and publish any incriminating evidence along with personal details online, subjecting their colleagues or acquaintances to trial by public opinion.

After the high school student was shot, in a teachers' group chat, some of Ho Sam's colleagues expressed that the students were too impulsive. "Honestly, they're too naive. They act without thinking about the consequences," a message from the director read. "Students shouldn't be involved in politics to begin with. They should focus on their studies," another teacher added. "What worries me most is that they're being used and don't even know it," a third chimed in.

These comments were screenshotted and posted online. The director and the two teachers were labeled as "pro-establishment." The school became a target as well. First, overnight, someone scrawled graffiti in red paint outside the gate. Then came the pranks: Two hundred unpaid-for pizzas were delivered to the school. The administration suspended the three employees involved in the group chat incident. Several meetings were convened in an effort to ferret out who had leaked the conversation. Fear gripped everyone. They could hardly trust one another. The offices were uncomfortably quiet.

When Ho Sam and Lee were alone at the office, Lee broached the subject. "Personally, I think exposing teachers' personal info was a step too far, but it's not a bad idea to give those who profit from the system a wake-up call." Ho Sam looked at Lee, who squirmed and hastened to add, "Just to be clear, it wasn't me who leaked the group chat. Don't look at me like that," he said. "You're actually pretty scary when you're not smiling." Ho Sam forced a smile.

The suspensions apparently weren't punishment enough. Netizens swarmed the teachers' social media accounts, hunting for more evidence. Nowadays, everyone was a detective. They examined each post for location and time stamps. They pieced together someone's background and social class from a few photos, or even an emoji in the post. Within a few days, the director's sins were laid bare: Last year, he went to the mainland for a dental cleaning; at a public forum, he shook hands with a certain legislator; in a social media post, he drank a can of cold brew from a certain foreign chain.

Ho Sam filled Chan Yuek in on this mess at work once caught up on the latest developments on an online bulletin board. "What's that coffee got to do with anything?" He was genuinely puzzled.

"You didn't know? That brand's authorized agent in Hong Kong also runs a real estate business. Remember last week, when a mall security guard refused to let protesters in? That mall belongs to the same company," Chan Yuek said.

"The connection between the mall security guard and this can of coffee is a bit remote, don't you think?" Ho Sam now felt thirsty and took out a can of coffee from the fridge. It happened to be the very same brand.

"Don't you get it? Our wallets are a way to vote." Chan Yuek snatched the coffee out of his hand. "We take a stand by exposing the offending parties and boycotting their businesses so they know to rein themselves in." Chan Yuek was even more agitated than Lee had been on this subject.

The whole thing was a bit off to Ho Sam. For one, despite his colleagues' smug comments about the students, Ho Sam didn't think they were even particularly against the protesters. "This kind of broad antagonization could hurt innocent people," he said.

Chan Yuek scoffed. "Innocent? We're at war. Who's out there feeling sorry for the kids on the front lines?"

She poured the coffee down the drain.

Among all the essays Ning Yuet had submitted, there was one that disturbed Ho Sam the most. The assigned topic was "A Difficult Decision." Ning Yuet wrote about a few junior high school students. On the internet, they discovered that the owner of a small eatery near their school had apparently insulted protesters and attended pro-police rallies. They decided to vandalize the shop with iron rods after dark to teach the owner a lesson. The essay was written in first person.

> *At first, I was terrified. I knew it was wrong. Growing up, I've always been a rule-follower. Destroying other people's property is a crime. If we got caught, we would end up with criminal records. On top of that, breaking things seemed wasteful. I felt guilty.*
>
> *But after talking it over with my friends, I made up my mind. I knew it was wrong, but I thought about those protesters who'd been arrested, beaten, and injured. Was the regime right? As an unarmed student, I won't be able to put up a fight on the front lines. Taking action against the shop was something I could do. I wanted to make the owner understand that supporting the police is wrong.*

Ho Sam thought Ning Yuet might have considered her pen as her only weapon. She expressed herself in these somewhat fictional accounts stubbornly and unabashedly. She wrote with so much conviction and so little baggage. Ho Sam wasn't sure what to say in his assessment.

Ho Sam had seen so many young people—his students, his colleagues, his girlfriend—grow angrier and more resolved as the demonstrations escalated. It wasn't that he wasn't sympathetic toward them. He understood they were made to feel powerless and they wanted to say something, or to do something. But he wasn't sure their chosen approach to expression or action was productive. He had seen teenagers hurling Molotov cocktails or shattering glass. The more resolved they were, the hollower Ho Sam felt.

After the next writing class, he asked to talk to Ning Yuet outside the classroom. She was visibly nervous and blurted out, "Mr. Ho, are you going to report me to the school?" He was taken aback. "Have you done something worth reporting?" Ning Yuet lowered her head and remained silent.

"What you wrote in the essay," Ho Sam said. "Is it real?"

"No. But I probably shouldn't have written something so . . . brazen," she offered.

"Do you think there are things you 'should' and 'shouldn't' write in an essay?"

"I showed this essay to a few classmates. They all freaked out and said I'd definitely get into trouble if I handed it in. But we already have no freedom out there, and if we don't even have the freedom to write what we want for a class, why bother writing anything at all?"

Ho Sam nodded. He thought he'd find an example to show her that freedom wasn't just the ability to vehemently express what was black and white but also to explore the different shades of gray.

Throughout the week, rumors swirled on social media. People were expecting new legislation to restrict the protests and plunge the city into a state of emergency. Some citizens speculated a curfew would be announced. Others feared martial law. On Friday, the answer came: an antimask law.

At a press conference, a government spokesperson invoked a colonial-era Emergency Regulations Ordinance. It bypassed the legislature and granted Hong Kong's chief executive the power to issue direct orders. Under the ordinance, a new law was issued to be effective at midnight. It prohibited people from wearing face coverings.

At noon, the school received an official notice from the Bureau of Education. It instructed all extracurricular activities to be suspended for the day. Students were required to leave school grounds immediately after classes ended. The school premises were to be closed. The bureau asked each school to print out flyers explaining the new antimask law and distribute a copy to each student to bring home for parental signature.

Before lunch break, teachers were informed of the notice by email. The air in the office was tense. Hardly anyone stepped out. Ho Sam felt a bit claustrophobic. Everyone was preoccupied by the notice.

> . . . it is neither customary nor reasonable for individuals to cover their faces in order to avoid being identified. In the course of normal daily activities, and when interacting with teachers and peers, there is absolutely no need nor any justification for concealing one's face.
>
> We would also like to take this opportunity to reiterate that the school is not a place to express political ideas. The school, together with its stakeholders, should work collectively to foster a safe, stable, and peaceful environment conducive to students' normal learning and healthy development. Students are further reminded to avoid contact with strangers outside of school, and under no circumstances should they engage in activities that may involve disorder, danger, or unlawful behavior.

After the last period ended, the principal made an announcement over the loudspeaker, ordering all students to leave immediately. All clubs, team practice, and dance troupe training were suspended until further notice. The campus would be locked within the hour. Once the principal finished talking, the loudspeakers blared a piercing noise. It sounded like a mixture of a fire alarm and a car theft alert. Ho Sam had never heard anything like it before. He had no idea the school PA system could make such a repulsive sound.

Most students were glad to take off earlier than expected. In no time, the building was almost deserted. Teachers also rushed to pack up and leave, anticipating congested traffic or roadblocks in light of the emergency law. Suddenly, an assistant burst into the office to report that a bunch of senior students refused to leave and were holed up in a classroom on the second floor.

This was above Ho Sam's paygrade, but he couldn't help but stop by the classroom on his way out. At its entrance were a few boys. They stood with their arms crossed. Slightly farther inside, a few girls clung to one another and sobbed.

Right outside the classroom was a small crowd of teachers. There was also a social worker. The vice principal was there too. He spoke loudly and forcefully at the students as if leading a hostage negotiation. "Please don't be like this. Please calm down. You're all very emotional right now. Being like this won't solve anything."

"Why are you kicking us out? This is our school, our classroom. We can't even stay here and cry for a little while?" one student said.

The social worker, a young woman in an athleisure outfit, spoke up in a soothing voice that sounded like it belonged on a children's TV show. "We're not saying you can't cry. We get it. We really do. Everyone needs time to process this. But your safety matters too. The longer you stay here, the more dangerous it gets outside. We're just worried about you."

"We'll be fine. We just want to be left alone and stay with our classmates right now."

Their head teacher, Mr. Chan, was also there to negotiate. "I know you feel powerless. But you're not helping anything. I've told you many times. At your age, you should be focusing on your exams. Only when you get into university will you have the bargaining power and opportunity to change society. Do you understand?"

"You're the one who doesn't understand! Look at what society has become—what's the point of getting into university? What does it mean to become a useful person?" a boy shouted at Mr. Chan. "One of our classmates was arrested, and you won't let him come back. We wore black masks to make a statement of solidarity, and you confiscated our masks. And now you tell us we're too emotional? Screw you!"

"We don't trust what you say anymore," a girl added.

"So what good does this do now? You tell me. Sitting here crying, refusing to leave. Are you trying to occupy the school? Do you think that will magically make what you want appear out of thin air?" the vice principal said, impatiently wagging his car key in the air.

"Stop pushing us like this. We just want the school to show some respect—respect our feelings. Students are humans too!" another student said.

Ho Sam stood in the hallway. He could see the campus emptying out and few cars remained at the school parking lot. He was pained by the sight of these wounded teenagers, who found no other way to relieve their own pain and now were being treated as a problem.

The school custodian went around and locked all the other classrooms before arriving with her cleaning tools and a ring of keys.

"Look, your feelings are causing trouble for others. Enough with this tantrum now. The custodian still has to clean up your classroom before she can go home. You need to think about other people for a change. Don't make things hard on everyone, all right?"

A boy at the door grabbed his schoolbag and charged toward the staircase. The others followed suit. They walked down the hallway and passed by Ho Sam. One of the girls turned around and shouted at the teachers, "I'll never forgive you!"

When the students were out of earshot, the teachers relaxed, clearly pleased that they successfully averted a crisis. "Whew, what a hassle," one of them said. Another rolled his eyes: "Talk about not forgiving. What is this, an elementary school breakup?"

"That's just how teenagers are. Weren't we all young once? They see adults as enemies. When they grow up, they'll realize adults have their own hardships too," the vice principal said as he gestured for everyone to get out.

After Ho Sam got home, he couldn't concentrate. Chan Yuek wasn't back yet and hadn't returned his texts. Normally, to unwind, he put a record on the stereo and leisurely cooked dinner. But he didn't feel like doing so that night. In this strange and restless pocket of time, Ho Sam flashed back to a few hours earlier, when the teachers had waited by the printer, queuing up like students to collect printouts of the Education Bureau notice. History, it seemed, had demanded that they sew their lips shut and stay in their place obediently.

While waiting for word from Chan Yuek, Ho Sam took out this week's essays from his students and read them carefully. He was surprised to see Ning Yuet's latest essay showed marked improvement. It was still about the protests, but no longer stuck in the rut of hollow slogans and self-satisfying moral victories.

Ho Sam had asked the students to imagine being someone other than themselves—or *something*, as Ho Sam now realized this additional possibility—by filling in the blank in the subject line of "If I were a . . ." Ning Yuet wrote her essay in six sections, each from the perspective of an anthropomorphized object: a bullet, a police uniform, a camera lens, a press conference microphone, a tree in the park, and a body part that had been shot. The six voices complemented one another, working together to reconstruct the police shooting of the student. Unlike before, Ning Yuet's tone was restrained, and the effect was quite ironic.

> *I am a bullet from a police officer's gun, always waiting to rid the world of evil. I often imagined myself being fired at a critical moment, successfully preventing a serious hostage situation or a criminal's escape. But when I was finally fired, I entered a small body, so full of life—wait, wait. Isn't—isn't this a child? I tore through his veins, and just before piercing his heart, I started to scream: Stop! Someone stop me! This isn't what I wanted! Just when the blood and tissue slowed me down, I felt a violent jolt. The body I'd entered had collapsed. God, won't someone help him? Please forgive me. This was never my intention.*

Another section began with:

> *I am a police uniform. When the bullet pierced that rioter, the blood bloomed across me like a glorious badge embroidered on my body. I felt a surge of blazing honor.*

Ho Sam was contemplating how to grade this unusual essay when the door opened. Chan Yuek came in limping. Apparently, she had gone out to protest and was caught up in police fire. A stray bullet grazed her right calf. She didn't want to go to the hospital, fearing police presence there. A paramedic at the scene had helped her to safety and roughly cleaned the wound before bandaging it up.

Ho Sam slowly unwrapped the gauze, revealing a patch of

open flesh soaked with fluid and blood. "We have to get you to the hospital," Ho Sam said. But Chan Yuek still refused. Her teeth were chattering, and her face was pale. She didn't even have the strength to speak.

Ho Sam felt so angry. He wondered if the police officer who fired the shot ever thought of his victims. Did his uniform get bloodied today? The line from Ning Yuet's essay rang in his head. *The blood bloomed across me like a glorious badge. I felt a surge of blazing honor.* "Honor," what a hollow word, Ho Sam thought. There was no sense in shooting people at a protest. Or being shot, for that matter. It occurred to him that Chan Yuek might take her injury and suffering as proof of her commitment, but that was beside the point now. He decided to call a trusted doctor friend for a private visit.

After the doctor left, Ho Sam put Chan Yuek to bed and sat down at his desk to finish grading the last few essays and prepare for the final class. He scrapped his original lesson plan. He wanted to do things differently now. No more video clips, corny jokes, or pointless writing exercises to fill the time. He would demand the students' attention and not let it slide when they dozed off or used their phones. He was no longer concerned about being the good guy.

Normally, if a student wrote an interesting essay, he would read it aloud in class. But in this new world, according to the notice, *the school is not a place to express political ideas.* He sneered at the thought of it. Sure, he wouldn't read Ning Yuet's essay to her classmates. He would offer some notes for improvement in private and encourage her to submit it to journals or newspapers.

For next week's class, he thought he would share an excerpt from *One Hundred Years of Solitude*. If questioned by his supervisors, he would make an argument that it didn't count as political ideas. He recalled a part of the novel vividly. After witnessing the banana company massacre, José Arcadio Segundo desperately tried to tell everyone about the blood and the bodies. But his fellow villagers treated him like a madman. They said it never happened.

Snoopy Friends

It was Tuesday, seven days since a sixteen-year-old boy at Sai Mui's school had been shot by the police. After class, Sai Mui noticed some stalls set up on the sports ground. It looked like a little market. People were handing out cookies, braiding friendship bracelets, and twisting balloons into animal shapes. There was also a booth with a sign that said FREE SPACE. A young woman with shoulder-length hair sat in the booth. Next to the sign, Sai Mui noticed, was a family pack of a popular brand of marshmallows in the shape of Snoopy. Each pack came with a sticker of a Peanuts character inside. She wondered which one was in this pack. It was a pity that her friends couldn't join her. They commuted to school from Shenzhen and had to rush off after class to catch the northbound train to get home.

Last Tuesday was National Day. A schoolmate was at a protest when a crowd of protesters surrounded a policeman in an alley.

Feeling threatened, he fired his gun. A bullet struck the sixteen-year-old close to his heart. He was rushed to the hospital. While undergoing emergency surgery, he was charged with rioting.

The next morning, school administrators called a press conference. It quickly turned into chaos. Reporters and concerned citizens flooded the campus, demanding that school management issue a statement to condemn police brutality and to pledge protection for their students. But the principal insisted on remaining "neutral," refusing to make any commitments. Most shocking of all was his remark: "It's like conflict in a family. If the parents make a mistake, does that mean their children have the right to smash up household items? Does being injured provide impunity for the children's actions?"

The live broadcast became the talk of the internet. Later that day, Sai Mui rewatched the conference with her sister, Panda.

One detail stood out to Sai Mui. A female teacher broke down into tears while talking about the injured student's condition. A sympathetic member of the audience offered her a packet of tissue. The teacher was just about to take the tissue when the principal, who sat next to her and was getting hammered by the attendees, snatched it and pulled out a sheet to dab at the sweat on his forehead.

"You can't make this up," Panda said.

For the rest of the week, the students' emotions ran high, and teachers struggled to get them to focus in class. Many graduates reached out to their alma mater, offering various forms of support. A group of alumni coordinated to create a space for students so they could release their stress and talk about things. That was what the booths were about.

As Sai Mui stood alone on the sports ground, the woman at the FREE SPACE booth waved at her and offered her a marshmallow.

"Shall we play a game?" she suggested in Mandarin, gesturing for Sai Mui to sit down.

"You can speak Cantonese. I was born in Hong Kong. I understand it perfectly well," Sai Mui responded in Cantonese.

At Sai Mui's school, about 70 percent of the students, including most of Sai Mui's friends, were either new immigrants from mainland provinces or commuters from Shenzhen. An average class only had a handful of local students. The common tongue was Mandarin and some students also spoke other Chinese dialects. After school, they messaged one another on WeChat. Many students struggled with traditional Chinese characters, as they had been used to the simplified version back home. During break, they chatted about mainland variety shows, internet influencers, shopping livestreams, and trending topics on Weibo.

To fit in, Hong Kong natives like Sai Mui made an effort to speak Mandarin. Their pronunciation wasn't perfect, and classmates made fun of them for it. In private, Sai Mui and her peers joked that they were a minority people.

That was just how things were in Hong Kong now, Panda had told Sai Mui. In the years since 1997, a booming industry emerged to help mainlanders migrate to Hong Kong, or to at least give birth there, so their offspring—the so-called anchor babies—would be granted legal status to live in Hong Kong and have better lives. Many young couples—parents of Sai Mui's classmates—had bought into the promises of quality education, health care, and the opportunities that came with a more advanced economy. They were convinced that as long as they managed to pass the border checkpoints and gave birth on Hong Kong soil, a bright future was guaranteed for their children.

About seven years ago, a mainland cousin from Mom's side became part of this birth tourism. Panda, who was a teenager at the time, had told Sai Mui their story. Mom went through quite the hassle to secure her a hospital bed. Once she checked in, Mom, Auntie Lan, and other family members in Hong Kong took it upon themselves to take care of her.

After a baby boy was born, the new parents made the painful decision to entrust him to a Hong Kong relative's family. Back then, they believed this sacrifice would prove worthwhile. They saw Hong Kong as a blessed land that would offer their child a higher standard of living, strong English skills, and easier pathways to studying abroad.

Just a few years after this fateful decision, however, the winds shifted. Hong Kong was no longer viewed as a prodigy child, the pride of the country. Instead, it had turned into the spoiled kid riding on the back of the motherland. As the mainland economy took off, the fortune of the cousin's family changed. Their farmland was bought up by the government to build a train station.

The poop-laden paths in the fields where chickens used to run were now paved over into a glossy shopping mall.

The cousin and her husband used the money from the government to open a restaurant that was so successful it became a chain. They owned multiple properties in Guangdong Province. They no longer needed to save up to visit their child in Hong Kong. They could easily afford frequent luxury expeditions to the city. They also began to think about raising him on the mainland.

When they looked into it, however, they found out their son wasn't eligible to attend any mainland public school, due to his status as a resident of Hong Kong. Their sacrifice turned out to be for nothing. The privilege they bought their son became a liability. So the son continued to live with relatives in Hong Kong and received money from his parents every month.

Mom had taken Panda and Sai Mui to visit the boy a few times. He was born in Hong Kong, just like Panda and Sai Mui, but he seemed to live a lonely life in the city. He didn't speak Cantonese well and longed to be with his parents.

At the booth, the woman switched to Cantonese. "You don't see many Hong Kong students these days!" She proposed a game. "How about we each share three things about ourselves? Two truths and a lie. The other person guesses which one is a lie. If you win, I'll give you another marshmallow."

Sai Mui nodded, and the woman volunteered to go first. "Okay, I'll start. One, someone I know recently lost his freedom, and it made me really sad. Two, I gave up a certain coffee brand. Three, I'm a man." She winked at Sai Mui.

"The third is a lie!" Sai Mui answered right away and winked back. "One, my big sister lives at home. Two, my best friend, Mei Yan, has been mad at me. Three, I once talked to the boy who got shot."

The woman tapped her chin. "*Hmm* . . . is the third one the lie?"

"Wrong!" Sai Mui was thrilled to have managed to trick a grown-up. She took another Snoopy-shaped marshmallow and popped it in her mouth as she continued speaking. "The first one's the lie. My sister ran away from home a few months ago. She started to come back to visit last month though. Once or twice, she even stayed overnight! As for the third, the guy who got shot was the head of a students' club. We said a couple of words to each other during a sporting event."

From there, the woman asked Sai Mui about her life. Why did her sister run away? How were things at home? Then, she asked Sai Mui to describe her feelings using colors. Sai Mui sailed through the questions and ate more marshmallow Snoopys in the process.

Of course, she glossed over some details she wasn't eager to share, such as the fact that her cousin Ah Mak had been fired from his job for some reason. Having nothing better to do, he visited her family every week. He often brought along his new girlfriend, a university student who helped Sai Mui with her homework. Sai Mui hadn't talked so much with anyone in a long time. She almost forgot how satisfying this felt. When she was leaving, the woman handed her the sticker—it was a Snoopy—and said the booth would be here for another couple of weeks and she was welcome to drop by again. She promised to bring another pack of marshmallows for her.

"Thank you, big sister. What's your name?" Sai Mui asked.

"I'm Chan Yuek," the woman said.

After spending an afternoon on campus, Chan Yuek was struck by the gloomy mood there. The victim, she learned from students coming to the booth, had been a cheerful, warmhearted person, a well-liked figure. His family moved to Hong Kong when he was in elementary school. He got on well with both local classmates and mainlanders. For the students' club, he organized workshops to teach the Cantonese romanization system and invited popular teachers to come share Cantonese slang and jokes.

After the shooting, his high school classmates left garlands of paper cranes, fresh flowers, and sympathy cards on his empty desk. His friends flared with anger like they had swallowed dynamite. In class, they provoked teachers, caring little when they were scolded or punished. They were simply looking for a fight. Many younger junior high students didn't fully comprehend what had happened. When they tried to ask about it in class, their teachers often brushed their questions off. The truth was they didn't know what to tell the children.

"Teenagers are the most helpless group in the movement," a volunteer in the alumni support group told Chan Yuek when she joined. "On the subject of politics and protesters, they often don't feel comfortable to speak candidly with their parents or teachers. There's a power imbalance. When they talk about it with their fellow students, it often spirals into raw emotion. It's not healthy to keep everything bottled up for too long. It's important for us to help them feel understood."

Each day that week, when Chan Yuek didn't have classes at her university, she staffed the booth. At first, she was assigned the post because she couldn't walk or stand for long stretches of time due to her leg injury, but she turned out to be quite good at the role. Each day, more and more junior high and high school students felt emboldened to stop by. She was humbled by how much each of them was carrying on their minds. One afternoon, a girl waited around and only walked up to Chan Yuek when the other students had left. After she sat down, Chan Yuek noticed a few scars on her arms. She was one of several school friends who had gone to the protest with the boy who was shot. "Why are we attending class like nothing happened while he's lying in a hospital bed?" she said.

The volunteer work made Chan Yuek think about her own childhood. Like when she greeted Sai Mui, Chan Yuek always initiated conversations in Mandarin to be welcoming. She spoke

Cantonese fluently now, but her first few years in Hong Kong had been filled with trepidation. She often stayed quiet to avoid exposing her poor Cantonese. At school, classmates always called her "the mainland girl." A few boys liked to mockingly imitate her accent. They said she talked like the auntie from the nearby rice noodle shop. In the bright, clean classroom, the boys buzzed around her annoyingly, reminding her of the flies she swatted in the dirt yard outside her grandmother's house.

She wanted to get rid of her accent so badly and devoted her free time to watching Hong Kong soap operas on TV. She rarely laughed or cried at these melodramas as she was too focused on mouthing the dialogue and memorizing phrases. She forced this new language down her throat as if swallowing a barely chewed date. Meanwhile, she tried to abandon the sounds of her old language. She rejected Mandarin with its words that made her curl her tongue. She diligently practiced enunciating her new language. The key was to master the Cantonese air puff. She pressed her lips almost closed and touched the back of her teeth with the tip of her tongue, enlisting her jaw muscles to force out a barely noticeable sound. Her new identity depended on it. In every sentence she spoke, every sound she made, she worked to erase her origins.

Nowadays, she was no longer the newcomer kid, and she had no doubt about her rightful place in the city. But the reflex to hide an aspect of herself in order to fit in had become entrenched in her so much that she felt an aversion rise inside her whenever she passed by a flock of Chinese tourists who spoke Mandarin loudly with no trace of self-consciousness.

At the booth, she was confronted by this ugly feeling again. Things had changed since her days as a student at this school. Many mainland students moved in packs and were secure in their collective identity. They didn't seem to shrink their Mandarin-speaking selves. For the first time, Chan Yuek saw the mental barrier she had built. For almost half a year, she spoke loudly to dismantle unjust laws, to dismantle the outdated views of people around her, but now she realized she had to dismantle her own prejudice.

A few weeks ago, Sai Mui's home had become a lot more crowded. First, Panda started coming back. Sai Mui had to clean up their shared bedroom and make space for her sister again, but she couldn't really complain. Then Panda started bringing her boyfriend, Ah Ming, over every now and then. On top of that, cousin Ah Mak and his girlfriend, Ah Lei, sometimes came over for dinner too. Occasionally the two couples were in the apartment at the same time and the place got quite lively.

One such day in October, Mom gleefully fussed over dinner prep. She had bought four boxes of char siu pork from a restaurant and steamed a whole fish. She asked the helper to debone it. After the meal, she took out various fruits from the fridge, including strawberries she had meticulously prepared for Panda. Panda checked her phone and suddenly said they had to leave. Sai Mui was secretly pleased: more dessert for her!

Mom was slicing fruit in the kitchen. She forced a smile as she turned back and asked, "Do you have to go now?"

"Sorry, but we agreed not to talk about things like this," Panda said curtly.

"All of you have already done enough, really." Mom couldn't stop herself. "The extradition bill has already been withdrawn. And look, there's a district council election coming up, isn't there? We should trust our fellow citizens to vote and let the elected officials handle things."

"Who said we've already given enough? Who's qualified to measure that? Elections are important. But we still need accountability for police brutality. The political prisoners are still waiting for trial. We still don't have real universal suffrage. To achieve these things, we need to work both inside the city councils and out in the streets."

"Aren't you all exhausted from the last few months? I heard the pro-democracy candidate in our district is looking for volunteers to hand out flyers and talk to neighbors. If you're up for it, I'll sign up with you tomorrow, okay?" Mom brought the fruit platter to the table and gave everyone a fork before taking her seat. "Just for tonight, indulge me. Stay and enjoy some fruit together. Look how fresh the strawberries are!"

Panda glimpsed the naked, seedless strawberries. She was unmoved. Sai Mui had hoped Panda's boyfriend might step in. He had a decade on Panda and worked at a software company. Even before Panda let Sai Mui meet him, she had praised him endlessly to her baby sister: He was experienced and had perspective; he had participated in the Umbrella Movement five years ago; he was always calm and collected; he always knew what to say. Or so Sai Mui was told. But Ah Ming said nothing. He popped a strawberry in his mouth and ate it.

Ah Lei tried to ease the tension. "It's true. I for one am pretty worn out from protesting all day. Maybe it's okay if we take—"

Before she could finish, Panda lashed out. "You still don't get it, do you? This isn't some fitness goal that once you hit your daily target, you can feel good about yourself, and sit back and relax. We have to keep showing up whenever we are needed." Panda stood up, her chair loudly scraping the floor.

"How are you supposed to keep going? Until when? What's your endgame?" Mom also rose to her feet, speaking in a harsh tone Sai Mui had never heard before. She stared at Panda, waving the fork in her hand. "For your so-called justice, you're slicing off your own flesh, giving up your own bones. But it's all a lie! This movement, it will eat every part of you until there's nothing left. Look at your cousin Ah Mak! For all his sacrifices, what did he get in return?"

Sai Mui was scared of this new side of Mom. Ah Mak lowered his head. Ah Lei gripped his hand.

Panda had a cold expression on her face. She looked straight at Mom. "Why shouldn't I get hurt? If everyone out there is cutting off their flesh and bone, why should I stop after just bleeding a little?"

This was typical Panda. Sai Mui felt irritated. Why did she have to push when Mom was clearly extremely upset? Sai Mui knew what Panda was doing. She was banking on Mom's love and betting it would make Mom give in. So sly.

Mom indeed backed down. "At the very least, please don't go out wearing black. The police will spot you."

Panda headed to their bedroom with Ah Ming to get her stuff. Sai Mui followed behind.

"I can shrug off other people's nonsense, but I can't stand it when it comes from my own mother. Why?" Panda said to Ah Ming.

"You've been resentful that she has preserved her normal life and stayed on the sidelines," Ah Ming said calmly. "But that's her choice. You have to allow that."

"If she loves me like she says, then why can't she love what I love, and stand with me? Why does she have to use her love to stop me?"

"Hung Yi, you can't demand absolute agreement in the name of love. Only dictators demand loyalty without questioning."

Panda flinched. "You always see right through me." The anger in her voice was deflated. He also always called her by her full name.

She rummaged through her wardrobe and found a blue T-shirt to put on. Then she found a black one and stuffed it into her backpack. Only then did she turn around and see Sai Mui. She hugged her little sister. "You've grown taller," she said, patting her head. Sai Mui, who had been mad at Panda just a minute ago, surrendered instantly. She hugged Panda back.

"Sorry I have to go again. Are you doing okay? Do you like seeing Ah Mak more often?" Panda asked.

Sai Mui wanted to tell Panda that Ah Mak seemed to be having stomach issues lately. She wanted to tell her about the time Ah Mak took her to eat at a cha chaan teng only to disappear into the bathroom for like half an hour. She wanted to tell her about her schoolmate being shot, about the booths on the sports ground. But Sai Mui knew there was no time. Panda was on her way out. The others were waiting for her. So she just answered simply, "Yes, it's very nice."

The next day, Sai Mui went to see Chan Yuek. She had only known Chan Yuek for a few days, but she had come to see this woman as a trusted friend. In between classes or after school, she stopped by the booth whenever Chan Yuek was free. Chan Yuek rested her wounded leg on a spare chair and patiently followed Sai Mui's reenactment of the fight between Mom and her big sister. "Do you blame your sister for what happened?" Chan Yuek asked after Sai Mui finished. Then, she rephrased her question. "Do you wish either of them had approached things differently?"

Taken aback by the frank question, Sai Mui paused to think.

She was programmed to please. She had trained herself to act obedient, to say things that Mom wanted to hear.

Now she wanted Chan Yuek's approval too, and instead of figuring out her true feelings, she considered what might win Chan Yuek over.

Just then, a boy came to the booth. He was a little taller than Sai Mui and didn't tuck his school uniform shirt into his trousers. "May I have one of these?" he asked politely in Mandarin, pointing to the marshmallows.

"Sure! Help yourself," Chan Yuek said. He fished out a Snoopy with his thumb and index finger and put it in his mouth. When he rested his hands by his sides, he held them in clenched fists.

"Why the fists?" Sai Mui blurted out.

"Try it. You'll feel powerful. It makes people afraid of you," the boy said.

"Why do you want people to be afraid of you?" Chan Yuek asked.

"When they're afraid of me, at least they still keep me in mind. Otherwise, they act like I'm nothing," he said.

"But isn't it better to be liked than to be feared?" Sai Mui retorted.

The boy relaxed his fists a little. Chan Yuek reached toward him and placed another marshmallow in his palm. "See, when you clench your fist, there's nothing inside. But when you stretch out your fingers, you can hold more."

The boy introduced himself as Zhiyuan. His class was next

door to Sai Mui's. Now that they'd become acquainted, he often joined Sai Mui and Chan Yuek at the booth. Sometimes he spoke his opinions at length in Mandarin. Sai Mui suspected he was probably just repeating what he picked up from Weibo or WeChat. He barely knew the protesters' main demands. She didn't feel like correcting anything. She had no interest in getting into an argument with him.

But once Zhiyuan got these grand statements out of his system, Sai Mui found him to be a pretty nice guy. He liked to tell Sai Mui about his favorite cartoons and TV shows. He was a Snoopy fan too! He also told her about the tasty dishes and fun trips he had with his parents when he was on the mainland.

Sai Mui had begun to feel that school and home were like two different countries. Every day, stepping through the school gate was like crossing a border. Once inside, she code-switched into another language and culture. Her classmates talked about their spacious apartments up north, about their parents driving them around to do things. Sai Mui began to think of China as a place full of secret sources of happiness. She had wondered why her classmates' essays often ended on a contrived uplifting note, such as "I'll grow up to be a useful Chinese citizen" or "I love my great motherland!" But now, she had begun to understand.

Sai Mui was well aware that it wasn't all glorious being a mainland kid. Many of them didn't know Hong Kong well. Their travels had been mostly limited to areas on the East Rail metro line, which made a stop at Sha Tin, the closest station near Sai

Mui's school. She soon learned that Zhiyuan had it worse than her cousin's child, who at least had relatives to stay with. Zhiyuan apparently lived alone in a luxury building near campus. He visited his family on weekends. And he was only twelve, just like her! Well, technically, he wasn't alone. His parents hired a domestic helper to clean and cook for him.

Zhiyuan's Cantonese was pretty pathetic, but he was trying. Sai Mui began to correct his pronunciation and to teach him phrases. "In Cantonese, when we ask people what they are doing, we don't say *ganma*, we say *zok maa ah*," Sai Mui said. She instructed Zhiyuan to study how her mouth moved and to repeat after her slowly. "Zok-maa-ah."

For Sai Mui and Zhiyuan, the booth truly became a "free space." A kind of equilibrium developed among Chan Yuek and these kids. Outside that bubble, however, tension was brewing.

In Sai Mui's class group chat, students split into two camps. One evening, a few nationalistic classmates brazenly reposted mainland propaganda, calling young protesters *feiqing*, *good-for-nothing youths*, and accused them of destroying the city while being "bankrolled by foreign forces." Students who supported the movement fought back, calling them brain-rotted Little Pinks. The chat devolved into a battle of insults. Half an hour later, the group administrator kicked out the involved students and posted a notice: "Please be mindful that this group is a neutral space. No political discussion allowed." The note triggered a mass exodus. In the end, out of a class of forty, only the admin, Sai Mui, and a few other classmates remained.

Things were wilder at the library. Some students scrutinized the catalog for titles they deemed problematic. According to them, all recent histories of protests were seditiously promoting the current movement and ought to be removed from the shelves. They reported their findings in a complaint to the Education Bureau and distributed leaflets to parents. The list they compiled was long and included not only books but also news clippings, essays, journals, and op-eds. The "problematic incidents" included a 2007 action to protect the historical Star Ferry and Queen's Pier from demolition and a 2009 movement to protect Choi Yuen villagers from being forced out of their homes to make way for an express rail. The bulk of the flagged books and documents, however, were about the Umbrella Movement from 2014.

Sai Mui tried not to think about this stuff, but she sensed that having opinions had become a dangerous thing, both at home and at school. When Chan Yuek asked her for her thoughts on the recent developments on campus, she blinked and said she wasn't sure. Zhiyuan was the opposite. He liked the attention and called the protesters names in Weibo posts. He sometimes sent her Weibo links to brag about the Likes and reposts he had received. He offered what he learned from experience: The more vicious his comment was, the more responses it received. Sai Mui didn't like what he was saying, but she also knew he'd probably say the opposite if that would bring him more clout. When he sent her such links, she usually replied with ambiguous emojis. She didn't want to know what her sister, Panda, or her friend Mei Yan might say about her new friend.

During lunch break one day, Zhiyuan stopped by Sai Mui's classroom. He called out her name in broken Cantonese. "Hang—Si—Ling!" Sai Mui's posture stiffened. She was embarrassed on his behalf and silently prayed that his mangled pronunciation wouldn't give her away. But everyone turned to look at her.

"Hang—Si—Ling," Zhiyuan repeated his erroneous call. Sai Mui steeled herself and walked out of the classroom. "Zok maa ah?" she asked impatiently in Cantonese.

"The cafeteria is selling cheung fun rolls today. Let's go, I'll treat you." Zhiyuan jiggled his wallet. Then he reached into his pocket and took out a sticker. "You're collecting these and missing Lucy, right? I bought several packs of marshmallows and finally found her." Sai Mui accepted the gift. Damp with sweat, Lucy's blue dress was a little frayed at one corner. Sai Mui softened. Zhiyuan was a good friend. Why should she care what others thought of him?

When they arrived at the cafeteria, it was already quite crowded. Zhiyuan said he would go line up for cheung fun and told Sai Mui to find them a seat. Then he walked across the dining area toward the end of the queue. He heard someone behind him. "Are you Zheng Zhiyuan?" the voice asked in Cantonese.

"*Hai, zok—maa—ah?*" He turned around and saw a few tall, buff high school students. For a fleeting second, he was flattered that these older local boys had come looking for him.

When Chan Yuek and several school staffers arrived at the cafeteria, Zhiyuan had been beaten so badly that his face was swollen and blood was spilling out of his mouth. A middle-aged director charged into the melee and tried to pry Zhiyuan from the others. The grown man himself took a few punches. "Stop it!" he shouted. A few faculty members joined him, and they finally managed to pull apart the high schoolers.

Apparently, a classmate had taken screenshots of Zhiyuan's posts on Weibo and posted them on a local online bulletin board. He had also shared Zhiyuan's photo and personal info. The buff teenagers were friends of the shooting victim. When they came across Zhiyuan's inflammatory posts, they were furious. They believed it was the same rabid sentiment that had almost killed their friend. Society and school had failed them. They decided to take things into their own hands.

Sai Mui watched a limp Zhiyuan being carried into an ambulance. She was in shock. None of the people in the cafeteria—not even Zhiyuan's friends, who were presumably among the crowd—stepped in when the teenagers jumped the twelve-year-old. Neither did Sai Mui. She froze and watched her friend get beaten up. Sai Mui was excused from classes that afternoon. Chan Yuek took her to pack her bag, and they sat at the booth while waiting for Sai Mui's family to come take her home.

"Am I a coward? Why didn't I do anything?" Sai Mui asked.

"Don't think like that," Chan Yuek said as she held on to Sai Mui's shoulders and looked into the girl's eyes. "Listen to me: It's awful that things turned out this way. But it's absolutely not your fault.

"It's not your fault," Chan Yuek repeated softly, this time to herself, the little girl who couldn't save her dog.

The Outside World

On a damp and chilly November morning, Ah Lei left her dorm and walked down a tree-lined road toward the campus gate. The birds were still everywhere—on the roads and bridges, off the path. They must have fallen from the trees. There were different species. Ah Lei recognized the sparrows, but she couldn't name the others, including the ones that had purple and yellow feathers. Ants and little bugs crawled all over these tiny lifeless bodies. Ah Lei navigated her way around them and avoided looking at their glassy eyes, wondering when a city agency or the campus sanitation department would come to remove them.

The avian carcasses first appeared two days ago. Early that morning, university students across the city began occupying the main boulevards outside their campuses in what had been dubbed the "Daybreak Action." By choking off traffic, they intended to disrupt the economy, hoping to force the government to respond to their demands. The action was desperate. It had become a different world since early June, when hundreds of thousands of people first demonstrated against the extradition bill. By September, when the protests finally forced the government to withdraw the bill, numerous arrests, injuries, and several deaths had occurred. The movement intensified. People demanded that the chief executive step down, the police be held accountable, and for broader democracy in Hong Kong.

At Ah Lei's university, students carried trash cans, fences, and other objects from the campus to the roads outside the main gate and the south gate. There were smaller side exits, but as they faced narrow streets, there wasn't much traffic to begin with, so the students left these alone.

Soon, dozens of police officers arrived at the main gate and the south gate. They removed the objects from the road and began a standoff with the students. The university announced that all classes were canceled for the day. Panda and Ah Lei hadn't been involved in the roadblock action. They woke up to the alerts and decided to shelter in place before figuring out what they could do to help.

The police-student confrontation centered around the south gate, which was next to a metro line. A footbridge connected the school gate and a metro entrance, overlooking the train rails. Students had occupied the bridge and tossed barriers onto the tracks, paralyzing the metro line. Throughout the day, the police tried to occupy the bridge, firing tear gas and rubber bullets. The students' defense was equally fierce. After several students were arrested, their teammates called for backup, and their peers on campus began to send them Molotov cocktails.

Near the main gate, the police fired more than two thousand rounds of tear gas onto the open spaces on campus, driving thousands of faculty members and students to flee through side gates.

Nevertheless, a few hundred student activists decided to stay. By that evening, people across the city who had read about and watched a livestream of the events arrived to drop off food and supplies. Some of them came straight from work to show support for the students. Around eight, the police fired rubber bullets and deployed crowd-management "water canon" vehicles. Some of the visitors decided to hunker down with the students.

Ah Lei and Panda's dorm was not far from the south gate, and students transported the injured to their dorm lobby, which became a makeshift first-aid center. Young men and women trickled in with bloody limbs from being hit by rubber bullets. Others were turned blue by the chemical spray from the water cannons. Some of them were carried in, others leaned on friends. More than ten volunteer medics—many of them medical school students—gathered and attended to them.

The usually empty lobby was now packed with dozens of people. Residents moved chairs and sofas from their rooms to accommodate the patients. Amid this mess were caged pets and plants left behind by students who fled. In the early hours of that morning, mainland students who got wind of the imminent action decided to evacuate in anticipation of violent clashes. Ah Lei read news reports that said large numbers of mainland students had packed the train station in predawn hours to board early northbound trains for Luohu, Shenzhen. Those who didn't manage to get on the train rushed to the pier at Pak Shek Kok, where hometown associations and other mainland groups had arranged boats to take them away.

That night, hundreds of Molotov cocktails later, the police stopped their attack at the footbridge. Students on the bridge took turns to rest and sought help for their injuries. In the next two days, the confrontations continued. The university president announced an early end to the semester. Various public figures called on the students to evacuate the campus. Some students left, but some nonstudent supporters joined those who remained.

And yet, once Ah Lei left the university grounds, on the city streets, life seemed to be carrying on as usual. Ah Lei caught a cab to a nearby station and took the metro to see Ah Mak.

As she approached Ah Mak's public housing compound, she stopped by a modest siu mei restaurant with a row of roasted ducks in the display window and picked up a lunch box. Nearby, a district representative candidate was speaking into a megaphone, asking passersby to exercise their civil rights to vote. Ah

Lei recognized her as a member of a pro-democracy party. "Only if we elect enough pro-democracy candidates to the legislature and local offices. . . ." the candidate went on. One of the campaign volunteers handed Ah Lei a flyer that promised the candidate would use the power of serving as a district representative to get the government to respond to the citizens' demands.

While waiting for the elevator in Ah Mak's building, Ah Lei checked her phone. She had received a few messages from Sister Ka, the organizer who had helped rescue Ah Mak after his arrest at the end of the summer. Since then, Ah Lei had been aiding Sister Ka's group. In the messages, Sister Ka asked Ah Lei to help replenish some urgently needed first-aid supplies and shared a shopping list. "Dropping off lunch for Ah Mak now. I'll get to these right away," Ah Lei wrote back. The elevator came. Stepping in, Ah Lei saw her reflection in the metal surface. She looked muscular and tan from all these months of running around under the sun. Who was this woman of action? What happened to the passive and depressed Ah Lei? She chuckled to herself, feeling a surge of optimism.

Ah Lei took out a key and unlocked the door. The living room looked exactly the same as when she left last week. It was as if no one lived there. The sink was dry. A half-eaten bowl of strawberries from Panda's mother was left out to rot. She threw away the fruit and washed her hands, then spread out the election flyer on the table like a place mat and put the lunch box on it.

She nudged open the bedroom door and slipped her hand into

the gap between the cabinet and the wall on the right. The light flickered on, revealing Ah Mak, who was curled up in his bed, his back toward her. Ah Mak didn't move.

"Time to eat! I got you a char siu and roast pork combo from downstairs," Ah Lei said.

She sat down on the edge of the bed. "Things have been crazy at school these past few days." Then she realized such news wouldn't help coax Ah Mak to get up and have lunch. She gently tapped him. He was unyielding like a rock.

In September, Ah Mak was released on bail after two days in detention. The police kept his cell phone for evidence and took away his passport so he couldn't leave Hong Kong. He was required to report to the station twice a week, and if he was found at another protest, his public defense attorney warned, he would be in violation of the bail terms.

When Ah Lei picked him up at Sham Shui Po Police Station, she saw bruises on his face and limbs. Ah Mak never talked about what happened to him when he was locked up. In the following months, Ah Lei stopped watching the news on TV when Ah Mak was around because when police appeared on the screen, he always rushed to the bathroom. Once at a restaurant, upon hearing police sirens, Ah Mak puked on the table.

He was dismissed from his contract position at the railway company. Suddenly jobless and unable to join the protests anymore, Ah Mak became unmoored. Panda's mother often invited him to dinner or made up excuses for him to babysit Sai Mui.

Otherwise, he spent all his time at home watching the DVDs he had collected over the years: B movies, art films, animation, sci-fi, detective flicks.

At first, Ah Lei joined him every now and then, thinking he just needed a little time to unwind. Then she realized he wasn't taking a short break but was instead seeking lasting refuge. The TV in the living room was on all day and all night, even when he went to bed. Ah Mak didn't shut his bedroom door, allowing the lights and shadows on the glowing screen to keep him company as he slept.

Sometimes, he lay in bed all day and skipped meals and water, letting time pass by. Ah Lei forced herself to perk up. If both of them stared into the darkness, they would end up in the abyss together.

She remembered that terrifying night when she hunched outside the police station not knowing what would happen to Ah Mak. A drunk man stumbled past her, jeering at the helpless, anxious crowd of family and friends of detainees.

"Shoulda known you can't beat the Communist Party. If you could, your ol' pa and ma wouldn't have come down here. You think Hong Kong has such good prospects?" he said in Cantonese.

People glared at him. He stumbled across the street and shouted, "However much you have lived it up, that's how much you are about to suffer! All of it's gotta be paid back!"

An unfamiliar furor took over Ah Lei. She stood up and

charged toward the man. She screamed at the top of her lungs, "What do you care, you motherfucker!" The man let out a laugh and carried on walking away.

After leaving Ah Mak's place, Ah Lei went to a pharmacy to pick up supplies on the shopping list: saline solution, aloe moisturizing lotion, and alcohol wipes. But the shopkeeper told her everything was sold out. She dialed Sister Ka's number.

"All gone? Anything else in stock?" The line was a little noisy. Sister Ka was clearly in the middle of something.

"There's still Vaseline, dressings, bandages, liquid bandage spray, and medical tape on the shelves." Ah Lei circled the shop. "Oh, and rubbing alcohol—a one-liter bottle."

"That's okay. We've got too much of those already. Hang on." Ah Lei heard Sister Ka apparently talking to other volunteers. Since the first evening, she had set up camp at Ah Lei's university to help support students. "Do you have a white shirt, size medium? Who delivered these lunch boxes? Can someone take it to the teaching building?" Ah Lei waited patiently. "Sorry, things are a little chaotic over here. Could you try the upscale mall nearby? The one that attracts lots of tourists. I remember there was a whole floor of duty-free drugstores."

Ah Lei hesitated. "Sister Ka, I don't have that much cash on me."

"Don't worry. I know someone who lives in that area. Mr. Lam. He'll cover it for you."

Ah Lei waited about fifteen minutes in front of the fancy duty-free shops in the mall. A middle-aged and slightly burly man approached Ah Lei and introduced himself as Mr. Lam. He wore a light-colored dress shirt, slacks, and shiny black leather shoes. On his wrist was an expensive stone-inlaid watch. Judging from his outfit, Ah Lei didn't think he was on his way to a protest. But the fact that he was able to show up here on such short notice in the middle of the day probably meant he wasn't at work, either. Ah Lei wondered what he did for a living.

Inside a Japanese drugstore, she found what she was looking for, but the price was several times higher than usual. She briefly considered giving up some of the items. Mr. Lam took out his credit card and said, "Don't worry, I've got this. We all know what you're going through is a war—it must be hard." Ah Lei thought that it was quite an emotionally charged comment, and guessed that he was addressing her as a representative of the poor young protesters out there. The injured among them urgently need the creams and medicines to soothe their pain, and he was here to save the day. Ah Lei thought the word "war" was rather heavy-handed, but since Mr. Lam was the one paying the bill, she didn't say anything. She respected his right to imagine all kinds of horrifying scenes, all kinds of people needing his generosity.

Mr. Lam looked at Sister Ka's shopping list and cleared out the stock at the Japanese pharmacy. He led Ah Lei to two other stores on the same floor where he bought more first-aid items.

Ah Lei looked away when he paid. She didn't want to know the astronomical total amount.

They loaded the bags into the trunk of his Subaru. On their way to the university, they made small talk.

"You must be so terrified," Mr. Lam repeated. "It must be hard on you all. Hong Kong appreciates everything you've done."

Ah Lei was used to this kind of remark. In the last two months, Sister Ka had often brought her along to pick up supplies from various donors. They came from different walks of life. Some were business owners, others were professionals or retirees. But they all wore the same awed expression when handing Ah Lei their donations. "It's really not that dramatic," Ah Lei told Mr. Lam.

"Right. So how did you meet Chiu Ka?" Mr. Lam asked.

In fact, Ah Lei didn't even know Sister Ka's surname was Chiu—just as she didn't know Mr. Lam's full name, either. Since the movement began, people had grown used to not exchanging personal information. The less you knew, the better for everyone. Ah Lei learned to withhold details as well. "She helped a friend of mine a while ago. Now I do some volunteer work for her."

"Help" felt like an understatement. After Ah Mak was arrested, Sister Ka made countless phone calls before tracking him down at the Sham Shui Po Police Station. Ah Mak's disappearance was so traumatic to Ah Lei that she couldn't bring herself to join any protests. Instead, she started running errands for Sister Ka.

"That's great. So what do you do? Anything special?" Mr. Lam's curiosity made Ah Lei feel like an animal in a zoo.

Ah Lei gave him an abridged version: arranging accommodation for kids who had run away from home, buying white shirts for arrestees to wear in court, ordering meals for those held in custody. . . . She had learned to do some of these tasks when Ah Mak was detained.

Once again, Mr. Lam offered his sympathy. "You're all truly amazing to have kept going this long." While waiting at a red light, he opened his wallet to show Ah Lei a photo. "I want my child to be as brave as you." In the family portrait, a boy who looked to be two or three was riding on Mr. Lam's shoulders. His smiling wife stood beside them. They all wore white T-shirts. Behind them were fundraising booths run by political groups and a crowd of marching protesters—a backdrop brimming with fervor.

As he drove, Mr. Lam reminisced about "the old days." His family had been attending various marches in the last three or four years. Unlike those undisciplined people who showed up late or joined halfway through, he said, they had always been punctual. Each year, he felt proud that they were living up to their civic duty. These events were typically on public holidays, and they could have driven up to the mountains for a hike or taken a trip to the outlying islands, or visited Ocean Park for aqua-theater shows. But they chose responsibility over leisure. "I've since learned about the mistreatment of animals, so we aren't doing that anymore," he added hastily. At the end of a fulfilling day, he always treated his family to a nice dinner. Their post-protest meal of choice was sushi in Causeway Bay.

After returning home, he and his wife always regretted accepting far too much printed material. They were too exhausted to study all the ideas on these leaflets and pamphlets, but it felt wrong to toss them into the recycle bin, so they glued them on the wardrobe door in their son's room. "We thought of it as our own Lennon Wall. We dreamed that once it was covered by leaflets, Hong Kong would finally become a true democracy," he said wistfully.

The car reached Kau To Shan, where mountains cradled luxury residences. It was only two in the afternoon, not yet rush hour, but the road was becoming congested. The narrow and winding lane was packed with vehicles. When they were near a university side gate, the traffic came to a halt. People got out of their cars, hauling take-out bags, umbrellas, and bottles of water. That's when Ah Lei realized that they were all coming to support the student activists.

Mr. Lam parked his car too. "At the start of this movement, I was full of hope. I thought we might be able to welcome freedom before my son's wardrobe-door Lennon Wall was full." He rolled up his sleeves and split the load with Ah Lei. They walked down the street, each of them carrying an armful of supplies.

"But after July, we didn't dare go out again." He smiled bitterly. "My wife thought the movement had gone off course and that democracy couldn't be achieved through violence. That's when I reached out to Chiu Ka." After seeing news about the university, he took a day off and told her he and his car were at her disposal. "I didn't even tell my wife that I took today off. I just pretended I was going to work like usual.

"Do you think I'm cowardly?" Mr. Lam said. Ah Lei couldn't see his expression behind his designer sunglasses. She knew he was asking for affirmation, but she wasn't sure she could offer it.

In recent weeks, Ah Lei was increasingly confronted with different opinions among supporters of the movement. On the second night, dozens of students and supporters gathered outside her dorm building to make Molotov cocktails. Panda and Ah Lei joined the group. They scoured all the dorm rooms, pantries, and cafeterias for ingredients—sugar, laundry detergent, towels, and glass bottles. They sent requests for gasoline in Telegram groups. Soon, several supporters showed up on motorcycles and ferried gasoline in their fuel tanks from the nearby gas station.

They mixed the ingredients for the fuel and poured them into glass bottles. They cut towels into thin strips and twisted them into wicks. The finished products were collected in boxes. Each time they filled up a box, it was handed off and delivered to the footbridge outside the south gate.

Just past ten, they were running out of glass bottles. A small team was dispatched to rummage through trash cans and recycling bins across the campus. The effort didn't yield much. Again, they asked for help in group chats. In twenty minutes, sedans began to arrive. The students helped drivers off-load crates of bottled beverages. There was bottled milk, beer, soda, juice, and tea. For a moment, Ah Lei felt disoriented by the sight and felt as if they were hosting a party. The tired students popped open some sodas and juices to drink. But there were more drinks than they could possibly consume, so they dumped the liquids down the storm drains.

Milk, rust-colored soda, and bright orange juice all went straight into the gutters. Only in a city like this, Ah Lei thought. These products weren't used to hydrate or to comfort but to be dumped so their containers could be filled with explosives for Molotov cocktails. To become fire. To be hurled at others.

Panda picked up an emptied, curvy soda bottle. "Look, through the bottle, the world looks bloated."

Ah Lei tried it too. "And the moon becomes larger."

After midnight, the group disbanded. Students headed back to their dorms. In Ah Lei and Panda's building, some people gathered in the lounge, eating instant noodles and chatting.

Panda's boyfriend, Ah Ming, had arrived at the dorm building a little earlier. While waiting for Panda, he discovered an abandoned hamster near the elevator. Its owner must have realized it wasn't practical to bring the pet while evacuating the building. The little creature was curled up and trembling. Ah Ming tentatively reached his finger into the cage. The hamster bit him.

Panda and Ah Lei said hello to Ah Ming and joined a few others on the sofa. A balding, middle-aged man in a polo shirt spoke. "To be honest, I think the movement is becoming too extreme. We're losing public support. In the summer, I came out to demand accountability for police brutality. But now, at rallies, some people are wielding flags calling for Hong Kong independence. That really puts me off. I feel like the movement has been hijacked. Honestly, the only reason I came tonight was because the police firing tear gas all over campus was just too much. I came to protect the students. Otherwise, I really can't get behind the movement anymore."

"I actually think it hasn't been radical enough," a boy who looked no more than thirteen or fourteen countered. "That's why the government thinks Hong Kongers are easy to push around and keeps ignoring our demands." The teen's voice hadn't changed, but he spoke with the self-importance of someone far older. "This is a turning point for the movement. I'm telling you, I've been out there fighting since June, and this is the first time I've fought a positional battle. Before, it was all street-level guerrilla tactics, difficult to sustain, and morale scattered easily. Some of my friends have been kicked out by their parents. We figured, while we occupy the university, we can stay here, and build up resources."

Ah Ming took the hamster out of the cage and put it in the small bowl filled with sand next to the cage. The creature happily rolled in the soft mound. Panda glanced at Ah Ming and let out a sigh of exasperation.

"I disagree with you, little brother. Do you know why this movement has been able to last so long? *Be water, my friend.*" A young man cited the Bruce Lee quote that had been widely appreciated by protesters. He was trying to wipe the blue off his neck with a wet towel. "The essence of the movement is guerrilla-style flexibility. If we fixate on holding a certain ground, we stand to lose everything. The opposite side could surround us, and game over."

"Besides, if we occupy the university, how will students attend classes?" Ah Lei said.

After the hamster's sand bath, its fur was soft and glossy. Ah Ming found a pack of sunflower seeds and put a few in his palm and it climbed onto his hand and nibbled on the seeds.

"What kind of university student are you?" The boy jabbed a finger at Ah Lei. "Kids like us can't even go home or go to school anymore. And you're still worrying about university studies?"

"Wait—everyone, cool it," Panda spoke up. "Look at us. We're on the same side, but we're pointing fingers at one another. This is exactly why our voices of dissent are too fragmented, why the government doesn't take us seriously. If societal resistance is deadlocked, maybe it's time to return our attention to the legislature? We should focus our strength to elect representatives who will actually speak for us." Ah Lei noticed that Panda sometimes sounded not so different from her mother, but she'd never acknowledge it when it came from her.

"You think voting is going to bring about justice?" Ah Ming suddenly spoke without looking away from the hamster in his hand.

"We're fighting like cornered beasts and have tried everything else. Why not give elections a chance?" Panda said.

"But the movement had erupted precisely because of our pent-up frustration with the legislative and court system. We were forced to take to the streets because the resistance within the legislature had completely collapsed. Remember how the government arbitrarily disqualified candidates, canceled the seats of elected members, and how the political parties sold out their voters?" The bystanders struggled to read the situation, so they let the couple fight.

"But things are different now! Public opinion has shifted. Hong Kongers used to be politically indifferent, but now we are waking up," Panda asserted.

"Ha, the voters may have changed, but these politicians will never change. We can't hand the little power we accumulated from these months of sweat and blood to a few politicians."

"Whoa, the hamster just pooped in your hand!" the boy shouted.

Everyone turned to look and laughed. A few brown, rice-sized pellets rested in Ah Ming's palm next to the fluff ball of a hamster.

After receiving the supplies, Sister Ka asked if Ah Lei and Mr. Lam could help out with some additional errands. They left campus in Mr. Lam's car and did some more shopping. They were preparing to pick up an arrested student who was soon to be released. They bought white shirts of different sizes and some disposable underwear, toothbrushes and toothpaste, and towels. Ah Lei wondered how Sister Ka managed to maintain her hair on top of all her duties. She dyed her hair red and wore it cropped short, barely skimming her ears. Then they made a quick stop at an herbal tea shop.

"What's this for?" Mr. Lam asked.

"I just felt like having some. I've been breaking out lately," Sister Ka said.

It was a little after four. She led them to a congee shop while she waited for confirmation of the whereabouts of the young man. Mr. Lam and Ah Lei each ordered cold soy milk. They watched Sister Ka eating zha leung rolls. She dipped each fried roll in sesame sauce, sweet sauce, and chili sauce before stuffing the drenched thing into her mouth. When Mr. Lam went to settle the bill, Ah Lei asked him to get two tea eggs to go, then stepped outside with Sister Ka. Sister Ka lit a cigarette and told Ah Lei that Mr. Lam was a college classmate of hers.

"He was a straightlaced, goody-goody student. I was involved in activist circles and did sit-ins and occupied lecture halls. You know, back then, a decade ago, people were very conservative in their views about student activists. He and I didn't see eye to eye." Sister Ka blew out a puff of smoke. "Who would've thought? It's all very different now.

"Actually, I'm glad that you two met today. I've been meaning to introduce you," Sister Ka said. Ah Mak had been charged with unlawful assembly and destruction of property, which could lead to years in prison. Sister Ka and his lawyer reasoned that since he had no criminal record, if a trusted member of society familiar with his family background could write a letter to vouch for him, he could get a light sentence.

Ah Mak wasn't that well-connected, and Mr. Lam, who was now in management at a reputable NGO and had been a social worker on Ah Mak's and his mother's case, would be the perfect person to write such a letter. Of course, he would have to risk being publicly associated with a protester.

"Do you think he'll do it? It's kind of a big ask," Ah Lei said.

"Honestly, I'm not sure. But you saw him working so hard to help us today, so maybe something has changed now?" Sister Ka tossed her cigarette butt as Mr. Lam approached. "The kid is at West Kowloon Court. Let's go!" she said.

When they arrived at the courthouse, Sister Ka instructed Mr. Lam to park on the street not far from the entrance. Ah Lei saw a few journalists holding cameras roaming nearby. "Keep the engine running. I'll be back with the student shortly, and then we should leave right away. I don't want him to be photographed." She stepped out of the car with an umbrella.

It was just Ah Lei and Mr. Lam again. "Do you come here to bail out protesters often?" he turned to ask Ah Lei in the back seat.

"Only when no family members show up for them," Ah Lei said.

"What do you usually do? Should we take him somewhere to eat? What should we say to him?" Before Ah Lei could answer, Mr. Lam's phone rang. He finished the call quickly. "My wife told me to go home straight from work. She's worried these days," he said.

Then the car doors swung open. Sister Ka jumped into the passenger seat, and a tall teenage boy in a white shirt slid into the back. Several reporters swarmed toward the car snapping pictures.

"Shit, are they gonna get my license plate?" Mr. Lam panicked.

"Just hurry up and get out of here," Sister Ka said.

Sister Ka typed an address into her phone, then turned around to look at the teenager. "You can stay with me for the time being. We'll take you there now. I'll help you settle in, but I won't be around tonight. Do you want me to order dinner for you?"

"Are you going to be at the university?" he asked.

"You know you can't go there." Ah Lei slipped the tea eggs into his hand. "Eat them later. Don't make a mess in someone else's car."

"Don't worry about it. Eat them while they're hot. This old car isn't all that clean anyway," Mr. Lam said.

The boy peeled one of the eggs and took a bite. He seemed to be very hungry.

After dropping off the teenager and Sister Ka, Mr. Lam offered to drive Ah Lei back to the university. Ah Lei knew this was her chance to ask Mr. Lam the favor. The request was so important that she struggled to find the right words to broach the subject. She had no clue what it took to be persuasive. Should she plead humbly or pressure him with righteousness? Should she stay collected and let her emotions show? She felt she wasn't ready.

Now it was rush hour, and there was quite a bit of traffic. Waiting for the cars to move, Mr. Lam offered an unusually personal piece of information. "My wife has been thinking about moving abroad. We're fortunate to be able to afford it, and it's probably better for our son. But I don't know. This is our home, our community," he said, grasping the steering wheel tight. His phone rang again. Mr. Lam glanced at the screen but didn't pick up.

Seizing the moment of openness, Ah Lei gathered her courage. "Working with Sister Ka, I saw firsthand that so many protesters need help. And so many kind people like you stepped up. Whenever Sister Ka asks, people send us meals and supplies, or even hand us cash, no questions asked."

The car started moving. Mr. Lam's phone rang again. He declined the call.

Ah Lei began to feel her cheeks burn. "You're all good people. Sometimes, when I look at the abundant surplus of resources, I think to myself, wow, it's like there's no poverty in Hong Kong. You all have one condition: that we keep your involvement a secret."

Ah Lei forced herself to look at Mr. Lam. "Earlier, you asked me if you were cowardly. I don't know the answer." He kept his eyes on the road. She couldn't tell if he was putting his guard up again. She took a deep breath. "My boyfriend could really use your help. But it's not something you can stay anonymous about."

It was already evening by the time Ah Lei returned to her dorm room. Mr. Lam said he would get back to her, so the suspense wasn't over yet, but she was relieved to have managed to ask him. She turned on the light. Panda wasn't there. The place seemed forlorn. Panda's bed had been neatly made, not a wrinkle in sight. The desk, usually littered with makeup bottles, was clean. Ah Lei realized Panda wasn't coming back, at least not tonight. She felt a twinge of guilt. Maybe she shouldn't have argued with Panda the night before. Panda had fled home to avoid confrontations with her mom, and now, she had to escape the dorm again because of their fight. Everything had been okay just two nights ago, when they made Molotov cocktails, and debated politics with strangers in the lobby. Why was it so hard for people on the same side to accept their differences? Why were friendships so fragile?

Before the fight started, they were getting ready for bed and chatting. Ah Lei told Panda about a young girl she had recently visited with Sister Ka at a hospital. The girl struggled to eat lunch. The handcuffs on her wrists clattered as she maneuvered the chopsticks. In another bed was a boy, maybe fifteen or sixteen. A couple of police officers watched nearby. The boy was very thin and wore glasses with cracked lenses.

"I think this visit broke me a little bit," Ah Lei confided as she changed into her pajamas. "People say we are the generation of transition. Transitioning to what? I began to feel we have no place to stand in our own society. The kids younger than us are made to pay dearly for fighting for justice."

Panda nodded in agreement as she rubbed moisturizer onto her face. "Only when more people speak up will these kids be protected. Our parents' generation could really do more. I think they should feel guilty about the whole thing."

Ah Lei had known Panda was sensitive when it came to her mother, so she always avoided the subject. But having visited her parents' place lately, she increasingly felt Panda was being unreasonable. Suddenly, she couldn't hold back. "Your mom already can't sleep at night. What more do you want her to suffer?"

"Shouldn't middle-aged people feel even the slightest guilt about what's happening? About what Hong Kong has become?" Panda's agitation was now shifting to Ah Lei.

"What did they do wrong? Is this their fault? They didn't do anything." Ah Lei raised her voice too.

"Exactly! They didn't do anything!" Panda said, putting away the moisturizer jar and slamming the cabinet door. "In the last few decades, they could have stood up at any critical juncture, but what did they do? Horse racing. Dancing. Chasing money. Those who made enough jumped ship and emigrated. They did absolutely nothing. That's why Hong Kong is the way it is now," Panda said.

"It's not nothing! Your mom worked hard to raise you and Sai Mui, and now she is generously taking Ah Mak under her wing. When would it be enough for you? Are you only going to be satisfied when she takes a bullet on the street?" Ah Lei felt guilty as she recalled this. She was too harsh. What had gotten into her these days? Perhaps she should text Panda. She picked up her phone and pondered what to say. A message came in. It was from Mr. Lam.

"Ah Lei, it was nice to meet you today. I have great admiration for what you're doing. I'm so sorry to hear about Ah Mak's situation, but I'm afraid I have to protect my own family first in this tumultuous time. I'm sorry."

It wasn't terribly surprising. She shouldn't have allowed herself to hope otherwise. Ah Lei began typing a polite response. "No worries. I understand." She considered if she should add two smiling emojis to avoid coming off as sulking or too cold. But then the strange anger came over her again. Why should she make sure he felt good about his decisions? For disappointing her? Why should people who only contributed when there wasn't any risk feel they'd done enough?

She erased her message and put her phone down. Letting him feel guilty was her small, quiet revenge.

Be a Girlfriend

Election Day fell on the last Sunday of November. Panda didn't wake up until well past eleven. She had left a window open the night before, and the wind was rustling in through it. The dorm room was like a lush miniature zoo. Aside from the hamster, they had also taken in a tank of ornamental fish, a hedgehog, and several potted plants.

They had become custodians of these plants and pets since the mass evacuation. Thanks to negotiations, the standoff ended peacefully four days after it started. Panda and Ah Lei took turns watering the plants, cleaning the cages, and feeding the animals. They coordinated their schedules so if one of them was out on a date, having dinner with family, or spending the night at her boyfriend's, the other would stick around.

Before Ah Lei left for Ah Mak's place the night before, she reminded Panda to clean the fish tank and change the water.

By the time she finished tending to all the chores, it was

already past noon. Panda hurried to get ready. She threw on a black T-shirt and a brown skirt. She wanted to put on some light makeup, but when holding the eyeliner, her hand slipped, and the black pigment veered way off onto her lid. She swore under her breath and grabbed a cotton round to clean up. The more she dabbed, the messier it became. Looking at herself in the mirror, she understood why people made fun of smudged eye makeup as "panda eye." This was not her day. She removed it altogether and headed out to catch the bus.

She had a full schedule ahead: lunch with Ah Lei and Ah Mak, and then off to the polling station near her parents' to cast her ballot. Afterward, she would go to Ah Ming's place to watch the election results. The subject had become a source of tension between them. Ah Ming was reticent about the whole thing, while Panda had made it her personal mission to get him out to vote. Her last lobbying attempt got a little out of hand.

Ah Ming was driving and the car radio was on. News shows these days were all about the upcoming election: who had announced their candidacy, which power broker was backing whom. . . . He quickly switched the channel to a music station playing pop hits. Panda thought Ah Ming was becoming like her dad, avoiding political news and discussions.

"Why did you change the station?" she asked.

"I have the freedom to choose what I want to listen to, don't I?"

"What do you have against election news?" Panda laughed awkwardly, trying to lighten the mood.

"I've told you already. I'm not voting," Ah Ming said. "I thought we'd settled this. Why do you keep looking for any opportunity to push me to change my mind?"

"I'm not pushing you. I just don't understand. Why should you assume a bad outcome this year because of your disappointment with past legislative elections?"

"I'm not making any assumptions about the outcome. I simply don't have faith in the district offices, and I'm not planning to vote. Is that allowed?" Ah Ming snapped at her, ending the conversation.

But that was more than a week ago. Maybe she could try again, Panda thought. Aboard the bus, a TV was showing the latest polls. The numbers were optimistic for the slate of pro-democracy candidates that Panda was going to vote for. She pictured watching the vote tally with Ah Ming on his sofa. They were going to witness not just election workers counting ballots but a display of the people's resistance against the establishment. Then, Ah Ming would come to see: Things did change this year. The united power of voters would carry democracy activists into the legislature! Panda wanted to see his faith in elections restored. Perhaps, she also wanted to prove him wrong. Encouraged by this vision, she decided to urge him to vote one last time.

She sent him a message. "Are you really not voting? Come on, give Hong Kong a chance!" She stared at the chat window for a long time, but there was no reply. He was probably still asleep, she told herself.

The bus had left the New Territories and crossed into Kowloon. As it neared Ah Mak's home, the serpentine road was flanked by starkly different landscapes. On the left side were high-rise residential buildings; on the right was a stretch of jagged hills and overgrown woodland.

She messaged Sai Mui to check in on things at home. Sai Mui reported that Mom and Dad had planned to vote before breakfast, but when they arrived at the polling station just after eight, the queue was already spilling into the nearby park. Mom didn't want Grandpa to stand outside for so long, so they went for dim sum first instead.

"Mom knew you'd come back to vote. She bought something for you," Sai Mui texted mysteriously. Panda figured it was strawberries.

When Panda arrived at Ah Mak's, she found Ah Lei already in the kitchen, putting spaghetti into a pot of boiling water. Ah Mak was out on the balcony hanging up laundry. On the TV, *Sunday Theatre* was playing a Stephen Chow film. Panda called out to Ah Mak, "This is so nostalgic! The last time I saw this program was before college! Remember we used to watch it together every Sunday afternoon?"

Ah Mak finished putting the last few pieces of clothes on the laundry line and joined Panda. He was clean shaven and had a fresh haircut.

"Lately, I've been reminiscing about the past. Do you remember the summer before I started junior high, we all went to Ocean Park?" she said.

"Yeah. The tourists were so excited to see a panda, but it took a giant dump. It was hilarious."

"Ick! That's so gross," Ah Lei said. "Lunch is ready." They each sat down to a bowl of freshly cooked spaghetti accompanied by a soft-boiled egg on the side.

"I thought that panda was so cool. It didn't give a damn about expectations from others." Panda went to the fridge and found a jar of mayonnaise.

"Gotta respect the panda's free will," Ah Mak joked. He tapped the eggshell lightly against the table, cracking it into his bowl. Panda followed suit and mixed some mayonnaise into the spaghetti with her chopsticks. The strands were coated in a velvety, milky sauce. Panda loved the eggy aroma: sweet and salty.

"Carbonara for dorm living," Ah Lei said, picking out bits of egg shell from Ah Mak's bowl.

Ah Lei had been making the same dish when Panda returned to the dorm for the first time after their fight. Panda had come back to pick up something she had left behind, but as soon as she got out of the elevator, she bumped into Ah Lei boiling pasta in the common kitchen on their floor. The tiny space was thick with steam. Ah Lei was pulling her long hair into a ponytail with a red hair tie. Panda felt a little awkward, but when Ah Lei invited her to share the food, Panda obliged.

It was a particularly intense day out there. In the morning, students discovered that someone had broken into the chemistry department building. The unknown burglar had smashed the lock on the building and stolen chemicals from the lab, presumably to make a bomb. Then, a young man hijacked a campus bus to help transport students and supplies. He didn't have a driver's license and ended up driving it into the sidewalk. Luckily, it didn't cause any injuries.

"I don't feel good about what's happening," Ah Lei said as she slurped the noodles.

"It's getting wild. Thankfully, no one was injured by the bus," Panda said.

"I wonder what happened to all the Molotov cocktails we made the other night," Ah Lei said. They ended up making too many. A boy visiting campus somehow found the excess stash and threw one for fun. It caused a small fire, but students were able to put it out.

"I know," Panda said. "In the last few months, we've seen plenty of smashed storefronts and other damaged properties. I always told myself that these were necessary for the cause. But now that things are happening on campus, it hits different."

"It's really hard to weigh my decisions. Sometimes I feel that whichever path I choose, I might end up hating myself in the future," Ah Lei said. She finished her meal quickly and got up to leave. "Sister Ka asked me to bring her saline solution," she said.

"Go," Panda waved her off. "I'll wash the dishes."

After eating, Panda felt tired. She left the dishes and her unfinished noodles by the kitchen sink and went back to their room. She shut the windows and drew the curtains, and sank into her bed. These past few days, she had felt exhausted but couldn't leave the chaos behind. Even right now, Panda felt that she could hear people shouting. She could smell the faint trace of tear gas hanging in the air. She couldn't summon the strength to get up and go out there, but she couldn't fall asleep, either. Everyone had fought so hard for six months. What if nothing came of all this effort?

It used to bug her when Ah Lei acted like this. But their roles seemed to have reversed. In the aftermath of Ah Mak's arrest, Ah Lei snapped into focus. Panda, on the other hand, began to question the meaning of everything.

She turned to her phone. Five minutes, and she'd get up to wash the dishes, she promised herself. She doomscrolled on social media and hopped between group chats and news sites. She was seeking updates while dreading them at the same time.

Half an hour went by. She came across a clip showing the sports ground not far from their dorm building. The footage was shaky and often out of focus, but Panda made out a young woman who covered her left eye and sobbed. "It hurts so bad! I don't want to go blind! I just want to go home," she said.

Then the camera showed the woman's profile, revealing a ponytail with a red hair tie. Panda bolted upright. Was this Ah Lei? She rewatched the clip several times but wasn't sure. She called

Ah Lei. No one picked up. Her texts went unanswered. The last thing she had said to Ah Lei was offering to do the dishes. The conversation before that had ended with Ah Lei asking, "Would it only be enough for you if your mom took a bullet?" Panda regretted not acting warmer just now. She regretted holding back from completely reconciling. Did it take her best friend getting shot for her to get over herself?

Panda rushed toward the elevator. The plates were still sitting by the sink, unwashed. Her limbs felt weak. She prayed to every god she knew. The elevator door opened. Ah Lei emerged from it, seemingly unscathed. "The eggs must have been undercooked. I spent the last half an hour in the bathroom." Panda threw her arms around Ah Lei. "I'm sorry, Ah Lei. I'm so sorry."

Panda checked her phone again after leaving Ah Mak's place. Ah Ming had read her last message but didn't respond.

When they walked together hand in hand, she sometimes gradually loosened her grip, testing if Ah Ming would clasp her hand tighter or let it go. He never seemed to notice. If she turned around and walked away, she wondered, would Ah Ming come after her before she disappeared into the crowd?

Ah Ming's silence made her uneasy. She sent another message to press him. "What if I say that your unwillingness to vote means you don't love me enough?"

On the bus ride, her phone buzzed several times, but they were all election updates. By the time she got to the polling station in her home area, it was already past four in the afternoon. The line was still quite long. She called Sai Mui to let her family know she was here. When she came out of the station, she saw Mom carrying a couple of bags, waiting for her.

Mom opened one of the bags and began to explain things. "These sheet masks are hydrating ones. The weather's getting cold and the air is dry. These are lozenges—just let them dissolve, don't crush them. They'll soothe your throat. And here are some packets of dried fruits. They're naturally air-dried and healthy. Stop snacking on chips. They're so greasy." Before Mom finished talking, Panda wrapped her arms around her. When was the last time she embraced her mother? Panda inhaled her smell.

"Silly girl, what's wrong?" Mom stroked Panda's hair. "Are you tired?"

Panda murmured yes in response.

"It's okay. Everyone is getting tired."

Panda let go of Mom and took the bags from her. She noticed some new wrinkles on Mom's face. "Okay, it's getting late, I'll let you head to Ah Ming's. Say hello for me. Don't forget to eat the strawberries. I've picked out all the seeds."

As soon as Panda parted ways with Mom, her phone buzzed. She adjusted the bags so she'd have a free hand to check her messages. It was from Ah Ming. "Fine, I'll vote."

She yelped. Her hard work had paid off, her mission was complete. All is good. Now they were together, ushering in the change they wanted to see. In this buoyant mood, she hailed a cab.

At ten p.m., voting ended. Panda sat alone in Ah Ming's family's living room. The TV was on. Workers at polling stations across the city began counting ballots. There were journalists stationed at each district. Media outlets and the government website provided live updates. Ah Ming was playing video games in his room. His parents had gone to bed. Panda refreshed the news and social media apps on her phone frantically.

"Are you sure you don't want to come watch? It's so exciting!" Panda called out to Ah Ming.

"Enjoy," Ah Ming answered indifferently.

This wasn't quite what she had pictured. She had wanted them to experience this emotional moment together. But at least Ah Ming had voted, she consoled herself. That was what mattered. Numerous men and women had fought so hard for the last six months. They deserved a measurable victory. They needed it.

After midnight, the count was still going. Panda decided to take a quick shower. She really needed to shampoo her hair. As soon as she stepped out of the bathroom, she saw a map on TV where most districts were marked yellow—the pro-democracy camp had won in a landslide. It really happened! A complete reversal of power! She checked her phone for more specifics: among the more than five hundred seats spread across eighteen districts, challengers won more than 90 percent of them. They won in Panda's district, Ah Mak's district, and Ah Ming's district.

"Ah Ming, Ah Ming, we won! A total victory!" Panda dashed into Ah Ming's room to share the news. "Aren't you glad you voted? I have faith in human nature again!"

Ah Ming paused his game. He flashed a smile. Panda knew she shouldn't have doubted his intentions. She shouldn't have doubted their relationship.

He stood up and petted her wet hair. "Come on, I'll dry your hair." Ah Ming nudged her back to the bathroom and plugged in the blow-dryer. The hot air and noise drowned out all else. Whatever problems lingered between Ah Ming and her, Panda was confident she could fix them. They would work things out. Her frustration over the movement, her doubts about solidarity, dissipated.

She gestured for him to stop the blow-dryer.

"Aren't you just so happy?" she asked.

"No."

"Isn't this worth being happy over?"

"Not for me."

"Why are you acting like this?"

"Am I allowed not to feel happy?" Ah Ming said.

"I just don't understand. How could you possibly stay unhappy when something absolutely wonderful just happened?"

Ah Ming set the blow-dryer aside. "Do you remember telling me about throwing out your favorite skirt?"

Shortly after Panda and Ah Ming started dating, she told him a story from her first year of university.

It was the end of the semester. No one had time to spare. Everyone was stressed out from days of back-to-back exams. One evening, she emerged from a four-hour exam all sweaty. She had put on a red plaid skirt she really liked for good luck. The midi cotton skirt clung to her body, the hip and thigh area drenched from hours of sitting.

A group of classmates were going to pick up bread for dinner and then head straight to a study room. They made a pact to pull an all-nighter before the exam the next morning. Panda said she wanted to go back to her dorm room first. She needed to shower and to make herself some instant noodles. She would join them later.

"Ooh la la. Look at Miss Hoity-Toity here. You can't skip a shower or a meal like the rest of us?" a classmate mocked her.

Another nicer classmate pleaded, "Don't go! If you leave now, you definitely won't come back. Let's stick together and push through the night."

Panda couldn't defy the group pressure and stayed. She spent the night studying in the windowless, stifling basement study room. She felt sticky all over and her thighs were really itchy. She knew if she started scratching, she would never stop. She shifted her legs, trying to dispel the discomfort. The itch didn't go away, but a sour smell arose. She felt like rotting fruit.

She wanted to leave. What would she give to have a shower? But she knew what the group would say about quitting halfway. She endured what felt like the longest night of her life.

During the exam, Panda barely remembered a single thing from the night before. She ended up handing in her answer sheet early and ran back to her dorm room. She ripped her clothes off and tossed them on the floor. In the mirror, she saw red rashes spreading from the inside of her thigh down to the curve of her calf.

She stayed in the shower for a long time. She used a lot of body wash and scrubbed hard with a loofah, imagining she could scrape off the rash like removing scales from a fish, or purging rotten crops from a field. Afterward, she picked up the dirty clothes with a plastic bag and took them to the trash room.

"Just like that, my treasured skirt was ruined. Somehow, this was one of the most upsetting memories from that year," Panda told Ah Ming.

He nodded in understanding. "Sometimes self-righteous goodwill is more violent than outright malice."

When Ah Ming brought this up again, Panda was perplexed.

"What does that have to do with the election results?"

"Tell me, do you even remember how you did on that exam?"

"No. I guess what stuck with me wasn't the grade, it was how unbearable that night was. But why are you bringing it up now?"

"That night, your classmates, who might have had perfectly good intentions, demanded you to stay. Nevertheless, they forced their will on you, in the name of friendship. In a way, it was almost violent."

Ah Ming put his hand on Panda's arm before he went on. "Listen, I know you mean well, but in the last month, you pestered me endlessly about voting even after I explained my doubts about the effectiveness of elections and the legislative system. I feel you've been forcing your will onto me in the name of love."

"How can you lump these two things together?" Panda brushed Ah Ming's hand off. How dare he ruin this supremely joyful moment? She had let him in on this woeful memory. How dare he use it against her! But these emotions felt too vulnerable to share in this heated moment. "I've said this so many times already. We have to work within the system to gain resources and power. That's the only productive way to protect more people." She repeated her spiel.

"The standoff at your university was resolved quickly, but many students were still trapped at other campuses. What about them? What about the students who disappeared when they tried to flee through the sewers? What about all the people who died, who were arrested, who went into exile? What does an election victory do for them?"

Panda wanted Ah Ming to shut his mouth. To stop asking all

these pointed questions about the election. They made her feel like the floor was sinking. He was her lover. They had held each other close during their darkest hours. So why couldn't their happiness be in sync? Why couldn't her happiness be enough to make him happy too? Hope had become such a rare thing. If he couldn't share this night of euphoria with her, he should have at least allowed her to have it. But no, he was hell-bent on that damned prophetic high ground of defeatist nihilism. He just had to dismiss the electoral victory as nothing more than a collective delusion.

"And what have you done? Anything besides sitting here playing video games?" She grabbed the towel draped over her shoulders and threw it at Ah Ming.

She headed to Ah Ming's room to pack her things. He followed her into the room and lifted the game console, yanking out the plugged cables, and slammed the machine to the floor. The plastic shell split open. Parts flew in all directions.

"You want to force everyone to live in your reality!" Ah Ming shouted. "I doubt this election will actually change anything, and I didn't want to be part of it. But you just have to push me. Pushing me to vote and pushing me to perform happiness when I don't feel it. You hunted me down. I can't even escape into the world of games. Are you satisfied now?"

Ah Ming's parents were woken up by the commotion and came to check on them. Alarmed by the wreckage on the floor, they asked what had happened.

Neither Ah Ming nor Panda said anything. Mechanically, she collected her things. Ah Ming's mother tried to comfort her. "He's just like that. He normally doesn't make a fuss, but when he feels pushed, he lashes out like this."

Panda didn't respond, so Ah Ming's mother went on. "It's really not a big deal. Once he had even smashed a TV when he was fighting with his dad. It's all fine now, isn't it? Don't take it to heart. All couples fight and make compromises. As the saying goes, Lovers fight at the head of the bed only to make up at the foot of it. And it's too late for a young lady to wander through the street. Stay the night, and you two will figure it out in the morning."

The words were intended for peacemaking, but they only irritated Panda more. She picked up the bags from her mother and took off.

At four in the morning, Hung Yi stood alone by the roadside, waiting for a bus to come and take her away from this place. Half an hour later, she boarded the first one that appeared.

There were only a few other passengers. She sat down in a window seat. Her head throbbed. Her hair was still wet. A radio station was replaying election news. The bus started moving, passing buildings and telephone poles plastered with red and green campaign posters.

Hung Yi's phone vibrated. It was Ah Lei. She picked up and heard jumbled noises on the other end. "Hello?" she said. No one responded. She heard people shouting and laughing. She was about to hang up when Ah Lei finally spoke. "Panda? Ah Mak and I were so happy that we went out with a few others to celebrate at a karaoke bar. Would Ah Ming and you like to join us?"

Panda felt her cheeks burning, her hair damp and cold. Ah Lei's chirpy voice brought tears to Hung Yi's eyes. She began sobbing.

"What's wrong, Panda? Where are you? Do you want me to come?"

Where had it all gone wrong? Hung Yi had wanted nothing but justice and love. Were such pursuits meaningless in the end?

They stayed on the line until she finished crying. In a raspy voice, she assured Ah Lei she would be okay. She would fill her in later. Then she hung up the phone and wiped her face dry.

The bus passed through a tunnel and left the city behind. On the highway, it picked up speed, hurtling forward as if there were no tomorrow. Streetlamps emitted faint light, forming a trace of stardust. The roadside trees appeared sparse and barren at first, but they grew denser and taller, until they were about to leap into a run to keep pace with the bus, threatening to swallow the vehicle in the shadow of their groves.

In this strange landscape, Hung Yi no longer knew where she was heading to, or where she belonged.

She found the seedless strawberries Mom had packed for her. She popped one into her mouth. Her jaws shuddered, and she squinted reflexively. The fruit was quite sour.

Hung Yi pushed the window open. A cold blast wrapped around her. The trees seemed to let up. Through the seams of their canopy, twilight was slipping through.

Acknowledgments

I am deeply grateful to everyone who has helped bring this book into the world. My heartfelt thanks to my Taiwanese editor, Kuan-Lung, for his unwavering support and for cheering me on like the best kind of teammate, encouraging me to see this novel through. To my editor, Han, whose sharp and powerful insight polished the work and made it so much stronger—thank you. (The English-language edition of *Everyday Movement* is a revised version of the original Chinese manuscript.)

I am indebted to my translator, Jennifer, for her kindness and deep understanding, and to my agent, Kangqin, for her steadfast faith and wise guidance throughout this journey. My dear friend Crystal Chan kept me company through countless late nights as I struggled with the writing, and I could not have done this without her.

To my partner, Ting, thank you for giving me the time, space, and encouragement I needed to write. And finally, my deepest gratitude goes to the countless Hong Kongers whose courage and dignity inspired this novel in the first place.